YOUNG ART AND OLD HECTOR

by

NEIL M. GUNN

SOUVENIR PRESS

First published 1942 by Faber and Faber Ltd

This edition first published 1976 by Souvenir Press Ltd,
43 Great Russell Street, London WC1B 3PA
and simultaneously in Canada

Reprinted 1985
Reprinted 1993 (Copyright © renewed)

*The publisher acknowledges the financial assistance of
the Scottish Arts Council in the publication of this volume*

ISBN 0 285 62254 4

Printed in Great Britain by
The Guernsey Press Co. Ltd, Guernsey, Channel Islands

Young Art and Old Hector

By the same author

Novels

BLOODHUNT

BUTCHER'S BROOM

THE DRINKING WELL

THE GREEN ISLE OF THE GREAT DEEP

THE GREY COAST

THE KEY OF THE CHEST

MORNING TIDE

THE SERPENT

SUN CIRCLE

THE WELL AT THE WORLD'S END

Non-Fiction

WHISKY AND SCOTLAND

For

THE WOMAN OF THE HOUSE

Author's Note

The two traditional stories told within "Machinery" and "What is Good Conduct?" may be found in Campbell's *Popular Tales of the West Highlands*, to which acknowledgments are gladly made. Old Hector has his own slight variations on the themes.

Contents

1

The First Run of Grilse

"What now? What now? What now?" said Old Hector, spreading his legs.

"No! no! no!" screamed little Art, as he danced with rage at being stopped by the legs.

"What a noise!" declared Old Hector, lowering his bushy whiskers and laying hold of the small figure.

"Let me be!" yelled Art, struggling with all his force.

"Hots! tots!" said Old Hector. "Aren't you the strong fellow? Hush! look who's coming."

"There's no-one coming," cried Art, who wildly refused to look, for he had been deceived before now.

"But won't you just look?" suggested Old Hector.

"No!" shouted Art. All the same he slowly turned his wet eyes over his shoulder. When he saw no-one, he fairly kicked the earth. "There's no-one!"

"That's what the little hero said to the blind giant. 'What's your name?' asked the giant. 'No-one,' answered the little hero. 'I'll find you,' said the giant, groping about. In came a neighbour giant and asked, 'Who are you looking for?' 'I'm looking for No-one,' answered the blind giant. 'What's the sense in looking for no-one?' asked the other big fellow, and started laughing. And so——"

"I know that one!" bawled Art.

"If you do, then perhaps you know how many ladders it takes to reach the sky?"

"One, if it's long enough," spluttered Art, angrier still.

"Very good. Very good indeed. But ah, I know one you can't answer."

"You do not! Let me go!"

"Yes—I know one—one that I bet you even Donul doesn't know."

"You do not! You do not!" Art would not hear of it. "What is it?"

"What is the wood that is not bent or straight?"

Art danced again.

"Ho-ho, so you don't know it?"

"I do know it."

"What is it, then?"

"Sawdust," yelled Art.

"Clever! Clever!" nodded Old Hector. "But wait you, I have got one or two that no-one knows but myself, and if I tell them to you, then you could score over Donul. Wouldn't that be great? Wouldn't Donul then fairly be dancing? He would ask you—and ask you——"

"I don't want them!"

"Ah, but if you heard them, you would want them. Everyone in the world would want them, just as they want wisdom."

"Don't want wisdom."

"What's that? You don't want wisdom? Surely you never said that?" whispered Old Hector in an appalled voice.

Art did not answer.

"If you said it, I never heard you. Not properly," said Old Hector solemnly, nodding his whiskers so that they tickled Art's head. "But tell me, as one friend to another: why were you in such a hurry?"

"It was Donul—he ran off on me and left me."

"Did he, the rascal? Wait you, I'll put a few words on him when next I see him. Which way did he go?"

"He went this way and away off that way." Art now knuckled his eyes and hiccupped.

"Did he, indeed? Where do you think he was going?"

"Himself and Hamish—they're off to the River—I heard them, behind the wall."

"To the River! But that's miles and miles. What would they be going to the River for, anyway?"

"For salmon," cried Art.

"For salmon! Hush! What if the Ground Officer heard you? What would happen then?" Old Hector's voice was low as the wind in a bush.

"What?" asked Art awkwardly, not showing his face.

"He would turn you and your brother Donul and your brother Duncan and your three sisters and your father and your mother out of your home and off the land and away from this place, and you would be on the road with nowhere in the whole world."

"He would not," muttered Art.

"You know he would. You don't need to tell me you don't know that. Small as you are, you have enough wisdom for that. Wasn't it lucky, now, that I stopped you?"

"No," said Art.

"Otherwise the Ground Officer might have heard you and followed you, and so he might have caught Donul, and then——"

There was silence.

"If he caught Hamish, would you too——"

"We would. For Hamish is my son's son, and that would be enough."

"But I wasn't going to c-cry when I kept going."

"But how much better not to go at all!"

"I want to go!" Art's voice began to rise again.

"That would not be wise," declared Old Hector. "And if anyone's not wise he's no use; he's a laughing-stock, like Foolish Andie. Would you like to be foolish, like Andie? Poor Andie, who can only say 'Gu-gu——'"

"I would not."

"I should hope not, indeed," agreed Old Hector.

"Are you very wise?" asked Art.

"Well," replied Old Hector, scratching his whiskers, "well, now, what makes you ask that?"

"I heard Mother say that you were a wise old man."

"Did she, then? And to whom did she say that?"

"To Father."

"I see. Your father, perhaps—was not——"

"Your whisker," interrupted Art, who was beginning to look up at last, "makes a funny noise when you scratch it."

"Does it, though?" Old Hector smiled. "Would you like to have a whisker yourself?"

"Not yet," replied Art. "But perhaps some day I might have one. How does it feel like to have one?'

"Oh, it's fine and comfortable."

"Does it keep your face warm on a cold day?"

"It helps. I think you have a lot of wisdom in you for your years. How old are you?"

"I'm eight," replied Art.

"That's a fair age already," admitted Old Hector with a thoughtful nod. "You're coming on."

"I am," said Art. "It may not be so long before I'll have a whisker. But I'm not in a hurry for one."

"You're just as well," agreed Old Hector.

Art's eyes grew thoughtful, then glimmered. It was a difficult question to propound. "Is it possible," he asked, "to get wisdom without having a whisker?"

"Certainly, certainly," Old Hector reassured him at once. "I know a way whereby even you, young as you are, might get wisdom, but you would have to follow my instructions exactly."

"What way is that?"

"Well, I'll tell you. You have heard of Finn MacCoul, the greatest of all the heroes?"

"Anyone has heard of him. That's nothing."

Old Hector nodded. "Just so. Only it's more than nothing, because it's something. Do you follow that?"

"I follow," admitted Art reluctantly.

"Very well. Finn MacCoul was a great leader and warrior. He was the leader of the bravest men that the world has ever seen. He was the first of the famous fighting band, the Feinn."

"Was he the greatest fighter that ever was in the wide world?"

"As to that now, well, that's difficult. You see——"

"Was he greater than Cuchulain?"

"Ah, you've got me there. That's a searcher. You've fairly put me on my beam-ends now."

"Cuchulain was the greatest, easy," declared Art with quiet triumph.

"That is as may be," replied Old Hector doubtfully. "Perhaps you're only thinking so because Cuchulain was a small dark man, and you yourself are small and dark."

Even as Art repudiated the suggestion his eyes opened wide. "Was he like that?" he asked.

"He was," said Old Hector.

Art looked far away and smiled secretly. "Everyone knows," he declared, "that Cuchulain was a greater fighter than Finn MacCoul."

"Perhaps so. I'm not denying it, though I have my own opinion. A man is entitled to his own opinion."

"You are not," said Art. "He was the greatest! He was!"

"Very well so. All right. All right. He was a great fighter certainly."

"He could have—he could have——" Art paused to look over his shoulder. "He could have cut the head off the Ground Officer easily. Could he?"

Old Hector laughed. "Ha! ha! ha! Ho! ho! ho!" His head waggled. "Yes and twenty Ground Officers. And he wouldn't have cut them off, either. He would have put his finger against his thumb like that and—flick! off they were."

"It's a pity we hadn't him now," said Art.

"Never you mind," said Old Hector. "There's no saying who may grow up to be a Cuchulain some day."

Art's forefinger came of itself against the ball of his thumb and made a little flick so that no-one could see it.

"Why do you think Finn MacCoul was better?" he asked, when he returned from his thinking.

"Don't misunderstand me," said Old Hector. "I never said that Finn MacCoul was the greatest fighter. He was great, certainly, but there were greater than him. Answer me this, however. Why was Finn the leader?"

"Why?" asked Art.

"Because he also had wisdom," replied Old Hector.

"Cuchulain had wisdom too. He had! He had so!"

"He had some," admitted Old Hector. "But he had not the great wisdom. Only Finn MacCoul had that, as Finlay, the storyteller, will tell you. There is no denying it, and you have heard it yourself before now, and that's proof."

"I don't care if I have," said Art. "Wisdom is not that much."

"It is, and more, because it is that that makes a man a great leader. Now, if Cuchulain had had Finn MacCoul's wisdom, he would have been the greatest in the four brown quarters of the world. And yet Finn MacCoul got his wisdom simply enough."

"How did he get it?" asked Art cunningly. "Was it by a white serpent?"

"What way was that?"

"Don't you know that way? I made sure you would know that," said Art, "at least."

"Well, perhaps I have heard of it, but have you ever heard of a white serpent in this country? Answer me that."

"There might be one, though. Mightn't there?"

"I hope not," said Old Hector. "It wouldn't be a nice thing if anyone was going away off to the River all by himself and he met a white serpent. But, however that may be, it wasn't by a white serpent that Finn MacCoul got his wisdom."

"I didn't think it would be, myself," agreed Art. "That wouldn't be a right way. Besides, there isn't a white serpent here, is there?"

"Not so far as I know," answered Old Hector.

"And you know everything, because you're old and wise, don't you?"

"Perhaps so."

"What, then," proceeded Art, "was it that gave Finn MacCoul his wisdom?"

"It was a salmon."

"A salmon!" said Art, and he looked up with a clear wondering innocence that Old Hector thought more beautiful than Finn MacCoul's wisdom.

"It was indeed. And if you will stand by me while I sit on the corner of this dike, I'll tell you how it came about."

"I'll stand," said Art, and he leaned against Old Hector's knee.

. . . . .

"There was a time before now," began Old Hector in the storyteller's voice, "when there lived an old man who had the Druid's knowledge. In truth he was a Druid himself, but though he had the knowledge, he hadn't the great wisdom, which is the wisdom of all the ages. The only thing in the wide world at that time which had the great wisdom was a salmon that lived in a pool in a river. There were some hazel-trees that grew over this pool, and on the hazel-trees grew nuts, and these nuts were the Nuts of Knowledge. As the seasons came and the seasons went, time out of mind, the nuts would be falling quietly into the pool where the salmon lay. Well did the Druid know this, and he knew, moreover, that if only he could catch the salmon and eat him, then he would have himself the great wisdom of the salmon. But try as he would, he could not catch the salmon. Well, on a day of days, who should come along to the Druid to get lessons from him but young Finn MacCoul. He was only a lad then, maybe about the age of Donul. Donul will be fifteen, perhaps?"

"No," said Art. "He's only fourteen past. But never mind about him."

"Very well," nodded Old Hector. "Young Finn was a brave strong lad, and because he was fifteen or thereabouts he never cried any more. Oh, he was strong and supple and quick, and with his help at the pool didn't the old Druid catch the salmon! Well, there was the salmon at last, high and dry on the bank, with Finn's help. Now, the next thing was for the Druid to eat the salmon. But he must not cook it himself; he must get someone else to cook it, for that's how it had to be. So he told Finn to cook it for him. But remember, says he to Finn, you are not on any account whatever to taste the salmon yourself. Because, of course, whoever tasted the salmon first would get the wisdom. Do you see?"

"I see," said Art.

"Well, Finn was a fine truthful lad and the Druid knew he could trust him. So off Finn went to roast the salmon, for they often wouldn't be cooking it in a pot then as we do, but roasting it before the fire on a spit—that is, a thing you stick the salmon on and turn round so that all the sides get roasted. You have roasted a potato before the fire yourself before now?"

"I have," said Art.

"Well, it wasn't so long before Finn had the salmon ready. The Druid came in. He saw Finn's face. It was bright with the great wisdom. 'You have eaten some of the salmon!' he cried.

" 'I have not eaten,' answered Finn. And he was telling the truth, too. But he had got the wisdom. And do you know how? Well, at the last, when he went to turn the salmon, it was so hot that it burned his thumb, and without thinking didn't he stick his thumb in his mouth! And that was enough."

"Was it?" said Art, looking far away. "What did the Druid do to him?"

"Not a thing. It couldn't be helped. He was a fine old Druid, besides, so he just told Finn to eat the salmon, and then to be going away home, because there was nothing in the wide world that he could teach Finn any more. And ever after that, if Finn wanted to know something hidden from others, all he had to do was to stick his thumb in his mouth."

"Just stick it in his mouth?"

"Just as you're doing."

Art quickly withdrew his thumb from his mouth. "Tell me this," he said, looking at Old Hector's knee.

"Well?"

"Would it have made any difference if the salmon had

been boiled in a pot instead of roasted on that thing for turning?"

"Not a bit. Why should it?"

"I was only asking," said Art indifferently.

"I quite understand," replied Old Hector that same way. "The only thing about the pot is that a fellow would have to watch not to put his finger into the water and it boiling."

"Anyone can tell when water is boiling," said Art.

After a time, Art, who was exercised in his thought, said to Old Hector that he might as well be going home lest his mother needed him.

"That might well be," agreed Old Hector. "Hamish and Donul will lie low and start back on the edge of the dark."

"It's likely," said Art. "So-long just now."

"So-long," replied Old Hector, who then wandered down to the little barn, where he always had odds and ends to make or to repair. Thither in the mouth of the night came Donul and Hamish, and each from inside a trousers-leg pulled forth a grilse. The silvery bodies drew the last of the light out of the darkness, and Old Hector said they were more beautiful to behold than any other shapes in Creation. Donul and Hamish agreed with him, and their three voices were full of warm conspiracy and hushed delight.

"You're sure no one saw you?" asked Old Hector.

"You can rest assured that we took good care of that," answered Donul.

Old Hector nodded. "It was lucky I saw the keeper going west in the first of the day."

"Did Art try to follow me?"

"He did. But I took up his attention and then he went home. I'm thinking your father is not too well pleased about you going. He was miscalling me to your mother for a wily old poacher."

"He had little to do in that case," replied Donul. "Art must have been talking."

"But," continued Old Hector, "when men are at the age of both your fathers they become frightened, because they are so important. I have noticed that before now. You may as well go home first and spy out how the land lies. Your mother is a wise woman, Donul. You can whisper a word to her. When men are full of importance women have to be full of sense. And you too, Hamish. Both of you are soaking wet."

"We were wet," answered Hamish, "but now we're fine."

As they were leaving, Old Hector stopped them, asking, "Was it the first run of the grilse?"

"It was," said Donul. "We saw three more in the Hazel Pool."

"They'll wait there," said Old Hector.

Laughing softly, the two lads withdrew.

Old Hector sat down and gazed at the silvery luminescence in the darkness. The first run of the grilse! The words had the sound and the light of the first mornings of the world; they were younger than Art and older than Finn MacCoul; they held him to a trance that was bright with wisdom and sad with the sweet sadness of peace. He forgot his pipe and time passed over him. He would deal with Art's burned finger to-morrow.

2

The Knife, the Glass Ball, and the Penny

For two whole days the wide world was an empty place to Art, except for his craving, and it was wherever his eyes lifted, like a blackbird in a frost. Once he stole a knife from the drawer of the kitchen dresser, but when he tried it on a piece of wood down in the little barn, he told himself in bitter wrath that it wouldn't cut butter on a hot stone. This wrath so affected his hearing that his mother caught him. When she said that if ever she found him with a knife again she would give him a sound skelping, he had so far forgotten himself as to attack her and had received the first part of the skelping there and then.

Life was indeed very difficult. His mother could not understand that his only desire was to make a beautiful thing like a shepherd's crook, and there was no way of telling her. As if he would cut himself with a knife or fall on it and die! It was enough to make a pig laugh. So quietly the shepherd had sat carving the handle of his long crook into the loveliest shape. Art had run his fingers over the smooth pale surface, and as he got that queer delightful feeling, the shepherd had looked at him with his dark eyes and smiled. "What are you making at the end of it?" asked Art. "A serpent's head," replied the shepherd. "Are you?" said Art, and listened in wonder with the rest of the world to its farthest boundary.

The shepherd had a way of whistling, too; a small whistle with liquid turns in it, as he drew his head back, tilting it thoughtfully, and eyed what he had done so far, and the tune he whistled Art did not quite know but very nearly. Everything was a short distance beyond him, but he knew he would suddenly be in that place, if only he could get a real knife.

For the whole half of a day he had done everything his brother Donul had ordered him to do, but when he had asked at the end of it casually for the loan of his knife Donul had stretched his legs and said little boys shouldn't have knives, though Donul's own knife had only half a blade. Never to the end of time would he obey Donul again. Never.

Morag was more than two years older than Donul. She was seventeen, and of his three sisters Art liked her best. But when he saw her coming with two buckets towards the well, singing to herself as if the world was a happy place, his gloom took an edge of spite. Moreover he had heard that the shepherd had walked home with her one night recently from a ceilidh, and that she might be further in with the shepherd than he was himself did not help him at the moment.

"Hullo, Art," she called to him, her brown eyes glancing with mirth. She could balance herself so lightly at times, you would think she was standing in a wind. He turned his face away as if she weren't in it. "Still looking for a knife?"

"I know who you're looking for, anyway," muttered Art.

"What's that?" She came close. "What's that?"

"Shut up," said Art.

"That's not a very nice thing to say to your sister."

"I don't care if it's not."

"You're in a bad mood, surely."

"You're courting," said Art, and glanced at her swiftly in order to be ready for what might be coming.

The expression that went over her body and face alarmed him. She set down the buckets slowly and looked around in a scared way. Art took to his heels, but she caught him behind the barn. He struggled and yelled, but she smothered and in the end quietened him, for he divined an unusual state of affairs. He also became a little frightened of this strange expression on his sister's face. She asked him to repeat what he had said, but he remained dumb. She apparently could not repeat it herself. Quite suddenly she said, "Who?"

"Tom the shepherd," he muttered stubbornly.

Her pale face now flushed in a moment like a wild rose and her brows gathered in a terrible anger and her eyes darted fires. He tried to tear himself away, for now he felt deep in his marrow that he had said something that was terrible and wrong in a way that he never knew before, and as he could not admit this to himself, he cried wildly: "You are! You are!"

"You're wicked," she said. "I hate you."

Art didn't care, he said. "I'll tell at home, if you hit me," he threatened her.

Whereupon she had another startling change. Her voice came quiet and soft as a pigeon's, wheedling and playful. Dear little Art. There was no-one in the whole family she liked as she liked Art. She tickled him as though it had all been a game, and kissed him near the ear. Out of this he emerged shaken, but fairly whole.

"Will you promise me never to say that again, never to say it to anyone?"

He looked down and looked away, promising nothing.

"I'll give you something, if you promise."

"What?" he asked.

"I'll give you a bonny thing."

"What thing?"

"Wait till you see. You'll be surprised."

"What is it?"

"Promise me you'll never say it."

"Is it the little gold chain?"

"Would you like that?" she asked with some dismay. "It's only a lassie's bangle."

"Is it the brooch with the yellow stone?"

"What real boy would want a brooch?"

"I thought it might be that," he said. Then he looked at her in a way that could hardly hope. "Is it the round glass ball with the coloured threads inside it?"

She nodded, smiling.

"I promise," he murmured, embarrassed a little at last.

In the late afternoon of that same day, Art had got tired playing all alone with the coloured glass ball, and sat on the hard path lost in thought at some distance from his home. Towards him he saw his eldest brother Duncan coming with his face newly washed. Duncan was a tall man of nearly twenty and had a knife like the shepherd's. Art put the coloured ball in his pocket for safety.

"Well," said Duncan, "what are you doing here?"

"Nothing," said Art, head down.

"You'll be busy in that case."

"I know where you're going," said Art.

Duncan stopped. "What's that?"

Art silently kept his head over his secret. Duncan stirred him playfully with his toe. "Can't you speak?"

"I know where you're going."

"Where?"

Art gave him a quick glance. "You're courting." Then

Art felt the silence above him grow terrible. But he was prepared for that.

"Say that again."

Art did not say it.

"Say it!" commanded Duncan.

Art squatted lower, but the searching toe began to hurt him. "Stop it!"

"Say it!"

"Stop it!"

"Say it!"

Through his rage Art shouted: "You're courting Peigi Maclean."

The wallop he got in the side of the head flattened him to the ground. Duncan's face bent over more terrible than thunder and lightning.

"I'll tell at home," yelled Art.

"Will you?" said Duncan, and Art suffered on the other cheek.

"I'll tell Mother!"

"Will you?"

Art lay huddled, weeping bitterly.

"If I hear you say anything like that again," remarked Duncan, "I'll break every bone in your body. You remember that, my boy." Duncan was very angry, because though everyone in the two townships knew he was after Peigi Maclean, he himself fondly thought that no-one knew. He hesitated, wondering what more he could do to the broken figure. "You know I never break my word," he said at last in a cold fierce voice, and walked on.

As Art's pride was hurt more than his head, he could not control his weeping. Moreover, there was a horrid thing deep down that suggested he had brought this trouble on himself by trying to get a knife in a dubious way, and as he could not admit this his case was beyond relief.

"Hots! tots!" said a voice above, the voice of Old Hector who was driving the red cow home from the moor. "What's come over you at all?"

"Let me be!" cried Art, curling close to the ground.

"Well! well!" said Old Hector. "Who's been at you now?"

Art struggled against the lifting hands and Old Hector's beard went down his neck.

"It was Duncan," hiccupped Art. "He hit me."

"What? A big man like Duncan hit a little boy like you? I don't believe it."

"He did. He hit me three b-blows."

"I'm ashamed of him," said Old Hector. "He could surely find someone nearer his own age and size. Never you mind. When you grow big you can hit him. What did he hit you for?"

Art did not answer, but presently a desire to confess overcame him. "I said he was c-courting."

"Courting! Well, and what of it? Weren't you telling the truth?"

"I was," said Art, reassured at once by this astonishing fact.

"Everyone knows he's at the courting. It's no sin to tell the truth."

"No," said Art. "I just told the truth and he hit me."

"I can see you have been badly treated," nodded Old Hector. "But look! that old red besom of a cow will be in the corn patch if we don't catch up with her. Give me your hand."

Art gave him his hand and they walked along.

"What's courting?" asked Art.

"Well, now," said Old Hector, "that's not an easy one."

"Is it—is it something terrible?"

"As to that, it might well be."

"I thought so myself," said Art. "I thought it must be awful. Perhaps it's a sin."

"Do you think so, now?"

"Yes," said Art confidently and glad to be able to enlighten his old friend. "It's—it's like poaching—only worse."

"I think you're coming near it now. You're getting warm," nodded Old Hector.

Art looked up at him. "Did you ever court?" he asked.

"Och, I might have had a shot at it in my time, but that's long long ago."

"You wouldn't court now?"

"Not me," said Old Hector.

"I wouldn't court," said Art, "not if you gave me anything."

"You must have been putting your thumb in your mouth," said Old Hector.

Art looked up at him, smiled, and as he said, "No, I wasn't," he laughed.

The clear bright eyes of Art, gone all merry, made Old Hector laugh happily also. "If," said he, "you had put your thumb in your mouth instead of telling Duncan he was courting you wouldn't have got a walloping."

Art's merry eyes steadied thoughtfully, then looked up at Old Hector. "When I put my thumb in my mouth," he said, "I don't feel that I'm getting wisdom."

"You would have got it that time," said Old Hector.

"What," asked Art, "did Finn MacCoul feel when he put his thumb in his mouth and got the wisdom of all the ages?"

"What do you feel yourself?" asked Old Hector.

"I only feel my thumb," said Art.

"Good!" said Old Hector. "That's the beginning. By

the time you're Duncan's age you'll be all wisdom together."

"I should," said Art, "by that time. And for one thing I wouldn't be courting then. Would I?"

"You would not. Not if you were wise."

"I think it's silly, courting, don't you?"

"Very," agreed Old Hector. "But it's a thing that comes over people at certain times."

"What times?"

"Not at your age and not at mine, for which we ought to be thankful," replied Old Hector. "But there's a long while in between when girls and fellows have great bouts of it and go off their heads."

"Off their heads?"

"Clean."

Presently Art said weightily: "I think all girls are silly."

"Often they haven't much sense, I must admit."

"Did you ever have a great bout of it yourself?" Art asked.

"Come back here!" shouted Old Hector to the old red cow. "Run now," he said to Art, "and turn her or she'll be off on us."

Art ran and danced in front of the old red cow, who regarded him out of large brown eyes in her lowered head and then turned. "Gee up!" cried Art, and would have smacked her on the flank had she not switched her tail.

"She can wait here now getting a good bite until the milking," said Old Hector.

"She's a fine cow," said Art. "I like her."

"She'll do," said Old Hector, taking out his pipe. "Don't you think your mother may be missing you by now?"

"No," said Art. "It's early yet. She'll know fine I'm

with you. I heard her saying to Father that I would learn more from you than I would from him."

"Did she now?" said Old Hector, smacking hard at his pipe. "I have always had a great admiration for your mother. She's a fine woman."

"She'll do," said Art.

Old Hector laughed, tilting the rounded bush of his whiskers, and Art screwed his heel into the ground with busy embarrassment.

"Why are you laughing?" he asked shyly.

"You can make a good joke sometimes," declared Old Hector, settling himself more comfortably on the turf dike.

"It's easy," said Art. "I can make lots and lots of them."

"You do," said Old Hector.

"Do you like listening to me at them?" inquired Art, looking here and there.

"I do indeed," declared Old Hector. "I get more entertainment out of your talk sometimes than out of the talk of all the grown-ups."

"Do you?" asked Art, pivoting on his heel. "How's that?"

"For many reasons, but I'm not sure that you'll yet understand them. You have taught me to-day," proceeded Old Hector, "that all life is divided into three parts. The first is the period of childhood and it extends up to the courting age; then there is that age itself in the middle; and then there is the third age, beyond the courting, where I am myself."

"Do you like where you are yourself?" asked Art, regarding him solemnly.

"I do," replied Old Hector. "For now I know at last what is important and what is not. Long ago I would think things important that now I see had no importance at all;

and also I would think things of no importance which now I see were the only important things in it."

"Is courting important?" asked Art.

Old Hector's mouth opened, and remained open, while his right hand went up and scratched his beard with the crinkly crackly sound that Art never failed to appreciate.

"I don't suppose," said Old Hector, "that you have ever been courting yourself now, have you?"

"No," said Art. "Catch me! Why?"

"Because if you had, we might the sooner come to some agreement on this business. So perhaps meantime we could leave it until——"

"There was one time," muttered Art, putting his full weight on his heel and pivoting right round. "Isn't that a good hole?" he asked, taking his heel from the little cup he had made in the earth.

"Yes, it's a good one," Old Hector agreed.

There was silence.

"It wasn't anything," said Art, blowing the steam off a negligent energy.

"I don't suppose it would be," agreed Old Hector, negligent also.

"It was Mary Ann," said Art, smiling in a strained but still negligent manner. "You know, Hamish's Mary Ann?"

"The one with the red curls? I know her fine. She'll be about your own age?"

"She says she's four months older, but I don't think that's right. Do you? I think I'm older."

"As to that, I couldn't say exactly. But you're worth being older whatever. Besides, when she grows older herself she'll maybe not be so sure about it."

"She might have more sense then, mightn't she? She hasn't much just now. I know."

"How that?"

"It was like this," said Art. "I was coming along past the end of her house and she was standing there looking at me. I paid no attention to her, because girls are no use for having fun with. As I looked at her, do you know what she did?"

"No."

"She put her tongue out at me."

"Never!" exclaimed Old Hector, shocked.

"As sure as I'm standing here," said Art. "She put her tongue out at me."

"And did you put out your tongue back at her?"

"No," replied Art regretfully. "I wanted to, but I didn't like."

"My sorrow!" exclaimed Old Hector sadly.

Art regarded him apprehensively. "That wasn't courting, was it? It wasn't! I just walked away. Then I heard her laughing at me, and I picked up a stone."

"Did you throw it at her?"

"No," muttered Art. "I—I—didn't—I—I ran off home, but not in a hurry, just chasing a butterfly."

"I know," nodded Old Hector. "That was wise of you."

"I thought so myself," said Art, "but I wasn't very sure. I'll throw the stone at her next time, though."

"Do you think you should?"

"I'll throw it a little way whatever, just to let her see."

"On the whole," suggested Old Hector, "I think it would be wiser for you to chase the butterfly."

"There wasn't a real butterfly in it," Art now confessed.

"I suspected as much," nodded Old Hector.

"What," asked Art, relieved, "do you think is the finest thing in the world?"

"What?"

"A knife," said Art. "I wish I had a knife. If I had the whole world, guess what I would give it for?"

"A knife," guessed Old Hector.

"Yes," answered Art.

"I haven't a knife myself," said Old Hector. "I had one once, but young Hamish took it off me two years back. All the same, a knife is a queer thing. It cuts more than a stick. Your mother is a wise woman. For one thing it cuts love. If a person gives you a knife and you don't want the love between you to be cut, then you have to give that person a piece of money. Now I'll tell you a strange story about that, and then you'll run off home——"

"There's Tom the shepherd," said Art.

And Tom the shepherd it was, with his dark eyes smiling and his long crook. He was tall and old like Duncan who was over nineteen, but to Art he was quite different from Duncan, and Art always felt a little excited in his presence as if he was a hero.

Tom greeted them and Old Hector replied, but Art said nothing, listening. They talked about the sheep and the weather and the grass, and then an extraordinary thing happened to Art whose eyes were on Tom all the time.

As Old Hector was looking away at a thought, Tom looked directly at Art, closed his left eye in a deliberate wink, jerked his head sideways over his shoulder in the direction of the moor, and then as if he had not issued this secret invitation to Art to accompany him, he remarked: "Well, Art, still looking for a knife?" He laughed and added at once: "I must be off. If you're going home, Art, I'll see you part of the way."

"So-long, then, just now," said Old Hector to Art.

"So-long," answered Art, and he and Tom went away together.

When they had gone along the path a little way and dipped out of sight of Old Hector's house, Tom took Art up round a little hollow where no-one would see them.

Tom was very friendly to Art and told him he was in a hurry to round up the sheep or otherwise he would have gone along to his house. "But if I go," said Tom, "they'll be sure to keep me, and the only one I want to see is Morag over a small private business. I was wondering if you would do me a great favour and run home and tell Morag I want to see her, just for a minute. Only a minute. And I—I—don't want you—it wouldn't matter, but still, I mean, I don't want you to let any of the others see you telling Morag. Do you understand? I mean, it's nothing, but just I'm in a hurry and—and do you think you could do it?"

Art remained silent, his clear wondering eyes on Tom's face. Tom looked away, with a strange little laugh, and Art lowered his head.

"I'll tell you what," said Tom. "If you do it, I'll give you the loan of my knife for one whole day. And then, when you bring it back, I'll have a real hazel stick and root for you to carve at and I'll show you the way. I'll be up about the moors here for the next week or two." He produced his knife and showed it to Art.

Art could not speak. He would have done anything for Tom for nothing. He did not want anything. The knife held his eyes and his body in a small trance.

"I thought," said Tom, "that you would do a simple thing like that for me. It's nothing. It's nothing at all. But of course if you don't want to do it, I don't mind."

Art's hand came slowly out and closed over the knife.

"I'll wait here. Don't be long—but remember, don't let the others see you."

Art ran away with the knife gripped in his hand. He stopped only once to see if he could open the blade, and when the blade snapped back with a click his heart shivered with the fear of delight. He ran so fast that he fell, but he entered the kitchen with a casual innocence. His mother was very busy with pots, and Morag was mending. When his mother's back was turned Art held Morag's look, closed his left eye in a deliberate wink that screwed up half his face, and jerked his head sideways at the door, then he drifted out.

When Morag came out with the milking pail she heard her two younger sisters shouting beyond one gable-end, so she went quietly round the other. Her father passed her on the way from the byre to the house. With sure instinct, Morag found Art behind the barn.

When Art saw her eyes wide and round in her pale face he felt mysterious and told her hurriedly how Tom awaited her presence in the hollow.

Then she looked queerer than ever, and a little scared flush chased itself over her face.

"I can't go," she said to herself, "it's too late."

"It's only just for one minute," said Art. "Go on. Hurry up."

"I can't. No. I—no, I can't."

"Why are you frightened?" asked Art, gripping the knife in his pocket.

"I'm not frightened."

"You are. You're frightened."

But she did not seem to hear him. Her fingers plucked nervously at the brown jumper over her breast. She breathed. She looked here and there as if bogles were creeping in on them.

Art began to feel a little queer himself. Perhaps she was going off her head. Then her eyes came on him and he had the queerer feeling of being looked through like a glass ball.

"Will you come with me?" she asked.

"I will," he said.

And now she became extremely cunning about not being seen. Art would not have believed that a mere girl had it in her to be so cunning. But when they were away on the path she took Art's hand as if they were going to church. "We'll say that you said Hamish's sister Sheila sent a message for me," she said, gripping Art's hand hard.

"We'll say that," said Art, "if we're asked."

When they came near the little hollow, Morag stopped.

"Aren't you going?" asked Art.

"I don't know yet," said Morag, and Art saw her throat gulp as if she had swallowed a small bone.

"Come on," said Art encouragingly. "I'll take you."

"You run home," said Morag at last, "and wait for me behind the barn. I won't be long."

Art suddenly felt sorry for her, because now she was like one going on a sad and perilous journey.

"I'll go with you," he said valiantly, "and hold your hand."

She smiled down at him in a strange way, her eyes bright as if they were going to cry, and very softly said: "Dear Art," and fondled him, and said: "Now go."

He went and, looking back after a short distance, saw her still standing; then she turned and went into the little hollow.

If Art hadn't the knife to hang on to he would have thought life as queer as it was, and if he hadn't cut a salley from the burn with a twist to it like a tiny crook and tried to walk with it doubled up like an old man, he would have thought to himself that Morag was never coming back at all. But she came at last, and now she was quite different, and at once he grew afraid of her, she was going to be so kind. She said that Tom was just wanting to see her about a ceilidh. Her eyes were brighter than glass balls and her mouth redder than red berries, and she had a way with her that would steal the heart out of a fellow if he wasn't watching. But Art was watching, and when he should have been as weak as water, she said softly: "Art, will you do something for me, one little thing, and I'll never forget you, and I'll give you anything in the world I have?"

Art, very suspicious now, did not answer. His marrow knew it was going to be something awful.

"Promise me," she begged.

Art remained dumb.

"It's only a little thing, a little little thing."

"What?"

"I want you to run to Tom now and give him his knife back. Please, Art. To please me——"

It was too much. It was beyond even the worst. A sob got strangled in his throat. "No!" he said fiercely. "I won't! He gave me the knife! You have nothing to do with it!"

"Hush-sh-sh," interrupted Morag. "No, no, no. . . ."

Their mother's voice called through the faint gloom of the coming night.

"Hush-sh-sh," crooned Morag, softer than the evening wind. And then she said: "I did not know you loved the knife so much. Keep it—but wait for me here."

She came back after a time and slid to her knees before Art, her face all playful, and at once Art trusted her. She opened her hand and there on the palm lay a tiny silver coin with a hole in it.

"You can keep the knife but only on one condition," she said, in the voice of one telling a magic story there could be no denying, "and that is, that you run now to the little hollow and give Tom this threepenny-bit. Will you do that?"

"I will," said Art at once, and off he set.

He found Tom lying on his side in the heather, with his dark eyes slanting and smiling and waiting.

Art held out the threepenny-bit with the hole in it.

"Is this Morag's own?" asked Tom, taking it and looking at it with a careful wonder as though it were alive and might be easily hurt.

"It is," said Art. "And I knew she had it. She kept it with a little gold chain and a brooch with a yellow jewel and a—a round glass ball." He paused and added: "She kept them hidden in a wooden box, but I never opened it, though I knew where it was."

"That was right of you," said Tom. "Thank you very much."

Then Art made his great denial. He held out the knife to Tom the shepherd. "You can have the knife," he said, "and then I can take the threepenny-bit back to her."

Tom looked at him in such a way that his eyes narrowed and Art felt that what looked at him was not Tom but his mysterious smile.

"I never break a bargain," said Tom, not even glancing at the knife.

Art grew embarrassed, for now the mysterious smile seemed to be laughing at him. But Tom said: "To-morrow afternoon come here, and I will have the uncarved stick for you that is the finest stick that was ever cut out of the Hazel Wood above the Hazel Pool."

"You can rely on me," murmured Art, looking far away in his embarrassment.

"Sit down and give me your news," said Tom.

"It's not much news I have," said Art politely as he sat down.

"I'll tell you a queer thing that happened to me once," said Tom, and in a friendly voice he told Art of an incident on the hill that included a sheep, a lamb, an adder, and a raven.

The mouth of night was opening at last, but when Tom asked Art if he was frightened of the dark, Art said he wasn't, and Tom said he couldn't come with him because he would have all he could do to see his sheep on the moor.

"So-long just now," said Art.

"So-long," said Tom, tall and friendly, but with the pleasant mysterious smile on his face again as he looked down at little Art.

His heart in his mouth, Art ran off through the deep but still glimmering dusk, keeping a hand against each pocket lest the knife that was in one and the glass ball in the other might jump out. They might easily jump out, for things were mysterious and queer, and might be a little off their heads, too. Moreover, things might come out of the night, and things that came out of the night sometimes hadn't heads on them at all.

He was running along the grassy edge of the path so that his bare feet would make no sound, when all at once a low dark body without a head moved in front of him, and the heart fell out of Art's throat and went clean across him. Out of the grip of terror, he could neither go back nor forward. Then a light came into the midst of the dark body and Art saw that it was Duncan sitting on the grassy verge, lighting his pipe. But it was a queer Duncan, for as he threw the match from him he gave a little laugh, such a laugh as Art had never heard him give before, least of all to himself, for Duncan was the oldest of the family and ordered his brothers and sisters about and was often very stern. Then he lit another match, and after taking a puff or two out of his pipe, looked at the match and threw it also far from him with another little laugh.

Art saw now that he was off his head, and with a gulp

started forward on tiptoe but afraid to run. Perhaps he could steal past. But Duncan, swaying back in his strange mirth, suddenly saw him, and caught him by the leg as he leapt.

Art yelled as Duncan rolled him in the heather like a puppy dog.

Duncan laughed and tickled Art under the arms and between the ribs in front. Then he picked him up and stood him between his knees. "Did you get a fright?" he asked, and chuckled.

Art was panting but wary.

"Did I give you a walloping this morning?" asked Duncan like a fool with a joke. "Never you mind," he proceeded. From his pocket he withdrew a penny and handed it to Art. "That's for yourself and don't spend it all in the one shop!" Then Duncan got up and took Art's hand. "Come on," he cried. Clearly an uncanny happiness had taken possession of him since Art had last seen him. "And what," he asked, "are you doing out here at this late hour? Does Mother know? Never mind," he added, not waiting for an answer. "If she asks you where you have been you can say you were with me." And at that he laughed again.

Art took a sly look up at Duncan's head. It seemed to be in the usual place. The grip of his hand, too, was companionable and kind. To make sure that nothing more of an astonishing nature would happen to him, Art went along quietly, together with the knife, the glass ball, and the penny.

3

Machinery

Happening to turn his eyes, Donul saw Martha with the shaking head going towards the mill through the dusk of the evening. "Now run you home," he said to his little brother Art, "and if they ask you, say I'll be home in a short while."

But Art would not run home, and from being kind Donul's voice grew harsh and angry. "I'll wallop the face off you if you don't go this minute."

Art fell with the push he got, and Donul ran towards the mill. Yelling loudly, Art, from his knees and his little hands, got to his feet and ran after Donul as hard as he could.

Donul saw Martha lift up her head. Moving there across the land she was like a fearsome old scarecrow. He stopped, and Art stopped short of him. Donul picked up a stone and said in a low fierce voice to Art: "If you don't go home this minute I'll knock your brain out."

Art sobbed in little sniffs and picked his breast, his head down, but whenever Donul went on Art followed him. Martha had now gone into the mill. Donul looked around to make sure that no-one would see the terrible thing he was going to do to his brother. There was no-one, so he nodded grimly and strode back to Art. Art held his yell ready. "Will you go home?" asked Donul like thunder and lightning. Art did not answer, his eyes gleaming up once. "Will you go home?" cried Donul, and gripped his brother by the back of the neck.

Art yelled.

"Come on!" cried Donul, and began to drag him home. But Art would not be dragged. "So you won't come home with me?" demanded Donul in wild triumph. "You won't come home?" And he walloped Art. Art yelled as if he were being murdered, and though Donul now knew himself to be in the right, he crouched under that sound, looking over his shoulders. Art was sobbing, curled up on the ground. It's not one thing an elder brother has to bear. "Go on, keep crying," he said to Art; "keep crying, you mother's baby!" Then he jerked his brother into sitting up. "Stop it and wipe your nose, you little fool." Art heard the inner change in his brother's voice and tried to stop crying. Donul wiped his eyes for him roughly. "Come on," said Donul, taking Art by the hand, and they went towards the mill.

Art had cried so much and been obstinate because he was afraid to go to the mill and therefore wanted to go desperately. He had heard in his time many strange stories about the mill, and about more mills than this one. For there was a thing in the mill called machinery and it went round and round, with teeth on the edges of its wheels, and though one wheel was standing up and the next one lying down, their teeth would bite into one another like Art's own teeth, and woe and betide anything that came between them then. Donul had said they would bite your whole hand off and hardly notice it; your whole hand, right off. And if the iron teeth caught your sleeve they would "drag you in".

Art had seen the water-wheel outside going splash! splash! and had once drawn near to the edge of the black hole down through which the flood disappeared with such rumbling, gushing sounds that the earth under his feet had quaked. But he had never gone near it thereafter, because Kennie-the-kiln had appeared and said in a terrible voice that if ever he found Art about the mill again he would throw him into the black hole.

But the most awful thing about the mill was the going round and round. Three thieves had once broken into a mill, but the miller was clever, because he had shut the doors and sent the mill round and round. The thieves grew dizzy, and then they couldn't stand, and then they fell, and there they lay like ones dead and so were easily captured. And there was one story of a miller in the dead of night and of a man who came to murder him, but the man didn't murder the miller and instead got murdered himself. It was such a story as his mother wouldn't allow to be told before Art, but one day when Donul was wanting Art to do something for him, Art got the story out of Donul.

The mill was high, higher than three houses, and had cocked angles on it and little windows. There were hens round it and a water pool near the wheel where ducks floated. Men came whom Art didn't know, from places to which Art had never been, with sacks of oats in a cart, and backed in the cart below a door which was not like any ordinary door on the ground but high up in the wall. It was said that the machinery pulled the sacks up by the chain. And how could the machinery pull the sacks up unless the machinery knew how to do it? Darkly Art suspected that this machinery had more in it than men who laughed at him believed. They had better look out or one day it would catch and drag them in. He would have liked to ask Donul if it might, but his thought was not too settled yet, and, in any case, there were now no hens and no ducks and no carts, and—the mill was silent.

They passed under the little wooden bridge that

spanned the cavern to the top floor and approached the vast red-smouldering heap of husks which Kennie had thrown from the kiln fire. As they entered at the door, Donul shoved Art behind him, and Art followed like Donul's shadow.

It would have been dark inside but for the kiln fire, which put red gleams on the faces of bearded men. Many of them were laughing and their voices threw dancing shadows. They were so taken up pulling fun out of old Martha that they did not notice the boys come in. Donul sat down against the wall and Art crouched by him. Two other boys, as old as Donul, saw Art, and smiled to him in subdued greeting, but said nothing. Then the four of them looked at Martha, who was answering the men, her head nodding at a great rate. She sat on a full sack, with a loose neck coming up out of dark rounded shoulders, like the plucked throat of an old raven. Her head kept swinging back and fore on a well-oiled swivel. In this movement the boys found a terrifying fascination. "Hush!" said Donul softly to Art, who had said nothing.

Art might not have been able to understand some of the grown-up jests even if he had been able to listen. But words themselves had become queer sounds now. This was a ceilidh in a weird place. The shadows were peaked gnomes, very swift. In the bearded faces was a laughing glancing that was not in them at home.

"You can tie him up, as you did last time, and blindfold him," said Martha, "and you can say Smell that and Taste that," and she tried in her mirth to shake her head sideways, and so induced a complicated motion awesome to behold.

"We made the gauger so drunk that he was frightened to report us anyway, didn't we, Martha?"

"No, oh no," said Martha, whirring as if about to strike

a long hour. "He had only smelt and tasted and drunk himself under, but he had seen nothing on top, so what could he say he had seen?"

They liked their own joke to be explained to them by Martha and laughed with great pleasure, throwing their heads up, and some of them even nodding in sympathy with Martha, who was now nodding at a great rate.

"Well, if we made a good drop that time, the gauger couldn't complain but that we gave him his share of it. Eh, Martha?"

"There is a difference," answered Martha, "between him who has the boil and him who squeezes it."

Because the others were laughing, little Art now ventured on a smile himself. And soon the words he heard were more like the words he knew. And presently they asked Martha to tell a story, for it was a good way to put in the time while the grain was drying. "Hush!" said Donul to Art who had no thought of saying anything.

When Martha asked what story they would like, a man answered, "The Girl and the Dead Man."

"I have told that one many's the time," said Martha.

"It's none the worse for that," declared the man.

There was once a poor woman and she had three daughters (Martha began). Up got the eldest and said to her, "I am going off to seek my fortune." "In that case," said her mother, "I will bake a bannock for you." When the bannock was baked, the mother asked, "Would you like the little bit and my blessing or the big bit and my curse?" "The big bit and your curse," answered the daughter. She took the way before her and when the night was falling she sat against a wall to eat her bannock. As she ate, there gathered around her the birdbeast and her twelve puppies, and the little birds of the air.

"Will you give us a bit of the bannock?" they asked.

"I will not give it, you ugly brutes. I haven't enough for myself."

"My curse on you and the curse of the twelve birds, and the mother's curse is the worst of all."

The eldest daughter got up and went on, not having had nearly enough with the bit of the bannock. A long way off, she saw a little house, and if it was a long way off she wasn't long getting there. She knocked.

"Who's there?"

"A good servant wanting a master."

"We want that."

So in she went. For wages she had a peck of gold and a peck of silver; and every night she had to be awake to watch a dead man, brother to the housewife and under spells. Besides that, she had the nuts she broke, the needles she lost, the thimbles she holed, the thread she used, the candles she burned, a bed of green silk above her, a bed of green silk under her, sleeping by day and watching by night. The first night she was watching she fell asleep. In came the mistress and struck her with the magic club. She fell down dead and the mistress threw her out behind the midden.

Up got the middle daughter and said to her mother, "I am going off to seek my fortune and follow my sister." Her mother baked the bannock, and the middle one chose the big bit and her mother's curse, and she set off, and everything that happened to her sister before her, happened to her.

Up got the youngest one and said to her mother, "I am going off to seek my fortune and follow my sisters." When the bannock was baked the mother asked, "Would you like the little bit and my blessing or the big bit and my curse?" "The little bit and your blessing," answered the youngest daughter. She got that, and took the way before her, and when the night was falling she sat against a wall to eat her bannock. As she ate, there gathered around her the bird-beast and her twelve puppies and the little birds of the air.

"Will you give us a bit of the bannock?" they asked.

"I will that, you pretty creatures, if you keep me company."

She shared out the bannock, and they ate and they had plenty and she had enough. They clapped their wings about her till she was warm and comfortable.

The youngest daughter got up and went away. A long way off she saw a little house, and if it was a long way off she wasn't long getting there. She knocked.

"Who's there?"

"A good servant wanting a master."

"We want that."

So in she went. For wages she had a peck of gold and a peck of silver, the nuts she broke, the needles she lost, the thimbles she holed, the thread she used, the candles she burned, a bed of green silk above her and a bed of green silk under her.

She sewed and sat watching the dead man. In the middle of the night he got up and screwed a grin. "If you don't lie down," she said, "I'll give you one wallop with a stick."

He lay down. After a while, he got on his elbow and screwed the grin. The third time he arose with the grin, she hit him one wallop. The stick stuck to the dead man, her hand stuck to the stick, and off they set. They went through a wood, and when it was high for him it was low for her, and when it was high for her it was low for him. The nuts were knocking their eyes out and the sloes hitting their ears off. When they got through the wood they went back to his house. There she received the peck of gold, the peck of silver, and a vessel of balsam. She rubbed the balsam on her two sisters and they came to life. They returned home, and (concluded Martha) they left me sitting here, and if they were well, it is well, and if they were not, let them be.

Martha lifted her arms a little, like two wings; her curved hands came down, cupping her knees; her head nodded up and down with monstrous rapidity.

The miller went towards her, complimenting her, and giving her at the same time a discreet look. From under her apron she withdrew a small bag and no word was said between them.

When the others were talking to Martha, the miller went away and filled the small bag with meal, and left it outside by the door. Then he came back where the merry words were flying.

At last Martha got up and said she would not be keeping them any longer from their work with her old foolish stories. "My blessing on you, and on this mill, and may its best doings be ever hid from the eye of destruction." She went out and there was the little bag by the door. Putting it on her back, she set off for the small cabin where she lived alone.

Donul dug Art with his elbow. "Come on," he said softly, and put Art before him. Outside it was now nearly dark. "Give me your hand," said Donul.

Art gave him his hand and they walked along in silence. Presently Art asked: "Who is the birdbeast and the twelve puppies?"

"No-one knows," answered Donul.

"Are they all birds or are they all beasts?"

"No-one knows for certain. But that's the way they are in the story."

That made a difference. "I thought once or twice," said Art in a quiet voice, "that I just saw them."

"I have thought that myself sometimes," answered Donul. And then he asked: "What did you think they were like?"

Art gripped Donul's hand and in a low voice said: "I thought the birdbeast was like a great raven, and the puppies were little black puppies."

"I thought something like that myself," agreed Donul. "They are queer, anyway."

Thought of the queer engaged Art's attention for a little time. At last he said: "The machinery was quiet to-night."

"It was," nodded Donul.

"Was it doing nothing?"

"It was just lying in behind the walls."

"It would be dark where it was?"

"Dark as tar," said Donul.

"Does machinery sleep?" Art asked.

"No. It just waits."

"I know what it does," said Art. "It lies awake, waiting."

"Do you think so?"

"I do," said Art. "And then—and then—it springs with a roar and—and goes round and round."

"It goes," explained Donul, "when Kennie or someone puts the water on to the wheel. It waits for that."

"Does it?" said Art thoughtfully. And then he added: "And it always goes?"

"Always."

"And if you kept the water on the wheel, would it go for ever and ever?"

"For ever and ever," answered Donul.

"And all that time," said Art, gripping Donul's hand hard, "it's ready to drag you in?"

"It's the one thing it never forgets."

"Art!" called their mother's voice in the dark distance.

"That's Mother. Run! If they ask you, say I'll be home in a wee while."

"I'll say that," promised Art.

"You're not frightened of the dark for a little way?" asked Donul, his kind brother.

"I'm not frightened," declared Art. He started running as fast as his legs would carry him, shouting: "Mother, I'm here!"

4

Under an Old Gooseberry Bush

"Come on," said Donul to Art.

"No," said Art.

"Go on," pleaded Morag. "What a fine time you'll have staying at Old Hector's with Donul!"

"Will not have a fine time," said Art.

"But if you don't go Mother might never get better," said Morag, "and then you would be to blame. Wouldn't that be terrible?"

"Am not to blame," cried Art, stamping the earth.

"Hush-sh-sh!" said Morag. "Isn't it quiet that Mother must have, and there you go crying. Poor Mother!"

"I know what it is," said Donul derisively. "He's frightened to leave his mother. He's Mama's pet!"

Art danced in such anger that the tears bounced off him. The noise he made brought his father's face from inside round the door.

"What's this I hear?" asked the face; but it did not look angry, it looked sad, as though it had lost its way somewhere.

Morag now made a pleading round pout of her mouth to Art and her eyes implored him in silence. Many a one might find her difficult to resist when she looked so, but Art did not, because he wanted only to go to his mother, and they would not let him. When everyone was against him in this life and he was tired and maybe sore as well, then there was only one person in the world left. And now she was very ill and they were wanting him to go away from her altogether. It was not to be borne.

All the same, the sight of his father's face, so strangely quietened, as if he were in some way to blame, quietened Art a little, and when the face withdrew inside, Donul said to Morag: "Turn your back and don't look."

Morag turned her back.

Donul gave Art a secret wink, pulled some gleaming golden wire out of a pocket, hurriedly stowed it back, and jerked his head in invitation to distant adventure. Then he laughed derisively again, but silently this time and at the rest of the world that didn't know.

Art was visibly affected.

"Can I look round now?" asked Morag.

"You can," said Donul. "You're only a lassie."

At that moment Art saw old Betz, the black shawl round her head, coming towards their home. She looked more like a witch than ever and fear jumped on him with soft paws. He backed away and moved off from the house.

"I knew all the time you would come," said Donul in the friendliest tones as they proceeded towards Old Hector's, "because you would never be the one to stand between Mother and her good health."

"I was just angry—at Morag," muttered Art.

"No wonder," agreed Donul. "She would make a cat angry itself sometimes. Have you ever seen a cat angry?"

Art thought of their own cat by the fire and suddenly had a great longing for home again. "No," he answered in a low voice.

"Maybe you're thinking of a tame cat, but I'm thinking of wild cats on the hills, wild cats with flat ears and bare teeth and *fitzzz-kraach!*—like that—and then the spring!"

Art made no reply.

"I'll tell you a true story that Tom the shepherd once told me. It's about the size of the leaps a wild cat made in the snow, and it out after grouse and hares. Would you like to hear it?" asked Donul.

Art stopped and hung his head and began to cry. The sound of his crying was not fierce now as it mostly was, but broken and pitiful. "Want to go home."

The sound touched Donul inwardly and he pressed his brother Art against him and hit him little slaps on the back. "Never mind, Art, boy," said Donul. "Never you mind." He hit him gentle little strokes near the top of his head. "Never you mind," said Donul. "It's sore when it comes on you like that. I know."

"Want to go home."

"Yes, yes, hush now, I know. It once came on myself. And I cried and cried like anything. It was Duncan took me away. I remember it fine. But I went away. A fellow always has to go away at a time like that."

"Did—did you c-cry too?"

"Amn't I telling you? I cried far worse than you. You're hardly crying at all."

"Wh-when was it?"

"Long long ago. Just before you were born. Come now and blow your nose. It would be a pity for Old Hector to think you had a cry. Old Hector talks to you as to a grown man. And, boy, to-night won't we have the time of it! Do you know where we're going, you and me?"

"No."

"Hush!" Donul looked over both shoulders. "We're going to set snares," he whispered, "in the Clash."

"The Clash!" echoed Art.

"Yes. Beyond the ruins, on the edge of the birch wood, on the Ground Officer's own ground!"

"But—but Father——"

"Hach!" said Donul. "We're not staying with Father to-night. We're staying with Old Hector. We're free. Isn't it fine to be free?"

"Yes," said Art.

"Gives you a grand feeling, doesn't it?"

"It does," said Art. "I—I like being free."

"Of course! Who doesn't? And it's going to be a fine evening for it."

By the time they got to Old Hector's, who was sitting on the turf dike but Old Hector himself. As they drew near, he got off the dike and stood up straight to welcome them. His slow smile made a lot of creases that ran into his whiskers.

"Is this my friend Art," he greeted them, "come to pay us a visit?" He held out his hand, and Art, after glancing up into his eyes with grave shyness, took it. "How do you do?" inquired Old Hector as they shook hands.

"Fine, thank you," answered Art.

"And you, Donul?"

"Fine, thank you," answered Donul, shaking hands also. "I hope you are all well?"

"We are, thank you." Old Hector inclined his head. "And how are you all?"

"We are all as well as could be expected," answered Donul.

"That's good," replied Old Hector. "Come away in now so that I may present you."

Old Hector lived in a two-roomed cottage on the western edge of the croft that was once his but that now was run by his son Angus, who with his wife and family lived in the long new house at a little distance. Both houses were thatched, and at the end of each was a stack of black peat taken from the moor.

"Here are Art and Donul," announced Old Hector, "come to pay you a visit."

There were three women in their forties sitting round the fire, and one of them got up. She was Old Hector's unmarried daughter, Agnes, and she welcomed them as friends come from a far country. This pleasant formality from folk whom Art knew so well left him a trifle awkward, but he did not altogether dislike it. The other two women looked on with bright understanding. One of them was Hector's daughter-in-law from the long house and was the mother of, amongst many, Hamish and Mary Ann of the red curls.

The third woman was a stranger to Art and had black quick eyes. "Won't you give me a kiss?" she asked him promptly.

Art wriggled away at once and with some force.

"That's my hero!" Old Hector complimented him. "Women must always be at the kissing for some mysterious reason. Don't let them start on you, Art."

Art was silent, using Donul as a palisade.

"If I can read a face," said the dark-eyed stranger, "in ten years time he'll be kissing with the best."

"I don't think so," observed Mary Ann's mother, in order to help Art. "He has more sense."

"You're the one to talk there," said the stranger, and the three women laughed.

Hector then conducted his guests to the little barn where Donul produced his gleaming snare wire. There were three new stakes and several new cords required. During his expert examination Old Hector became so interested that he wanted a smoke but found he had left his pipe on the corner of the mantelpiece. "Run you in," he said to Art, "and Agnes will give it to you."

Art hesitated, but Donul gave him a look, so Art went,

yet slowly, for he was shy of the women and not a little afraid that the Dark Woman might still want to kiss him.

Very quietly he approached the door, and there he stood daunted, for the three voices were talking thirteen to the dozen and finding time for laughing as well. Then Art heard the name Mary and knew that they were talking about his mother. Talking and laughing, like witches in a hidden wood. Treacherous voices making mock of his mother, who was ill. Art grew angry and afraid. A trembling came upon him from a world slowly breaking asunder.

"How old is little Art now?" asked the Dark Woman.

"He's just eight past, for he's nearly ages with my Mary Ann," answered Mary Ann's mother.

"Eight years! And Mary herself must be—what?—she must be forty-five, anyway."

"She was forty-six at the last Lammas moon," answered Mary Ann's mother.

"Faith," said the Dark Woman, "it must have been a fair shot from the blue."

"Didn't we hear last Sabbath," said Agnes, "that the Lord works in mysterious ways?"

"Hmff!" said the Dark Woman. "There was more than the Lord at work."

Mary Ann's mother had a rich low laugh. Agnes was inclined to cackle a bit. The Dark Woman had bold flashing words, and now in four sentences she told a complete story, with such point in the last three words that laughter itself shook and sank. Mary Ann's mother's voice came up from where it had been drowned and said with a little ache of pain: "Oh dear me, I haven't laughed so much since the tinker's wife said yon to the minister's housekeeper."

"I hope there won't come a judgement on us for laughing and poor Mary in her trouble," said Agnes.

"Poof!" said the Dark Woman. "You were always a bit timid, Agnes. I remember when my own last baby was being born, and old Betz says to me—oh, she's a dry one, but capable—says she to me——"

"Hush-sh," said Mary Ann's mother. The three women turned and saw Art's pale face in the faint gloom by the door.

"God be here!" said the Dark Woman. But then in a moment she cried: "Why, it's only little Art himself, come, I warrant you, to give me that kiss!"

Art's pale face slowly drooped and turned away, and his body turned away, and in a moment or two he was not there.

"I hope the child didn't hear anything," said Agnes, as they all kept looking where Art had been.

"Hear anything your grandmother!" said the Dark Woman. "What could he have been wanting?"

"He was wanting his mother," said Mary Ann's mother.

"He was very quiet," said Agnes. And then they realized indeed that he had not made a sound. They listened and everything was very still.

"God be here!" said the Dark Woman, getting to her feet and going to the door.

"Is he there?" asked Agnes at her back.

"There's no sign of him," said the Dark Woman. "He must have gone round the house."

"That's queer," said Agnes.

As they were wondering what they would do next, Donul came round the house towards them. "Is Art there?" he called.

"He was here a minute ago," answered the Dark Woman. "Didn't you meet him?"

"No," said Donul, looking at their two faces. "Did you give him the pipe?"

"What pipe?" asked the Dark Woman.

"Old Hector's pipe," answered Donul, "on the corner of the mantelpiece."

While Agnes ran for the pipe, the Dark Woman laughed.

But when Donul got back to the barn with the pipe, Art was not there. Old Hector and himself looked at each other. "I know," said Donul. "He's gone away home."

"Didn't he want to come?"

"No," answered Donul. "He didn't want to leave his mother and her ill. I'll catch him."

"Do that," said Old Hector, and as Donul hurried away he slowly scratched his whiskers. Then he went out and up on to a little knoll, whence he saw something move by the low salley bush down by the dried-up stream. When he got there, Art was sitting half under the bush. Art saw him and began poking the earth with one finger.

"There's no water in the burn just now," said Old Hector. "The long spell of drought has dried it up except for a pool or two."

Art lifted his face a little way and his eyes rolled up to look at Old Hector, then looked down again. It was a strange detached look, and its pallor to Old Hector at that moment held the guilt of mankind.

"Seeing there's nothing in the burn," proceeded Old Hector, "you might as well come back to the barn. What do you say?"

Art remained silent.

"Come you," said Old Hector, and reached down his hand.

But Art, ignoring the hand, continued with a slow fatal detachment to poke the earth. He was like a changeling, cold and fey, and when next he looked at Hector his eyes remained on the bearded face, inscrutable and alien.

"Come you with Old Hector," said Old Hector, bending down. He caught Art's hand, gently but firmly, and Art arose and went with him. They crossed over the little knoll, where Old Hector paused and, picking up Donul in the distance, gave him a wave. As they went down towards the barn, the bodies of the three women were silently pressed together in the door of the house, watching them pass.

Old Hector talked in such an easy way to Art that there was no need for Art to reply. He talked about snares and the cunning ways in which they should be set, and explained how rabbits always kept to the same path, so that you could see their little hops on the grass.

When Donul came in, he demanded of Art abruptly: "Where did you go?"

"Never you mind where he went," answered Old Hector. "He's here now, and if you're going, it's time you went, for the shadows will be deep in the wood soon enough."

"Do you want to come?" asked Donul, staring strongly at Art.

Art lifted his face sideways and looked at Donul as previously he had looked at Old Hector.

"What's wrong with you?" demanded Donul.

"Why should there be anything wrong with him? Don't talk nonsense." Then he turned to Art. "Would you like to go away with Donul?" he asked him.

There was a short silence, then in a low voice of his own, Art answered: "I would like to go away."

Old Hector nodded firmly. "Certainly!" he agreed. "Hurry up now, both of you. And remember, Donul, all that I told you. You have your excuses whoever comes on you?"

"I have," said Donul. "And they could never prove them against me."

"That's the best kind," said Old Hector.

The Clash was three miles away by the cart road, but by the path over the moor it was barely two. It would be the longest distance Art had ever been from home, and because he had heard grown men speak of it and its past in solemn voices, it had for him a fabulous sound like the name Bethlehem.

Donul took his hand, because he felt that anyone seeing them walking so would know they were innocent.

Thus they journeyed together, and as they went their hearts lightened.

When they were out of sight of everyone, Donul stopped and exhibited himself before Art. "Would you notice by looking at me," he asked, "that I had anything on me?"

"No-one would notice hardly anything," said Art.

"Just a little bulge here? But look, when I keep my elbow like that—what?"

"That covers it entirely," said Art.

"I thought so," said Donul. "Give me your hand."

In time they came to the edge of the moor. "We go down this burn till we get to the ruins," said Donul. "The banks hide us," he explained. Art followed him on the difficult path, and twice Donul looked back with a smile and said: "You're doing grand. You'll yet be a great hunter yourself."

Art was pleased and took a little run to Donul's side. "Isn't this a strange place?" he asked, his eyes wide and bright.

"Does it feel like the back of beyond?" inquired Donul with a grown man's slow smile.

"A little bit," answered Art. "Does it feel a little bit to you?"

"A little," said Donul. Then Art smiled, too, and the moment was shared between them.

Soon they left the watercourse, climbed up a steep rocky bank, and there before them lay the ruins with green pleasant land beyond. Donul's brows gathered as his eyes swept what they could see, then he walked over to the ruins and lay down behind a small cairn of stones. When he spoke to Art his voice was low-pitched.

"We'll lie here to make sure there's no-one about. You've always got to lie a good while, because there might be someone down in the wood. You've got to give him time to come up."

"Yes," whispered Art. "Is that the wood down there?"

"That's it. We'll set the snares down below along the edge. There's plenty of time. We came at a good speed."

"I didn't keep you back, did I?"

"Indeed you made it faster if anything," answered Donul, "because it was like walking to a place."

"I like being here," said Art. "What heaps and heaps of stones! Are they 'the ruins'?"

"They are," answered Donul. "Not that ruin, nor that one, but the one up there—do you see it?"

"I do."

"That's where our grandfather was born," said Donul.

"Was it?" said Art and his eyes opened in a long stare.

"And do you see that one—in behind?—no, the other one, farther in?"

"I see it."

"That was where Old Hector was born."

"Was it?" said Art.

"It was," said Donul. "All the folk were driven out of here by the factor on order of the laird. The factor wanted the ground for sheep. You can see it's fertile land, and the birch woods were good shelter for wintering. There was great sorrow and hardship amongst the folk at that time."

"Was there?" said Art.

"There was," said Donul. "It was a dirty trick. The land they were driven to was then nothing but wild coarse heather-moor."

Art stared at the ruins. "How," he asked, "were they driven?"

"Like cattle," answered Donul. "And the factor's men pulled down their homes before their eyes."

"Before their eyes?" said Art.

"They did," said Donul. "And the little house Old Hector now stays in at home, that was the house his father built, for Old Hector was then only a little boy."

"Was he?" asked Art. "Was he once just little, like me?"

"He was," said Donul. "And he remembers all these times."

"He never told me," said Art, staring at Old Hector's ruins.

"No, for he bears no bitterness. He's like that. He's the last living of the Clash folk, and I heard them say at the mill one night that he's wise because of all the great hardships he has come through in his time."

Art had such a lot of thoughts in him now that he forgot to speak. As he stared at the ruins he curled up a little against Donul, whose eyes ran along the wood to the not very distant horizon, beyond which the Ground Officer had his home.

Presently Art said: "I can see something growing in front of our grandfather's house."

"That's an old gooseberry bush. But it's gone wild and

the berries on it are little. They wouldn't be ripe yet, anyway."

"Was it planted there long ago by our grandfather?"

"It might have been," said Donul. "I don't know how old gooseberry bushes grow to. But if that wasn't the first one, it would be a seedling from the first one."

"Where would the seedling come from?"

"From the berry, of course. The berry would fall under the old tree and then grow up."

"Would it?" said Art.

Donul broke the silence. "I think," he said, "we could perhaps risk going now. There doesn't seem to be a soul about and the sheep are settled for the night." He hesitated. "If, however, we were by any chance run into by the Ground Officer we would need to have a good excuse handy."

Art turned his staring eyes to his brother's face.

"I was thinking," said Donul, looking away busily and lowering his brows, "that we would say we were going for old Betz because our mother is ill."

"But we saw old Betz going to our house already."

"Yes," said Donul, "but if we had left a minute before we wouldn't have seen her."

"Did Father go for her in the morning?"

"Never mind whether he went or not," said Donul, with some impatience. "That's not the point. In any case, if anyone asks us, you keep your mouth shut. I'll do the talking."

Art did not answer. All the questions that would have leapt into his mouth fell dead. He had quite forgotten his home, and his mother, and Betz, because Donul had been so friendly. Now Donul wouldn't look at him.

"Come on," said Donul in a commanding voice.

Art went with him quietly, and Donul whistled under his

breath in a large unconcerned way as if going to the wood was nothing. But when Art stole a glance at him, he saw Donul's eyes darting about their sockets like weasels. Then Art was comforted for he saw that Donul was being a leader.

Once in the trees, Donul stood and listened so hard that his mouth opened. He stood for such a long time that Art, who dared not move, began to feel movement in the wood itself. The twisted branches had all they could do to keep still. Smooth fronds of fern curved over outcrops of grey-faced rock. Bunches of grass hung like beards, grey at the chin. A brown bee landed on a blue flower which swung at first but then bent down and shivered. Suddenly, as by magic, there was a little bird, blue and yellow and green, upside down on the branch before Art's eyes. It was the most beautiful thing he had ever seen.

Donul slowly looked down at the entranced face and smiled. "Your mouth is open," he whispered.

The bird flew away and Art looked up at Donul.

"What——"

"Hush!" said Donul. Slowly his smile deepened and he shook his head. "There's no-one here," he whispered, and over Art went a flush of such strange sweet intimacy that he could hardly bear it.

Donul hunted around quietly and got a fair-sized stone. "Come on," said his lips, shaping the words without sound.

Art followed close at his heels, sometimes putting a hand up against Donul's back. Donul now began looking about the close-cropped grass like one who had lost something. He paused and pointed to little steps not much bigger than his open hand. "See!" he whispered and showed with his pointing finger how the steps came down past them and went away. "It's a good run," he said, "not too old."

Midway between two of the steps and a little to one side, he began to drive in the small stake of the snare with the stone. He started softly, gently, but the ground itself caught the thudding sounds, and they ran up through the wood, and Art heard them going all over the world. The ground was tough from the drought and gentle strokes would not put the stake in very far, so Donul hit it harder, and as the sound increased in volume, hit it harder still, and, grown desperate, still harder. Then he set up the thin stick that was the size of a pencil, and in the notch in the top of it stuck the end of the wire next the cord, beyond which he smoothed the snare into a round noose, so that it hung between two steps or hops at a distance from the ground which he measured with his closed fist. As he stepped away from it, he put his head to one side and examined it like an artist.

"What do I care?" he said recklessly, referring to the sounds he had made. But he looked everywhere with his mouth a little open.

By the time they had set the third snare, their confidence was almost complete, and now wandering about in and out the wood was like wandering in an enchanted country, with the senses quicker than birds' wings. Donul made Art put one closed fist on top of the other, and that was a fair height for the snare. Art had his fists ready in good time. But Donul always kept him back from touching the rabbits' path, until Art felt that the path, like everything else in the wood, was alive. "They'll know," said Donul, "if we touch it."

Art nodded.

When they had set their ninth and last snare, they went up into the wood and lay under a leafy tree. The trees were nearly all birch and not very tall. "We can do with a rest," said Donul, "and then home. First thing in the morning, we'll be back, and then we'll see—what we'll see!"

"Yes," said Art. "Do you think we'll get many?"

"If we get two itself I'll be satisfied," said Donul.

"We might get three," said Art, "or maybe seven, you never know?"

"It's not likely. But no-one knows."

"No-one," repeated Art, and the sound was like the name of an invisible one far away.

"Do you like being here?" asked Donul.

"Yes," breathed Art. "Isn't it great?"

"It is," said Donul. "There's nothing in the wide world I like better."

"No, nor me," said Art, his eyes very bright.

"Old Hector said it was the first thing to make a man of you. And if you go about it the right way, there's no need to be frightened, because——"

The wood shook under the roar of a voice. A dog barked furiously. A rabbit shot past. The dog hurtled beyond them. The rabbit hit the top of their ninth snare with its hind feet, rolled over, squealed as the dog leapt, doubled to the right, and the dog, missing the rabbit, did a rapid somersault.

"Here, you brute!" yelled the Ground Officer's voice on the edge of the wood above them. He whistled and he yelled, in black wrath.

Art looked at Donul's face and saw it white with fear, but as the face made an intense movement, commanding silence, Art saw the lips part and tighten over closed teeth and the brows gather over frightened but fighting eyes. He huddled into Donul.

A stone came crashing down past them. The dog came up, saw them, and barked. "Here, you brute!" yelled the voice. The dog's tail went down, and, forgetting the lads in the more immediate expectation of a thrashing, he continued up through the wood with lowered head.

A sharp yelp from the dog, and the sounds receded.

"Rounding up his sheep," whispered Donul, smiling. "Wait here." He slid down to the ninth snare, set it up again, and came back. "When a rabbit is going at a great speed it leaps higher."

Within half an hour they were through the ruins and safely in the ravine.

"That was a narrow squeak!" said Donul.

"Wasn't it!" declared Art, who at one time had felt a little sick.

Donul looked at him. "Feeling all right?"

"Yes," said Art, risking a small smile.

Donul laughed. "You stood the test!"

When he got back to Old Hector's, Art would have been very tired if he hadn't been so proud of his exploit. Donul was anxious to see his friend Hamish (he had a good tale for him now!) so Art had Old Hector to himself, as Agnes was out. And not only once but many times did Art astonish Old Hector before the eating was over.

But when it came to the Ground Officer and his dog, Old Hector could hardly believe it.

"It's as sure as death," said Art.

"Well, that's sure enough," nodded Old Hector, and then Art realized he had used an expression for which his mother would have reprimanded him, but Old Hector never noticed a thing like that.

The time came when the tale was told and the questions asked and answered, and in the silence of the lull the world grew still. Suddenly it came on Art that he was in a strange house. Everything was strange. He was away from home.

Old Hector began talking, but when he had finished, Art

struggled against what he had to say, so it was the bare truth itself that came: "I want to go home."

"Ay, poor fellow, you're tired. You've had a heavy day. I don't know what's keeping Agnes at all."

Art did not want Agnes. There was only one woman he wanted, because into her all tiredness melted. She was full of comfort and soft as sleep. He felt the little whine and the cry welling up in him, but did his best to keep them down.

Old Hector saw the lip tremble. "I think we'll go to our beds," he said companionably.

"Want to go home."

"Ay, I know, Art. But you cannot go home to-night for your mother's sake. To-morrow she will be well and then you can go home."

"Want—go home." The head hung down, the little whine welled up and the cry came through.

Old Hector took him between his knees, and Art did not struggle but wept where he stood. Old Hector patted him gently and made little sounds but said nothing.

Presently when the worst of it was over, Old Hector said he would light the candle and that would brighten things up. Swallowing and doing his best, Art looked at the slow-flapping flames on the fire and round at the grey light in the small window. That light was lonelier than a grey face wandering in the night, and Art grew afraid. It could come for him and take him away. If he was in his own home with his mother, it could not come, nothing could come. For he could not believe that his mother was ill or that anything was different at home. His home and his mother could never change.

"Now," said Old Hector, "give me your hand and we'll both go to bed."

Art did not give him his hand but Old Hector took it, and with the candle in his other hand, he led Art into the second room of the cottage which was his own bedroom, for Agnes slept in the box-bed in the kitchen.

The strangeness of being away from home mounted into terror as Art came into this room where he had never been before. His desire for his own home with his own mother in it became so overpowering that he lost his head. But Old Hector's patience was wider than Art's terror and gently enclosed it. Though Art did not listen to him, he spoke of the hunter and the hunter's courage and of how Art had now proved himself and would one day be a grown man, and as he spoke he took off Art's jersey and asked him a little private question, and Art faltered, "Yes."

Presently Old Hector tucked him into the shake-down bed and sat beside him with his back against the wall. Art's eyes were very wide open and glistening with thoughts and emotions, and though he was not now crying, anything might happen to him in a moment.

"What's wrong with Mother?" he asked in a queer voice.

"She's just not very well," said Old Hector. "So it's better to give her all the peace she can get."

"I know what it is," muttered Art.

"Do you?" said Old Hector calmly.

"It's—it's a baby," said Art, and he drew in a breath in two quivering parts.

"Who told you that?"

"I know," said Art, with a valiant swallow.

"Perhaps you do then. There's no saying but it might be."

"I—I don't want a baby," said Art.

"Don't you cry now, for indeed I don't blame you. If I were you I wouldn't want one myself. But when it comes, what can you do? You've got to make the best of it."

"Wh-where does it come from?"

"That's not an easy one to answer always."

"Did—did old Betz bring it?"

"I wouldn't put it past her," said Old Hector. "She's always meddling about."

"I don't c-care for her," said Art. "Do you?"

"I have had nothing to do with her for many's the long day, and I'm not likely to bother her now. So we're both in the same boat in that respect."

"Where—where does she find it?"

"Och, some say one place and some another. They'll tell you here that she finds it under a cabbage, but I have heard it said that she finds it under an old gooseberry bush. You can't always believe what you hear."

"An old gooseberry bush," repeated Art. His eyes grew wider than they had yet been, and he saw a vision, and the truth of the vision was beyond doubt. The crying fell from him.

"What now?" asked Old Hector.

"There's an old gooseberry bush," said Art on a hushed note, "in front of the ruin of my grandfather's house in the Clash."

"So there is," agreed Hector.

"That's the one," concluded Art, with profound conviction. "I know now."

"Glory be to Himself," said Old Hector. "With your mind at rest, maybe you'll now say your prayer."

Little Art got to his knees, and faced Old Hector, and over the young head the protective whiskers nodded time to the sing-song rhythm. After which Art said: "I'm not sleepy," but the words hadn't gone very far when he was after them.

Donul came in, and spoke to Hector for a while, and fell asleep beside Art. But Agnes did not come.

At the second hour of the morning, Old Hector heard

the outside door open quietly. Then there was a hand at his own door—and a whisper: "Are you sleeping?"

"How is she?" he asked.

"She's fine now. It's a boy. But she had a hard time," said Agnes, taking a step into the room.

"Well, I'm glad it's over for her. She's a fine woman."

"Yes," murmured Agnes, Old Hector's only unmarried child. "It's a heavy boy."

"I'm glad of that."

"Yes," murmured Agnes dreamily. "A lovely child."

"You go to your bed now," said Old Hector firmly to her.

There was a sigh, then Agnes went out and closed the door gently behind her.

5

The First and the Second Childhood

"Do you think I should waken him?" Donul asked Old Hector in the morning.

"I think you should."

"I could be much quicker by myself," suggested Donul.

"Perhaps," said Old Hector. "But you promised him, and a promise is a promise. Besides," he added, "you know that we're just helping him over a difficulty. We all have to get broken in to man's estate."

Donul looked down with a hesitant expression. "If you think so," he said.

"It might be as well," nodded Old Hector. "He'll have enough disappointments for one day."

So Donul tried to waken his little brother Art, but it was early in the morning yet, and Art did not want to open his eyes. In the end, however, and quite suddenly, his eyes opened wide and looked around the unfamiliar room. His peevish protests stopped on a catch of breath.

Agnes had the porridge ready, as well as a kind welcome, and when breakfast was over the lads set off.

"Isn't it a fine morning!" cried Donul to the wide world.

Soon the last trace of sleep was gone from them both, and a rare friendliness took its place. It was lovely to be walking across the moor in the early morning. The moor was fresh and clean, and cool, too, having come naked out of sleep. A cock grouse got up.

"Do you hear him, the old fool?" cried Donul.

"*Go-back!* yourself," cried Art, imitating the bird.

At that they laughed, their eyes bright and cunning with the morning's mirth. When Donul walked fast, Art made a little trot.

Oh, it was lovely walking over the moor, with long shafts of light, and the legs of their shadows opening and shutting like scissors. The sky was a young tender blue, and when they came to the highest point, Donul stopped. "The sea!" he said, and yonder it glittered under the sun. Listening, they heard the faint far calling of gulls. The world itself was far away and near at hand. Their hearts quickened and their bodies were filled with a bounding energy. The world was full of light.

Soon they were through the ravine and behind the cairn. While Donul studied the landscape carefully, Art stole a look up at the old gooseberry bush. A queer feeling came over him and he brought his eyes away carefully.

"Come on," said Donul, and off they set.

They could not find the first snare, and then there it was, as they had left it. Donul had to hit the head of the stake first to one side and then to the other before he could get it out.

The second snare was vacant also. "Dash it!" muttered Donul. "I made sure there would be something in that one."

The third, the fourth. "Nothing!" He had no hope now. Finished. "Might as well not visit the rest," he said, the beauty of the morning drowned in primeval spite. And then in the fifth snare, sudden as magic, there was a living rabbit.

Art stopped, and his breath also. When Donul leapt, the

rabbit leapt against the noose. The rabbit stopped struggling as Donul caught it, but when he tried to loosen the noose off its neck, it began to struggle and squeal. Donul couldn't get a grip of the noose, it was sunk so deep in the fur. "Shut up!" he said angrily to the rabbit. But the squealing was too much for him, and lifting the rabbit by the hind legs, he hit it smartly behind the ears with the edge of his open hand. After two or three sharp blows, the rabbit dangled loosely. Then Donul took the noose off, glancing over his shoulders as he did so. His face was dark with excitement, his eyes glittered, his hands shook a little. Art saw this exultation of the hunter and was deeply moved by it. The fear of that which might pounce upon them was there too. "Feel that," said Donul in harsh triumph. Art tried to feel the width of the fleshy back, and though it did not convey much to him he nodded in great astonishment.

There was a rabbit in the next snare. Donul danced in. There was a rabbit in the seventh snare, stretched dead from a headlong impact. Donul laughed noiselessly at Art and over his shoulders at the wood. Fortunately the last two snares were empty or their excitement would have weighed them down.

Once in the ravine, Donul took off his jacket and stuck his sweating head in a pool. Art did the same. They laughed at the faces they made through the trickling water. They ran about, shaking their heads. They sat down, and Donul felt deeply moved toward his little brother Art, and Art loved Donul.

"I'm glad we have one for Old Hector," said Donul. "And then two for home. Morag will make a grand stew for Mother. And Mother needs it. Isn't it fine?"

"It is," said Art. "It's the finest thing in the wide world."

"It just couldn't be better," said Donul. "But mind,

whatever you do, don't tell them we were here, or Father would take our heads off."

"I know why he's against poaching," said Art.

"He's frightened we'll get into trouble, and the Ground Officer would make a case of it before the Court."

"And then we'd be on the road," said Art, "the whole of us."

"And the baby, too," said Donul, trying not to look unusual. "And it can't walk yet."

If Donul did not look at Art, Art did not look at Donul. But the strength of the moment was in Art, and if his smile was a trifle awry, still his manner was fairly large. "What kind is it?" he asked.

"It's a he one," answered Donul, and his grin broke into a rough laugh.

"Ho! ho! ho!" laughed Art also, forcing the sounds to their rough work.

"Ay," repeated Donul, "it's a he one."

"I don't care," said Art, "supposing it was a she one."

Donul leaned back with the laughter that came on him, and hit the ground with his heels. Art repeated his witticism twice, it was so good, his mirth rising higher each time until it shrilled, and all his body was an eel for energy.

"Oh! oh!" groaned Donul, "aren't we having fun out of it!"

"We are," cried Art. "And I could make more fun any time."

"Don't," pleaded Donul, "or goodness knows who'll be hearing us."

In the end Art's excitement grew to such a pitch that Donul had to smother him in the heather.

When they were wiping their eyes, Donul said: "Oh dear, my belly is sore, laughing."

"Did I make it sore?" asked Art.

"You did," said Donul.

"Mine is sore, too," said Art, "there."

When they had agreed on the location of the pain, they resumed their journey.

Donul carried the rabbits between the lining and the cloth of an old jacket that was a little too big for him, being an heirloom from his elder brother, Duncan. He now stood before Art for inspection, and Art felt important as he suggested the shifting of the bulges a little this way or that. At last, in agreed formation, they took the moor.

When they came to the highest point, there was no-one to be seen but the sea, and the glitter had left it and it was at once calm and playful.

"I would like to go to the sea," said Art.

"I'll take you some time," promised Donul.

"Couldn't we go to-day?" asked Art.

"We'll see," said Donul.

"I'd like to go to-day," said Art, with a little trot, for he did not want to go home.

"Keep in your place," commanded Donul. "We must face up to things like men."

Not a soul did they meet, for it was still early, until they saw Old Hector himself by the corner of the barn. There he was, standing quietly, alone. As Art drew near, he saw the smiling lines run into the whiskers, and then Old Hector's arms came out a little from his sides, like two wings. Art ran forward, trying to keep his eager voice low: "We got three!"

"Never!" said Old Hector. "Not three?"

"Yes," said Art. "And all their backs are broad."

"God bless us," said Old Hector, glancing at Donul's face to see what had happened. Then he took Art's hand and they went into the barn.

. . . . .

A little later, Art and Donul prepared to return home.

"Leave the boy alone," said Old Hector firmly to Agnes. "Men don't like to be fussed over."

"It's the first I have heard of it," said Agnes.

"Well, you're hearing it now," said Old Hector. "So-long."

"So-long," answered Art and Donul, and they set off.

As they went on their way, their minds were so full of the thought of returning home that they did not speak. When at last Art saw his home, it came pressing against him and slowed up his steps.

Donul looked down at him. "Come on," he said with a jaunty air.

Art hung back a little, but he went, too. At the door he could hardly enter. "You go in," whispered Donul, "and I'll go round to the barn with this." Art said nothing, but when Donul had turned away, Art ran after him.

"Go on in," said Donul firmly. "And tell Morag I want to see her."

Just then, Neonain, who was two years older than Art, came to the door and saw them. "Here's Donul and Art," she cried in a loud voice.

Donul glanced at Art fiercely and Art turned towards the door. Neonain backed away and cried again that Art was here.

"Will you shut up?" said Morag to her in a hissing voice. Morag's face was flushed with the housework and her responsibilities. Over in the off corner where it was warm, Janet stood upright, continuing to rock the cradle gently with her foot as she gazed at Art's face in the faint gloom behind the door. The two young girls were excited over the return of Art and regarded him in a concentrated way.

"Here's Art," said Morag. "Come in! What are you standing there for?"

"Is that Art?" asked his mother's quiet voice from the box-bed.

"Come in," repeated Morag, catching him by the shoulder and pulling him forward.

His mother had dark eyes and black hair and a smooth face, which was paler than he had ever seen it. She regarded him with a curious distant smile. "And how did you like staying the night at Old Hector's?" she asked.

Art's head drooped and his eyes glanced out of their corners at this place which was no more as it had been and from which he felt himself an outcast.

"What are you gaping at?" said Morag to her young sisters. "Get outside and play. You're only in my way."

Janet and Neonain went slowly out.

"Were they kind to you?" asked his mother.

Art could neither move nor answer.

"Come and see your baby brother," Morag invited him. "But don't make a noise, for he's sleeping." She pushed him towards the cradle, then she bent down and drew the clothes back from the tiny chin. "Isn't that a nice baby brother to have?"

Art did not like the look of what he saw, and all at once experienced such an extreme loneliness that he wanted to cry. Before the crying could overcome him, he turned for the door, hearing his mother's voice saying: "Never mind him. He'll get over it."

At that a hot flame of anger in him did not know whether to switch the tears on or off, but the feeling of being a hunter who had slept away from home came to his aid. He drifted round the corner of the house to find Janet and Neonain standing together, looking at him. Janet had something in her arms, over which her shoulders were hunched. Art's eyes regarded them with a hostile stare. The situation being clear to all, no-one spoke. Janet turned her back on Art and deposited what she had in her arms on a little bed of grass and then moved away to fetch two pieces of wood with which to box it in.

Art drew near and regarded what lay on the grass. It was a narrow flat stick, all wrapped in brown cloth except for three inches at the top, which bore two black spots for eyes, a down stroke for a nose, and a cross stroke for a mouth. Art put his foot under it and kicked it over the green.

Janet charged him like a fury, swinging a hand that hit him such a slap that he sat down heavily. Three full seconds passed before the yell came.

Never had he yelled more mightily, and, scrambling to his feet and thus getting his full wind, he even increased the volume as with blind instinct he turned for protection and comfort to the door of his home.

But his father, coming round the lower gable-end, intercepted him and told him to stop his yelling this minute. Art danced with rage and fear. "If you don't stop it," said his father angrily, "I'll give you a good skelping."

"No," screamed Art, all sense drowned in this vision of terrifying indignity.

"Will you stop it?" demanded his father.

"No! . . . Y-y-yes!"

"That's better," said his father, withdrawing his hands from a certain place. "Now run away and play."

Art stumbled brokenly round the corner of the house, to find his two sisters grouped again in conspiracy. Janet regarded him with hostile satisfaction, as she nursed her wounded treasure. The sight was too much for Art and bellowing a warrior's rage, he went straight to the attack.

Janet, holding her ground, hitched away her treasure,

and dealt Art at the same time a stinging buffet in the region of the left ear. If a final incentive was needed, this provided it. Art became the terrifying male rampant, screaming his war cry, and leapt to grip and tear asunder and destroy the treasure. Janet gave ground. Neonain yelled back at him, but gave ground. They both gave ground. Before the awful spectacle of the berserk male, they broke and ran.

Art pursued them for a little way and then returned to the victorious field. As they screamed indignities at him, he strutted over the green. He saw the little bed of grass and scattered it in a series of running kicks.

"I'll tell Mother on you!" cried Janet, making in a wide arc for the door.

"Tell away!" chanted Art. "Tell pie! tell pie! sitting on a tree!"

"I'll tell what you did!"

"Only an old bit of stick!" yelled Art with superb sarcasm.

But as his sisters, outflanking him, approached the door, he decided to withdraw. At the same time a great hunger came upon him to be once more with Donul, to be with Donul and to go away and never more come back home.

But Donul was not in the barn. "Donul!" he called in the dim silence as though his brother might be hiding. Nothing moved. Everything was listening. "Donul!" Art went out and round to his own hiding place at the back of the barn. Donul was not there. Donul was nowhere. The world was empty and he was alone.

It was round about the midday meal when Morag put her head in the low door of the little barn and asked Donul, who was skinning the second rabbit, if he had seen Art anywhere.

Donul paused to look at her. "No," he answered.

"We haven't seen him since he came back with you in the morning."

"Haven't you?" said Donul. He pulled the skin over the shoulders. "I shouldn't worry," he suggested calmly. "He'll have gone to Old Hector's."

"I thought you went there?"

"No. I just promised to let Hamish know what luck we had."

"Then it'll be all right, you think?" asked Morag, who had many worries on her head at the moment.

"Of course," said Donul dryly. "What do you think was going to happen to him?" And he went on with his work.

But immediately Morag had gone, he stopped and thought. Then he attended to the rabbit again, using the half blade of his knife delicately, because it is a ticklish business pulling the forelegs through the reversed skin when a boy wants the skin whole. He used much more force than usual, and when the job was over he stood listening. The bunch of old hay with which he had wiped his hands he threw impetuously against the floor and went to the door. There was no-one about. With the air of going nowhere in particular, he started for Old Hector's.

But no, Old Hector had not seen Art.

"It's Morag, she's sort of upset with one thing or another," explained Donul.

"Was there a bit of a shindy when he got home?" asked Old Hector.

"There was," said Donul. "I heard enough yelling at least." He looked away with a strained smile.

"You'll find he's not far off," said Old Hector at last, nodding to his own thought. "He's probably gone out a bit and lain down behind a hillock. He'll be wanting himself to be missed."

Donul glanced at Old Hector with a real smile. "That will be it!" he declared, nearly laughing.

"You go back," said Old Hector, "and have a hunt round on your own."

"I'll do that," nodded Donul and he hurried off.

But though he made a wide circle round the house, looking behind every hillock and into each likely hole, he found no trace of Art. At last he could not ignore Morag's summons to dinner, particularly as the cry was taken up by Janet and Neonain, and he went towards the house, wiping his hands with a bunch of grass as though he had only just completed the skinning.

"Isn't he a young rascal!" said Mother, when Father had blessed the food.

"Maybe he'll not want to come home from Old Hector's now," said Janet hopefully.

"You be quiet," said Morag.

"It wasn't me," said Janet, "it was him."

"You helped," said Morag.

"I did not! I did not! He—he hit my dolly!"

"Oh be quiet!" said Father. "Cannot we have a little peace in this house when we're eating itself?"

"We're doing fine," said Mother, calmly and pleasantly. "And this is a good stew, Morag. It's a tasty bite."

"I'm glad you like it, Mother," said Morag, her lovely brown eyes glancing with pleasure.

When the meal was over, the men went out. As his father was lighting his pipe at the end of the house, Donul went up to him and said awkwardly: "I don't know where Art can be. He's not at Old Hector's."

His father looked at him. "Not at Old Hector's?"

"No. He's not at Hamish's either. I searched everywhere about."

His father kept looking at him. "Where do you think he's gone?"

"I don't know," answered Donul.

"God bless me," said his father, "is this the next of it!" His voice was anxious and the eyebrows gathered over the eyes in a way Donul's own did at times. "Have you no idea at all?"

"Well," said Donul, "the only thing I can think of is that he has gone to the sea. He asked me to-day if I would take him to the sea. I said I would some time. He said he wanted to go to-day."

"Did he?"

"He did."

His father looked over his shoulders as Donul had looked at the wood. "Let us go quietly," he said.

Donul felt friendly to his father at that moment. Though the family was not very big, the ground was poor and not a great deal of it. The long spring they had come through was always the worst time. Soon his father and his eldest brother Duncan would be leaving for the summer herring fishing as "hired men," and they would bring back a few pounds. Then if the harvest was reasonably good, they would be snug enough after that. But these were anxious days for a father who hadn't many shillings to lay his hands on. Porridge and milk is a good food, and folk should be grateful to have it twice a day, but a stew is a delicacy that inspires men with strength.

They walked away together. They never spoke, and presently as they came over a rise they saw down to their right the black lochan or tarn called Shivering Eye. As his father's footsteps slanted that way, Donul's heart moved up a little in his breast.

"He would never go there," he said, not wanting to go himself. "It's a place I made him frightened of."

"That's good," said his father, in a companionable voice, but holding to his course.

The water looked blue-black. It was difficult to tell the exact depth of the lochan because even a delicate hand could not be sure of the moment when a long stick first touched the invisible bottom. A finger-tip could sink the stick a couple of feet in ooze. With a quick glance round the edge, Donul, however, could see that the water had not recently been disturbed. Then his father stood still as a heron, staring at the ground. The heart moved up in Donul as he saw, under his father's eyes, imprints in the black peat of two small bare feet.

"I think they're old," said his father.

"Yes," said Donul. "There's an oily scum on that one. They're at least yesterday's."

"I think so," said his father.

"I'm sure," said Donul, his heart beating thickly.

A breath of wind made the Eye shiver.

"Let's cut down this way to the sea," suggested his father, "and then we can go along the shore and ask at the cottages."

Though his father's eyes were keen and the gathering of the eyebrows made them appear far-sighted, his manner was calm and sensible. This helped Donul a lot. Down by the broken sea rocks, his father paused and shouted, "Art!" They listened to the silence above the sound of the sea. "No, he's not there," said his father.

When Donul had shouted "Art!" once, he found it easier to shout the next time.

There were three cottages standing back a little from the simple slipway where a few boats were hauled clear of the tide. Of a woman at the first door, the father asked: "You didn't happen to see little Art about?"

"No," she answered slowly. "Has he gone missing on you?"

"Well, you know what little boys are. If you see him, will you send him home at once?"

"Has he been long gone?"

"No, no, just an hour or two."

By the time the woman had got answers to more questions, she looked uneasy. When they left her, Donul said: "I'll go and get hold of Hamish. He's probably at Old Hector's by this time, anyway."

"Do you that," said his father.

After walking a few paces, Donul began to trot, and then, out of sight of his father and the cottages, ran like a hare. He was so breathless when he met Old Hector that for a moment or two he could not speak.

"No," Old Hector answered the look on his face, "Art hasn't been here yet."

"I—I thought he might," gulped Donul, ashamed to be gulping so much. He tried to smile. "I'll—get Hamish."

"Where have you been?"

"Father and I—went down to rocks—then along to the slipway. No sign of him."

Old Hector stood still in thought.

"I'll get Hamish," said Donul, "and we'll go off the way of the River. He often asked about the Hazel Pool."

Old Hector, looking at Donul without seeing him very clearly, nodded absently. Donul ran off. Agnes came out at the door and anxiously asked her father for confirmation of what she had clearly overheard. He paid no attention to her, and she retreated hurriedly, saying: "I'll get on my things." Anxious faces would come to many cottage doors at word of the lost child.

. . . . .

Old Hector turned towards the moor and the track that led to the Clash, going slowly at first, but presently with more decision. And this was curious even to himself, because the farther he went, the more time he had to think, and the more he thought the more foolish seemed his vision of Art's body lying curled up in sleep under the old gooseberry bush that stood in front of the ruins of his grandfather's house.

There was just no sense in it, however he looked at it. First of all, it was very unlikely that Art would think of going back alone into the region inhabited by the Ground Officer. That unseen figure of wrath hurtling the stone through the wood—many a queer nightmare would come to Art from that yet. And the old gooseberry bush—what could Art expect to find there? And even if he found it, he wouldn't want it. It was just the one place, surely, that a timid frightened child would wish to avoid, taking all that had happened into account? Surely, surely, thought Old Hector to himself, proceeding with more decision than ever.

Then a strange sadness descended upon him with a weary smile. It was no later than last night that he had heard the visiting woman, the black one, saying to his daughter-in-law and to Agnes as they sat round the fire, shortly after the two boys had left for the Clash: "Well, what do you expect? He's back with the boys of his youth. Your father, my dear, is just like any old man of his years —he's in his second childhood."

And as he walked along, Old Hector admitted to himself that what she had said was true. He was in his second childhood. A slight bitterness, an arid feeling, swept his mind in a dry wind, and he realized that in the woman's heartiness there might be knowledge but not too much understanding. For the greatest difference between first childhood and second childhood was not a matter of experience, of knowledge; not a mental difference so much as a difference of sheer time. To a child, "next week", "next Saturday", were doors opening to adventure, to growth. The same terms in second childhood meant a week less of the few that were left, and they would, in the silent moment, strike the mind with a faint shrivelling panic.

And when they thought he understood children and was kind to them because he was in his second childhood, that, too, was not the whole truth. In the prime of his manhood, children to him were all pretty much alike beneath their differences. Now he saw that they were more distinct, one from another, than grown men. Some of them wearied him very quickly, though he might not show this. And if he tried to be patient, it was not only because it was expected of him, but also somehow because he expected it of himself.

Yet the wonderful thing was the resemblance between the two states. When a young boy was alone with you, talking quietly and asking questions, he rarely grew obstreperous, as he so often did before an audience. And then suddenly, all in a bright moment, you would see the open wonder of his mind. It was there before you, as a bird or a rabbit might be. And for a time the companionship would be pleasant and take on little extravagant airs and sensible follies. That early rapt wonder, which had been lost for so many years, opened its own eyes in you once more and beheld the world. But now it was not the same wonder, not quite, for it had grown selfless and was altogether clear vision. It asked for nothing. This vision of the circle completing itself was all the mind desired, so marvellous it was, and supporting the vision came a feeling of such well-being that panic or time could no more intrude.

Little Art had brought some pleasant moments to Old Hector, and, whatever the reason, he would rather have to listen to his questions than to those of any of his own grand-children, and he had more than a few.

Yet all that being so, why he should now feel that little Art had gone to the old gooseberry bush, either to see what he could find or to crawl under it, was beyond him. As it was beyond sense. So, if anything, he increased his pace, and he could still walk with some of the buoyancy that had always been in his balance, though he was much nearer eighty than seventy.

He left the ravine higher up than the boys had done and, coming down the hill-slope, saw the ruins spread below him. Involuntarily in the quiet afternoon he stood and looked upon them in their quiet still desolation. Perhaps it was because he had been driven out of here with his folk, at about Art's age, that the mind of Art in its fears and quick imaginings could touch him so naturally now. He remembered—ah, how he remembered! He remembered so vividly that it seemed to him his young body flashed by in a half light round the walls and corners of a legendary place.

Here was the green mound, the hill of the fairies. One night his elder brother (last seen on the Gold Coast fifty years ago) and another grown lad had come down in the deep gloaming and said in quiet voices that they had heard music inside the mound. Hector had stood listening with the rest. He would never forget that moment of extreme, half-terrifying, half-inviting enchantment. But no-one had ventured to go up.

Many years had passed since he had been here last, and then, in the fullness of his manhood, the place had seemed smaller than his childhood's memory of it, smaller and less important, though he had known again the ancient anger at the loss of the good land. But now the place did not seem small and unimportant. It was as big as it had ever been, but because of the young life that had once run there, and still ran inside his own mind, it appeared to him more desolate than at any time before. Force, brute force and greed, had passed this way and raped the living houses, and the grey lichen began to creep, and was still creeping, over their bare bones. Outspread they lay under the sky, and, entering into communion with them, he forgot for a time why he had come back.

As he awoke and remembered, a grey smile went over his face, for he had come to find youth—on the hearthstones that had lain cold for nearly three generations.

It was hardly a surprise to him when he found no trace of Art under the old gooseberry bush, though a touch of spite did dry and embitter his mouth. There could be no doubt now about his being in his second childhood. None. He stood staring over the tumbled stones, like the trunk of an old tree whose branches had gone.

"Well, well," said his voice to itself at last, and his head turned, and his eyes looked about them. Yes, this was the home of little Art's grandfather, who was a boy like himself when they played together around the walls, in the fields, and down in the birch wood. Beyond their fathers were their grandfathers, and he could remember them clearly, and that was going back a long time.

This long memory touched Old Hector and his eyes grew warm, measuring the walls of the house. He turned his back on the gooseberry bush and approached the walls, which were still some three to four feet high, for they had been so thick in their time that a man could stroll round the top of them by the edge of the thatch. Often indeed a small beast had grazed up there.

Watching his feet as they stepped over the pile of tumbled stones in the narrow doorway, he came into what had been the living-room. His head had scarcely started to lift when it stopped and he stood very still.

Rushes, broad-leaved docks, weeds of many kinds, including some with flowers that grew out of the brown clay in the heart of the wall and nodded in the moving air. All was tumbled confusion save in the centre of the room where the fire had been. There it was flat and covered with a pale, almost fawn-coloured grass that grew to the height of a foot or so. Curled up on this bed, sheltered from the wind, with the warm sun falling on it, was the body of little Art.

"God between us and all harm," muttered Old Hector's voice under its breath. Had he come upon a fearful and fabulous beast, sunning itself in an unexpected place, his expression could not have been more arrested. Then he went forward, and stooped, and studied the face that looked tender and fragile as a wild bird's egg. Passing in and out between the parted lips went the breath of life. He watched its movement for a time and then straightened himself. It was God that was good, too!

His old legs feeling suddenly weak, he sat down beside Art, and his expression was gay and full of wonder, and God was lost in it.

There was no hurry now, for the little fellow was tired with the travelling that had been on him, not to mention his other worries. As he rested in the afternoon sun, Old Hector's thought went so deep that his eyes closed and he had a small snooze.

He felt the better of it, and, when he wakened Art, was able in a pleasant voice to overcome the boy's first fears. Nor did he put questions to him, but took all that had happened as natural.

Art, however, was quiet, and spoke little, and that in a low voice. Once or twice Old Hector glanced at him, for he seemed to have changed, and it's only into a changeling that a child can change. He let Old Hector carry him on his back without protest.

"Look you," said Old Hector, trying to interest him, "do you know what place that is?"

"No," answered Art.

"It's the Hill of the Fairies."

Art stared at it, and slowly rubbed his cheek where the brush-past of Old Hector's whiskers had tickled it.

"There's no need to be frightened of the little folk," said Old Hector. "For the little folk are the good folk, they are the men of peace. They were always fond of music and dancing. I could tell you many a wonderful story about them."

Art kept looking back at the mound, the cold pallor on his face and his eyes alien.

"Of course," said Old Hector with sly humour, for he was anxious to get mortal warmth back into the child, "sometimes they would be playing pranks on people and would even take a little child away when they got the chance. But you have no doubt heard as much?"

"Yes," said Art in a quiet voice, and added after a moment: "did they hurt the child?"

"No, oh no," answered Old Hector. Then he told Art a story of how a child was taken away and a changeling left in its place, and Art listened to it from a little distance.

Soon Old Hector grew tired with the weight of Art, and put him down, and when they had gone some way they rested. They were now both in the quietened mood, when the last questions may come out and look about.

It was in this mood that Old Hector asked Art in a calm low voice: "Why did you go away to the gooseberry bush?"

And Art answered, "I don't know," and hung his head.

"What put you into the house of your grandfather to sleep there?" asked Old Hector.

"I don't know," Art answered again.

Old Hector looked away. "I couldn't put words to it either," he said at last thoughtfully, "yet we both know or we wouldn't be here."

Art stole a look at him. Old Hector turned and the smile came and ran on each side into his whiskers. "Now," he said, "give me your hand and we'll go back to our own mortal folk. There's warmth there and you'll be laughing soon."

Art gave him his hand and they set off over the moor.

6

The New Jersey, the Fluke, and the Whispering Reeds

Little Art was in a very complicated condition and it was Saturday morning. Saturday was different from all other days of the week because it did not belong to the school. When you awoke in the morning—suddenly, like a bluetit on a hazel branch, it was Saturday.

Since the arrival of Henry James (for so he would write his name in English one day at the school), Art had ceased to be the baby of the family. War there was for a time, but out of it Art had gathered some important spoil. For one thing, as Morag had put it, "You are no longer the baby now, you are grown up;" whereupon he had stamped the earth in his rage, and attacked her, even as the words fed him honey. Being a rampageous warrior on the outskirts had its points, the principal one being an enlarged freedom and mastery of action. He could also be derisive, like Donul, and twist his mouth. For example, when Janet was nursing Henry James outside—an occupation which to Art's astonishment she seemed to enjoy—and Henry, from pleasant cooing and gurgling turned, for private reasons of his own, to high-pitched notes of clamour and alarm, then Janet would become deeply concerned and croon over him and murmur: "Hush! my little Hen."

"My little hen!" Art would echo her. "My little hen!

Ho! ho! ho!" and double up in his harsh mirth and twist his mouth to one side.

On such occasions Janet exhibited remarkable powers of forbearance. Even when Art began to throw small peat-clods not directly at them but still pretty near them, all Janet would say was "Stop it!" and stare at him with a face as still as stone.

But this Saturday morning, life was complicated far beyond the usual. Henry James, who had been ailing for a few days, was definitely peevish and sick. Art had seen him being sick, and had not liked it. Particularly he had not liked his mother's concern, her deep concentration upon the little pale face in the cradle. "He's not like himself. I don't know what's come over him," she had said on a queer low note.

All the same, if his mother was as afraid as all that, why had she turned on him when he had got up and thrown the old ragged jersey at him and told him to wear it, instead of the new one of which he was inwardly so proud? It was funny that a woman could find time to think of an annoying thing like that if she was really upset. Very funny. He refused to put on the old jersey.

"Very well," said his mother. "Go without."

As if he could go outside without his jersey! It was past speaking about. It could make a fellow so angry that he wanted to weep. So Art slapped his porridge rather than ate it, and drops of milk scattered in a small shower from his blue bowl and fell on the table.

"You're running on it, my lad!" threatened his mother.

"Am not," said Art, holding himself with difficulty. Then he happened to glimpse Janet's silent censorious face. It was too much. He missed his mouth with the overladen spoon, which thereupon discharged its contents upon his undervest. His mother dried him, and shook him, and gave him one slap, and threatened to thrash him soundly then and there.

"Have you no thought of your little brother?" she asked. "Haven't you done enough already, without adding to his illness?"

At these words, Art lost control of himself. He denied them vehemently, he danced, he yelled, he hit blindly at his mother, in a storm of passion far wilder than any he had ever yet indulged. She ran him out of the house, but now he would not leave go of her, tried to hang on, until she lost her temper, and, turning him over, gave him three good spanks.

"There!" she said. "And if I hear any more noise from you, you'll catch it much harder." She closed the door behind her. He attacked the door, pounding it with his fists and bare feet, but did not open it. All at once he saw Neonain standing quietly looking at him. She had observed the dreadful indignity of the spanking. Mountain torrents! As he approached, she backed away, saying: "I know where Morag's gone." Her air was not mocking, it was mysterious.

"You do not!" he cried, although in point of fact he had not observed Morag's absence.

"I do," answered Neonain. "She has gone for old Betz."

That stopped him. That brought the world to a standstill. "She has not," he said from habit, but there was no conviction in his voice. His eyes caught his undervest and he felt naked. Neonain looked at his undervest in the calm way a girl can. The world slid away from Art leaving him naked at its dead centre.

For this business of the jersey was nearly the biggest complication of the lot. No later than last Saturday afternoon, Duncan had returned from his job on the new road over at Clachdrum, not only with good money in his pocket but with a present for his mother and the jersey for Art. There had been no present for anyone else. Nothing for Janet or Neonain. Even Henry James had been ignored.

It was a triumph for Art and he could afford to laugh at jealous eyes. Even if it was a surprise, still one had only to think of it for a moment to see the reason, namely that Duncan liked Art best. And what was there to wonder at in that? thought Art.

And the jersey itself—oh, it was a beauty! None of your home-made, loosely knitted, crotal-brown things, that bunched and bagged, but a real fisherman's jersey, dark blue, firm, and fitting so lithely that you needed someone to skin it over your head (just as your father did) when you wanted it off. Even Donul was not old enough to have one like it yet.

At school it had been the envy of eyes, no matter what the words spoken. Twice on the first day it had been pulled from behind, and Art, turning smartly, had hit the offenders over the head and pursued them. Even Mary Ann had stopped dead still and looked at it, as Neonain had looked at his undervest, only far more so. "What are you gaping at?" he had asked her. She did not move, nor did her expression change, but her eyes—only her eyes—lifted from his jersey to his face and looked at that. Whereupon Art had charged away, making loud derisive noises.

Now on this Saturday morning, Art wanted to have his jersey on to show it to Old Hector. He knew that Old Hector would admire it properly. Not, of course, that that mattered very much, but the great thing about Old Hector was that you could talk to him frankly, without feeling that he would laugh at you if you asked anything out of the way, for indeed it was often very difficult to tell beforehand what was "out of the way". With some people you could hardly open your mouth but you were "out of the way". In truth you had to be very sure of your man before you could ask even such a simple question as: "How does a bee make honey?" But with Old Hector it was different. You could ask him anything. And if he didn't know the answer he would scratch his whisker, and while he was scratching his whisker, you might think of an answer yourself, and then Old Hector would say that perhaps you were right, and at that you would not think less of Old Hector but more, and maybe tell him something else he didn't know.

Furthermore, his father and Donul had gone to sea very early this morning in the small boat to try to catch some fish. And it had been allowed last night that if Old Hector was going down to the slipway to meet the boats coming in—which it was certain he would do—then Art could go with him, but not otherwise. And now, because of not being able to get his new jersey, Art would be late, and there was nothing he more passionately desired than to walk down with Old Hector and see the boats coming in.

There was one last and most terrible complication, but it lay so deep that Art would not let himself think about it. And no wonder, for it plumbed the uttermost abyss of crime, as may presently be seen. The marvel is that he could still stand on his own feet, though the whole world was falling away from him.

Neonain lifted her eyes from his undervest to his face, and the deeps of womanly pity, that forever save the world when appalling crime has shattered it, gave a small stir within themselves. Perhaps, too, Neonain had been having a thin time of it for many weeks, because of the ruthless way in which Janet had arranged exclusive dealings in Henry James. However that may be, she now asked quietly: "Why haven't you on your jersey?"

It was a staggering question and brought the murderer

up into Art's eyes. But Neonain was not dismayed. With a simple yet profound cunning, she nodded. "I'll get it for you."

Art did not speak. He stood gaping after her as she drifted innocently into the house. When he saw her emerging with the blue jersey, he still stood. But she ran swiftly past him on her toes round the gable-end. And if she did, he wasn't long catching her up.

"They never saw me!" she whispered gleefully. She told him about how she managed it, even while she was pulling the narrow neck down over his ears. But though his ears were hurt and his breath choked, he merely exhibited a slight impatience. And even when it was on, she gave it a pull here and a final tug there, then looked him over and said: "Now you're fine."

"I won't forget you for this," he observed gruffly, and took to his heels, leaving her standing there.

But he was late. Old Hector had gone a good while ago, Agnes told him, eyeing his jersey. Yet before even her comment could issue forth he was off again.

Too late! too late! Here was Old Hector coming up the path. Art stopped, wriggling slowly upon himself.

"Well, well, so here you are at last!" cried Old Hector. "What came over you this morning?"

"I was kept late," replied Art moodily.

"Hots! tots! that was too bad. And what's this I see? Eh?" Old Hector laid down the string of fish the better to regard the new jersey. "Man, that's a fine one. That's a real fisherman's one." After wiping his fingers on his trousers, he felt the texture. "And who gave you this?"

"Duncan," replied Art, all at once wanting to cry.

"That was kind of him. That was a real good present to get. Indeed it was. You must be a favourite of his surely."

"I am," said Art, but uncertainly. His eyes filled. "Wanted—to see the boats—coming in," he explained.

"Certainly," agreed Old Hector. "It's natural you should. Certainly. I'll take out my pipe and have a smoke, and a sit-down for a minute, too. I'm a bit tired. You're not in a great hurry yourself, are you?"

"No," muttered Art.

"That's fine. Yonder's your father and Donul going home by the brae-face. You might still catch them."

"Don't want to catch them."

"Why would you?" agreed Old Hector, nodding. By the time he had his pipe going, Art had got the last gulp down.

"So you've got a brave new jersey. Aren't you the lucky fellow now?" And Old Hector smiled through the thick smoke.

"I am," murmured Art, smiling a little, too, but not yet at Old Hector.

"It will be a grand one for the sea, that. Some fine afternoon, when you get your long holidays, you and I will have a row by ourselves in—in the little Norwegian pram."

"Will we?" asked Art, looking into Old Hector's eyes.

"We will that, and more," said Old Hector, nodding lightly.

"I'd like that," said Art, "better than—than anything."

"And we'll fish, too, for flukes. You don't need to go far out for flukes. You get them on the sandy bottom of the bay. You can see them coming to the bait."

"Can you?" breathed Art.

"You can. And then they take the bait and you haul them up."

"Just haul them up and into the boat?"

"Just that same," nodded Old Hector.

"I'd haul them," said Art, making motions with his hands, "very quickly."

"That's the best way," agreed Old Hector.

"If you didn't haul them quickly, would they get off?"

"They would, often. A good fisherman is always quick."

"Would this be quick enough?"

After Old Hector had studied Art's rapid hauling, he nodded. "That would be ample. There would be no need to be quicker than that."

Art straightened himself, and his shining eyes, glancing everywhere, landed on the fish. "You have some flukes here!" he cried.

"Two or three. And fine ones they are."

"Look!" cried Art. "Look at that one! Look at his red spots!"

"Yes, isn't he a beauty?"

Art stared at the vivid red spots on the glistening brown back. They looked for all the world as if they had been stuck on. He glanced up into Old Hector's face, a wary smile in the centre of his earnestness, and asked: "Will they come off?"

"I don't think so," replied Old Hector reasonably. "But you could rub them and see."

Art got down on his knees and scraped the spots with his nails. "They won't come," he cried.

"I thought not," said Old Hector.

"No. And look at his mouth! Isn't that a queer twist it's got?"

"Queer enough."

Art withdrew his finger from under the twisted mouth, and contemplated the spots again. "Aren't they bonny!" he exclaimed fondly.

"They are lovely indeed," agreed Old Hector.

From this joint worship of beauty, Art stirred and in a

wondering voice asked: "How is it that the spots came to be on him?"

"I believe I could tell you that, too."

"Could you?" breathed Art, and he stared up at Old Hector.

"There was a time before now," Old Hector began, "when all the fish in the sea gathered to choose a king. Now the fluke here thought he would have a better chance of being chosen as the king if he would dress himself in a way that would be noticed and admired. So what did he do but deck himself out in these red spots. He took so long over doing this, however, that by the time he arrived at the great gathering he was late and the other fish of the sea had already chosen the herring as king. The fluke looked at the herring. 'Hmff!' he said, twisting his mouth to one side, 'a simple fish like the herring, king of the sea!' and his mouth has been to one side ever since."

Art would have laughed, had he not been held in such wonder, such wonder—and something else. He took a sidelong look at Old Hector's expression, but the smile was running innocently into the whiskers. Art lowered his head.

"It wasn't—wanting the new jersey—that made me late," muttered Art in a low voice.

"What's that?" asked Old Hector. And he asked it again, but Art would not answer.

"It was—Henry James."

"Henry James, did you say?" asked Old Hector, inclining his head. "What about Henry James. Eh? Isn't he well, or what?"

"Morag has gone for old Betz."

"For old Betz!"

Art turned his head slowly and gave Old Hector one of his strange looks.

"God bless me, what's wrong?" asked Old Hector anxiously.

"I don't know," murmured Art, and he lifted his eyes again and looked at Old Hector.

Old Hector suddenly laughed, waving his beard like a flag. "No! no!" he said, "you needn't worry. Old Betz won't be bringing another baby."

But Art did not laugh, though Old Hector had an extra laugh on top of the first one. His eyes were merry and they tried to reassure Art and bring him into their orbit.

Art did not come in. He seemed indeed to be going farther away and downward. His big toe slowly scraped a runnel in the earth of the path. "Mother said—he's not himself," he muttered in a low voice. His face had the alien look, cold and distant. It was the pale look about the withdrawn glitter of the eye that for some reason always made Old Hector feel that the guilt of humanity through all time was here descended upon the child. It was man the outcast, strange in himself.

Old Hector lowered his head, the better to hear. "Is Henry James not well?"

"He's changed."

"He's what? Is he sick?"

"He is. He's not like himself." Art raised his eyes and looked at Old Hector, not frankly, and yet with a stare. They might have been the glass eyes of a living idol. Then the lids fell and the head drooped.

Old Hector stared penetratingly at the child. His mouth gathered thoughtfully, his head rocked up and down very slightly.

"So they sent for old Betz," he said. "Well, what better could they do? That was wise indeed. For old Betz knows —about those things."

Art slowly looked up and away.

"Yes, you can trust old Betz. Don't you worry any more. Old Betz will find out all about it, and then Henry James will be himself again."

"How will she find out?"

"She'll find out. We can leave it to her."

"Will she tell——? Who——?" muttered Art, the end of the sentences hidden.

Old Hector looked at him more narrowly. "All you are thinking are just fancies. It has nothing to do with you or with me. Never you mind about that. It will soon be all right, you'll see. Now, will you come home with me for a while?"

Art did not answer and went quietly along with Old Hector, but as they approached the house, he said: "I think I'll go home now."

"Very well," nodded Old Hector. "I hope you'll manage over to see us in the afternoon, just to tell us that Henry James is all right."

"So-long," said Art quietly.

"So-long just now," said Old Hector, and he stood looking after the child.

From a little distance, Art turned his drooped head slowly and looked back. The face was so pale that Old Hector, his heart touched, waved cheerfully. But Art did not wave back. Withdrawing his grey look, he continued on his way.

He was apparently in no hurry, for he often stood and slowly gazed here and gazed there. Any man watching the child might well have grown tired of watching, and then, looking up again—Art would have vanished.

For Art had turned up the hollow where Morag and Tom the shepherd had once met under Art's guidance. But no emanation from that red-berried turmoil came to him now, and presently he went up over a broad lip of ground and lo! before him, more still than a dream, quieter than sleep, was the Loch of the Rushes. There was the main clump of rushes as it had been before, *tom luachrach*, under which was hidden the big pot of the Feinn, according to legend, as Tom the shepherd had told him. Tom and himself had sat here on two afternoons while Art did his best with Tom's sharp knife to carve the hard block of hazel wood into the slender curve of the shepherd's crook. His hands had not been strong enough, but Tom had said he was shaping so well that in one year's time, when his hands grew bigger, he would be the youngest and finest carver in the two townships. On the second afternoon Morag appeared to take him home. But Tom said he would make a race of it and give Art a start. And Art had run so well that he was at home nearly an hour before Morag. But he did not tell on Morag, and when she appeared all flushed with running and said that Tom had started telling her something and she did not like to interrupt him—for it was bad manners to interrupt anyone—Art agreed that perhaps she had not been given a fair chance, but he had looked at her closely.

There was no one here now, though, and the memory of Tom and himself having been here made the loneliness of this quiet place lonelier still. It was as if everybody had just left and so, in a sense, were invisibly present. Everyone knew that fairies lived in green mounds, like the one Old Hector had shown him at the Clash. But not so many knew, Tom had said, that they also lived where the rushes grew by the side of a loch; and if not in every rushy loch, at least in some of them, and this was one.

It wasn't a very big loch. It was, indeed, quite a small one, but it had an importance of its own because the ground sloped upward all round it, so that when you stood near its edge you were in over the brink of a world shut off, with a new little world around you.

Art felt himself shut off and was afraid to approach the rushes by the water's edge. He stood as still as the spears of the rushes themselves. His hair was dark but not black, for the family was a mixture of black and brown. It had not been cut for some time, and his brown eyes stared from under the thatch that invaded the fragile brows. He had a slenderness built for growth, but, with the promise of strength in his shoulders, was no taller than need be for his years. The blue jersey narrowed his body lithely, and the huddle of brown cloth that was his kilt hung around his bare legs. Standing so still he looked wistful enough, but there was a reserved expression in the brown eyes that turned them dark and mysterious, and there was a persistence, over these still moments, beyond the persistence of the heron, for he was afraid.

Slowly, with his mind intense as in a dream, yet with an aloof air, he approached the rushes. The peat grew soft under the influence of the water and yielded to his toes. His eyes were on a mass of close-growing clumps. To them he would bend down and say what he had to say.

At last the moment came, but, as he stooped, the face of the loch darkened, and all the rushes said: "Hush-sh-sh-h-h-h!"

They were alive, slenderly jostling each other to listen. He felt the active ardent life run in them. It was a terrible moment, but he held against the inward panic, and said: "I never meant it. I—I did not want you to—to take Henry James away."

"Ah-ah-ah-h-h-h!"

"M-make him as he was. Please. Please do." His voice was rising.

"Hiss-ss-sz-zz-zzz!"

"Please! Please!" cried Art, losing control of himself, starting upright, pressing against his feet. Now the outermost foot had sunk an inch, and as he made to draw it back, it held so that he had to put his other foot farther out in order to keep his balance. This other foot, his left one, sank at once to the ankle.

The world-old panic of the reeds had him now.

In his violent struggles, he felt the soft hands of the little folk drawing him down. They had a grip of him. They were not letting go. He yelled: "Let me go! Let me go!" And at that there was a high cackling sound and a rush of small brown bodies upon the water, as a mother wild duck and her young scuttered away, but Art did not see what they were, for he had fallen and was madly clawing toward the dry land.

At first the little folk would not let his feet go, but at last yieldingly they did, and when he got upright he ran, squawling and screaming, ran up over the lip of that hidden world, and down into the hollow of his own world. When he fell for the third time, he lay, and had there been anything in his stomach to put up, he would have put it up; but there was nothing.

He was trembling all over, though the crying was now dying, for even at this most dreadful moment, he did not want to have to tell what had happened to him. It was once, many days ago, after a bitter humiliation in his own home, that he had gone down behind the barn and asked the fairies to deal with Henry James, just to show everyone! He had had a queer feeling after he had spoken the words, for the fairies, as Old Hector had said, and as everyone knew, were always ready to take away a human child and leave one of their own, a puny peevish changeling, in its place. However, as the days had gone on and nothing had happened, Art had felt relieved, particularly when he was happy. In fact he made himself believe that he had never really done it at all, and even if, so to speak, he had done it, it was only in fun. And then—it happened to Henry James.

Presently Art found that he was all wet and shivering, and then he found that his new jersey was plastered on one side with peaty slime. His new jersey itself. His kilt was bedraggled. His legs and feet, and particularly his knees, could hardly be blacker. He drifted to a little pool in the dried-up stream.

An hour or so later he approached his home circuitously by way of the barn. While he was lingering there to see what was going on, Morag appeared—and stopped short at sight of him, for he was not a very good washer at the best of times. Looking on his face, she did not, however, say what she was going to say.

"Where have you been?"

"Nowhere," answered Art.

"Dear me," she said, regarding his clothes and legs. "The fish is cooked and eaten—but I kept a special tail for you in the pan."

She looked free from real concern. There could not be much wrong at home.

"Did old Betz come?"

Then Morag laughed, as if she understood everything now. "No," she said. "She wasn't at home. She was away off at another house, where they are expecting—at another house, a long way off. And Henry James is better. He is his old self again. Isn't that fine?"

"When did he get better?" asked Art.

"Not so very long ago," said Morag, lowering her voice and looking all around. "And do you know what we think? I'm telling you this privately, so don't mention it. Mother and I think that Janet gave him some of that sticky stuff she had in a packet some days ago—remember? She wouldn't give you any? And it was that that did it, we're thinking. Janet said she didn't give him any, but she cried whenever she said it."

Art's expression did not change. It was quiet and pale. He turned his head and looked far away in the direction of the Loch of the Rushes. Morag regarded him narrowly.

"I'll have to try to clean up your jersey," she said gently, "before you go in."

"Go and bring me out the old one," said Art.

Morag, after another glance at him, went at once.

Art looked slowly about the old familiar barn and light seeped into his eyes. His right hand of its own accord wandered across him feeling for his stomach. If it had run away on him through the backbone, as it sometimes did, the fish would find it, and bring it back. Waters from the well of hunger came up and ran under his tongue. His bright eyes never left the gable-end round which Morag would come rushing in a moment with a happy breeze about her.

7

Nowhere and Somewhere

"Get back," said Donul to Art, "or I'll knock your teeth down your back throat."

"Will not," mumbled Art.

"Won't I?" said Donul. "You just watch if I don't." And he began to move away sideways. Art's feet appeared to be stuck, so Donul swung his face front and walked rapidly, but in an instant he swung it back.

Art stopped.

"You moved!" shouted Donul, his face working with the rage of a Fingalian hero about to give battle.

Art looked up through his eyebrows. He hadn't yet begun to cry.

"If you try to follow me," yelled Donul, "I'll flatten you to a pancake." He moved on; he turned swiftly.

Art stopped.

Donul came back in a little run and gave Art a wallop. Art yelled where he sat, and Morag suddenly appeared.

"Ah, you big bully," cried Morag. "For shame! Go and hit someone your own size."

"I'll do that," cried Donul, tearing up a lump of turf. With a piece in each hand, he swung his right arm. Morag ducked. After that feint, Donul let go the turf and it hit Morag hard astern. As Morag straightened herself she got the second piece of turf in the neck. Then Donul took to his heels.

Art stopped crying to listen to the things Morag called after Donul. "It's all down my neck," she said to Art, and doubled herself up until her hair was on the ground.

After Art had watched her contortions for a time, he turned and saw Donul fast disappearing. The sight made him cry out, and so great was his sudden rage that he stamped the earth round and round in a circle.

"Stop doing that," said Morag.

"Will not stop!" cried Art.

"Don't stamp the earth like that," said Morag in a peculiar voice.

Art stamped for a bit longer, but then stopped to look at the earth as Morag did.

"It's nothing!" he yelled, taken in by a trick.

"Nothing you can see," said Morag.

"Nothing!" yelled Art, his rage now directed against Morag.

Morag looked at the earth without appearing to look at it. Art had a quick look himself.

"I'm going," he cried.

"It's no good going now," said Morag.

"I know the way he went."

"That way leads to Nowhere."

"It does not," said Art.

"Where does it lead to, then?" asked Morag.

And Art saw that in truth it led nowhere.

In the pause that followed, Morag looked at Art's eyes trying to find Nowhere. The bare hillside up which Donul had disappeared led to tumbled ground and peat hags on the other side, and, beyond that, to broken rocks and wild cavernous places of the sea. Art's eyes were so clear and bright in their far contemplation that Morag could not take her own eyes off them.

"He wasn't going there whatever," said Art at last.

"Going where?" asked Morag, sitting down.

"Nowhere," said Art, with an embarrassment that made his voice moody.

"Where then was he going?" asked Morag.

"He was pretending," said Art.

"Was he?"

"He was. He was pretending to go nowhere, but when he got over the top, he would then turn and go somewhere."

"Do you know, I believe you're right!" declared Morag.

"Of course I'm right," said Art. "Any fool would know that."

"Not any fool," replied Morag. "A fool would never think of it. A fool would just set off looking for Nowhere."

"He would never find it, then," said Art. "That's sure."

"Do you think not?"

"How could he find Nowhere? That's silly."

"If he wandered on—and on—and got lost . . . where would he be when he was lost?"

As Art had no answer to that one, he asked: "Where?"

"He would be nowhere then."

"But if he found his way back?"

"But if he didn't?"

"But if Old Hector went away and found him, then he wouldn't be nowhere no more?"

"But if Old Hector couldn't find him?"

"I don't think," said Art, after a thoughtful moment, "that Nowhere is a nice place. Do you?"

"I don't," replied Morag. "I would rather be somewhere any day."

"So would I," said Art. And then he remembered: "Donul is somewhere," and his voice threatened to become urgent again.

"But where is Somewhere?"

"It's somewhere," said Art, growing impatient. "Everyone knows that."

"Of course. But where?"

"I know where it is." He was suddenly tired of the talk, and angry.

"I wish you would tell me where it is," said Morag lightly. "I'm only wanting to know."

"It's away off at the River," said Art. "That's where it is. And Donul has gone there and left me."

"Hush!" said Morag. "You're not quite certain that it's there. It might be some other place. There are many places in Somewhere."

"Are not!" said Art. "He's off at the River."

"But you can't be certain. You have been deceived by Donul before now."

"Have not!" And because he was telling a lie he stamped the earth.

"Don't stamp the earth," said Morag in a peculiar voice.

Art got so enraged that he stamped the earth round in a small circle.

"The poor earth!" said Morag. "What has it done to you?"

"Plenty," said Art, and he took a quick look at it through the angry water in his eyes.

"It never has done a thing," said Morag. "you know that."

"Don't care," said Art.

"Very well," agreed Morag, putting her arms round her knees and drawing them up until her chin met them. She then looked at Art sideways with a teasing smile.

Art gave her a wallop, such a hard one that it hurt his own hand, and when she cried out he ran off. At first he thought she was pretending to be weeping, but in a little while he wasn't so sure, because the tingling in his arm was more sore than the wallop Donul had given him before then. She was lying on the earth, little heaves in her shoulders.

He circled closer, and presently Morag caught his leg, and when she had him down she tickled him, until his laughter pierced through his anger in a fierce tumult.

"Will you hit me again?" demanded Morag.

"Y-y-yes!" yelled Art.

"Very well," nodded Morag remorselessly and went on with the tickling.

When they were exhausted, and were accusing each other of having started it first, Art said: "You said I was stamping the earth."

"So you were," said Morag.

"What's wrong with that? I can stamp it if I like."

"Certainly," agreed Morag. "But why take out your spite on the poor earth? It's a lovely earth." Tilting her head sideways, Morag caressed the green turf with her hand, for she was in love with the earth and many other things at that time.

"Lovely your grandmother," said Art.

"All life grows out of it," murmured Morag.

"I don't, whatever," said Art, and laughed out loud at his own cleverness.

"You do," said Morag. "For you would not be alive at all if you had not the things to eat that grow out of the earth. The earth is the mother of all living things."

"Is it the mother of cocks and hens?"

"What do cocks and hens live on, if it's not the corn, and the meal, and the potatoes that are left over?" demanded Morag. "And where do such things come from if not out of the earth?"

As he worked it out, Art began to see there was something in the idea. "And cattle and horses, too," he said, "for they live on grass?"

"Yes, and sheep and lambs also," nodded Morag—and paused. A warm flush stole over her face and made her eyes extremely bright.

Happening to observe this phenomenon, Art stared. "You're blushing," he said. But as his mind had immediately thought of Tom the shepherd, whenever the words "sheep and lambs" were spoken, it now made the extra link between Tom the shepherd and Morag's blush in a flash.

As Art, however, had run secret messages between Morag and Tom, he could not now very well give way to a derisive laugh, so he just continued to regard the blush with deep interest.

"I can blush if I like," challenged Morag, her chin tilting.

He had heard it said that Morag was "good-looking". Suddenly he saw what was meant. He saw that Morag was good-looking even though she was his own sister.

"You're good-looking," he said to her.

"Am I?" said Morag, with a smile that made her strange and at the same time twice as good-looking. "You're not a bad-looking fellow yourself."

"Amn't I?" asked Art shyly.

"Even though you do stamp the earth."

"Will the earth be angry with me?"

"Ach," said Morag, "the earth is a kind old mother and she won't mind a little stamping at an odd time. Perhaps, now and then, she likes it."

"Do you think——"

"Morag!" called their mother's voice.

"Oh lo!" said Morag in swift consternation. "I clean

forgot. Mother is wanting you to run a message and sent me for you."

"Who? Me?" demanded Art.

"Yes, you. Now please Art be a good boy and run."

"But why me? Why——?"

"Janet is watching Henry James, and Neonain has gone off to ask after Widow Morrison who is poorly. And I'll tell you what!" said Morag swiftly and brightly.

"What?" asked Art dubiously.

"You know how Old Hector sometimes scores over you with a conundrum——"

"Art!" cried their mother's voice.

"He's coming!" cried Morag. "Well, you cut across after your message," she continued, "and ask him: Where's Nowhere? That'll stump him."

"And where's Somewhere, too," said Art.

"And No-one and Someone," said Morag.

"And Nobody," said Art.

Morag laughed at his wit, and gave him a push, and though he never did anything but walk slowly to take a message, he was now so delighted at thinking of Nobody that he ran.

8

The Thimble of the Fairy Woman

Of women generally, Art was beginning to have no very high opinion. His mother was still useful at times, though he often had difficulty in getting all the food out of her he wanted. Moreover, she was not inclined to stand what she called "any nonsense", and as little boys like Art wore the kilt in the ancient traditional manner, that is without the complication of the undergarment called trews, he was, in a moment of stress, immediately vulnerable.

"Women," Old Hector had once said, "are notoriously unfair in the advantage they never fail to take of a man's weakness." And Art, seeing his point, had stopped sobbing and felt better.

Morag, of course, was different; but if so she was the only one. And once leave the grown-ups and come down to girls round about his own age and, well, the very way, for example, two or three of them would band together, interlocking their arms, and walk or run, giggling foolishly, during play-time at school, was enough to make boys scoff openly.

In truth, the boys often did more than that; they would barge roughly into the girls as if they had not seen them, and break up the interlock. The girls would screech angrily and shout: "You cheeky things!" whereupon the boys would give utterance to gruff bear-notes of laughter.

Sometimes two or three girls would turn upon a single boy and attack him. He had then either to run and risk being laughed at or face the attack with reckless daring; and the best manner in which to face the attack was to swing a strap of books in a way that would knock their brains out if they did not scatter, so generally they scattered.

Nothing is perfect in this life, however, and Art, to his secret and often, indeed, bitter humiliation, had a weak spot in the heel of his mind. She was Mary Ann, the young sister of Hamish, and, as everyone knew, Hamish was the greatest friend of Donul. Donul and Hamish, being over fourteen, had, of course, left school, but Mary Ann was round about Art's own age, though they said she was four months older.

Now one of the worst features about Mary Ann was that she had curls and that their true colour was red-gold. Red is a colour one can laugh at, and gold is no doubt attractive in a pretty fashion, but red-gold is full of challenge and fire. Derision may be expressed in the way a fellow pulls a girl's hair, but it is rarely the hair that first moves him to the pulling. In Mary Ann's case the hair was enough. In the most peaceable and innocent circumstances, it would ask to be tugged. A boy's eyes filled with daring at the mere sight of it. And it added zest to the fun to know that if there was one thing Mary Ann hated more than any other it was having her hair pulled.

Now Art never had had the courage to pull Mary Ann's hair. Other boys could do it as they rushed by, but not Art. Always when he was just about to do it he was invaded by a queer feeling that weakened him, and he would run on making loud derisive noises, as though he had more than done it. Then one day, carried beyond himself, he did it. At once she swung round and hit him a stinging slap in the face. He made excellent derisive noises as he rushed away, but he had been staggered inwardly even more than outwardly, and the memory of the experience haunted him for many days.

Mary Ann had another feature, and they were her eyes. Not the colour of her eyes, but just her eyes, and some time after his experience, Art by an unlucky chance found himself being looked at by them. Her body remained perfectly still and her eyes never wavered. They just kept on looking, and slowly he twisted and broke and ran away, doing his best to run carelessly.

This trouble so hung in his mind and so annoyed him secretly, that he made it, very indirectly, the subject of a discourse with his friend Old Hector. And Old Hector found himself in deep water at once.

"That's a very difficult one," he answered. "But girls are just girls and that's the difference."

"Yes, but how are some persons made girls and some boys?"

"You know who made us all," replied Old Hector. "And if girls are girls they cannot help it. It wouldn't be fair to hold that against them."

"Were they just unlucky?" asked Art, thoughtfully.

Old Hector made a cloud of smoke as he reclined at his ease on the corner of the turf dike. "Perhaps they don't think so," he said.

Art looked at him with some wonder. "Don't they?"

"Perhaps not. How can we tell?"

"Perhaps they don't know any better?" suggested Art.

"There may be something in that."

"I'm sure there is," said Art, who was always glad to help out his old friend. "I'm quite sure. I never heard yet of a boy who would like to be a girl whatever. Did you?"

"No, I cannot say I have. But did you ever hear of a girl who would like to be a boy?"

Art was clearly surprised. "No, but anyone knows a girl would like to be a boy if she could. She must," said Art.

"It doesn't follow," said Old Hector.

Art laughed, his eyes bright and merry. "That's the funniest thing I ever heard," he said, twisting on his heel, "that a girl wouldn't like to be a boy!"

"I can see you don't believe it," nodded Old Hector. "But there are strange things in the world. And consider. Isn't it a good thing that girls like to be girls—a good thing for us, at least, because that keeps them quiet?"

"They're not often quiet," said Art.

Old Hector laughed, tilting up his beard. "The holidays have gone to your head," he said. "And it's good weather you're going to get. Isn't it a lovely morning?"

"It is," said Art. But weather was a thing he did not notice very much, so he added: "There's one thing, and that is that men can do what they like in the broad world, they are the masters, but women——"

"Father!" called Agnes.

"I must be going," said Old Hector, quickly. "Look in any time you're passing, and so-long just now."

"So-long," answered Art, as he stood watching his old friend hurry away.

Art knew what he would be hurrying away for: to do some job that Agnes had ready for him.

There was always a lot of work to be done about a croft, and Art did not like doing work. No-one should have to work on his holidays. Toiling at the same thing over and over for a long time was very wearisome. If he went back home, they would be certain to have something for him to do. And there was always that awful "I want you to run a message." So he drifted over the knoll above Old Hector's cottage and down to the little burn. He had hardly reached the salley bush, when who should appear from behind it but Mary Ann. He stopped and she looked at him.

"Hullo," she said.

"Hullo yourself," he answered largely, holding his ground.

To-day there was something different about her eyes. "Where are you going?" she asked quite simply.

"Oh," he answered at random and more largely than ever, "I thought of going away off to the River."

"The River!" she repeated, deeply impressed. "But that's a terrible way off."

"It's nothing to me," said Art. "I have gone farther than that when I was little."

"Have you?"

"I have. It's only over two miles, but the Hazel Pool is three. And there are always salmon in the Hazel Pool."

"Are there? I have never", said Mary Ann, "been to the River. I have never seen the Hazel Pool."

"Haven't you?" remarked Art lightly as if he knew the pool well.

"No," said Mary Ann. And then she smiled to Art, and turned her head away slightly, and her head drooped, and red-gold curls fell by her brows, and she shook them back and examined a salley leaf, and she picked the leaf, and she looked back at Art.

Art was suddenly charged with boundless energy. "Haven't you?" he asked. "Not even as far as the River?" It was incredible, but he refrained from laughter.

"No. I would like to go," she said with an innocence as fair as her skin, "if someone showed me the way."

Art hesitated, for all in a moment he realized how desperate the situation was. To be seen was to be accused of courting Mary Ann. If the cold sweat could have come to his forehead it would have come. He looked slowly about him.

"No-one knows I'm here," said Mary Ann confidentially. "Is this the way to the River?"

"It is."

"Come on!" And she smiled to Art for the second time, a friendly, conspiring, daring, and inspiring smile. So far Art had not encountered anything like it. In somewhat similar circumstances, Donul could smile daringly too, but there was a great difference between Donul's smile and Mary Ann's.

As they went on he was torn in many directions, and could not make up his mind whether to go or not. It was an awful risk. "Stay here," he said at last, "and I'll see if any-one is coming."

"I'll stay," said Mary Ann obediently.

Art crawled up the short slope like a hunter and lay flat. He saw Hamish in the distance cutting bog hay and he saw Old Hector and several others moving busily about the landscape. They were all working and Art suddenly felt safe and remote from them. It was a fine feeling, and when he slipped back to Mary Ann he was nearly laughing. "Come on!" he said, and started running.

Mary Ann could run well. Art jumped over a ditch. Mary Ann jumped, too, but she fell. "Did you hurt your-self?" asked Art.

"No," answered Mary Ann, smiling. "It's nothing."

The next time he carefully selected the jumping place, and he jumped, and Mary Ann jumped, and she didn't fall.

"That's better," said Art.

"You know a lot about everything," said Mary Ann.

"I'm used to it," said Art negligently. "I've done things that would frighten you."

"What things?"

"Many a thing," said Art mysteriously. "But I couldn't tell a girl because it must never be known."

"I like that!" said Mary Ann.

Art glanced at her with some astonishment. Her face was hurt, her eyes bright, her lips petulant. She did not look at him and slowed up her walk.

"I did not mean anything against you," said Art, bewildered. "I only meant—just that—that——"

"You did so," replied Mary Ann. "You said that I would tell."

"I never did," said Art. "I never did."

"You did so."

"I did not."

"You did so."

"I did not. Am I a liar, then?"

Mary Ann did not answer, and at the sight of her lips which appeared to tremble, Art experienced the vague weight of a burden of misery and guilt. If he could, he would have run off home.

"I only said I mustn't tell, because if it was known, we—we would be had up before the Court and put in jile," he explained.

She regarded him with round eyes. She seemed a softer, more peculiar being than the girl, ever ready with her fist, whom he knew at school.

"Will you say, 'Cut my throat and burn my breath'?" he asked awkwardly.

"Cut my throat and burn my breath," she replied, drawing her finger across her throat as Art had done.

Art nodded and glanced about him. "Wait here," he said, "till I have another look."

"Can't I come?" she asked.

"No," he answered. "Wait till I see first."

She waited. Presently he turned his head round and beckoned her. She crept up close beside him.

"Look!" whispered Art. "Look at them!"

Mary Ann looked, and quite far away she could see figures on the land and about the houses.

"They're working!" explained Art.

"Working!" repeated Mary Ann, joining in Art's low laugh.

The spectacle of humanity engaged in toil induced a merriment all the greater for the recent cloud that had shadowed their relations.

"That's Sheila chasing after little Henry Ian!" declared Mary Ann.

"And yon's Hamish on the scythe!" declared Art.

They began to roll with laughter, the red-gold head by the dark. Humanity was funny when you saw it solemnly at work in the distance. Life had never before presented them with such an amusing and exciting and comprehensive moment. Their sarcasms at the expense of a bowed humanity increased their mutual friendship until they all but rolled down the bank.

They ran after that, and leaped, and then began to talk quite solemnly, as Art realized for the first time in his life that he was a leader. Mary Ann obeyed him. What a pleasure, therefore, it suddenly was to tell her, under the oath of secrecy, his experience away in the Clash, snaring the rabbits, with the Ground Officer shouting on his dog and sending the stone smashing down past them in the wood!

Mary Ann's eyes grew bigger than ever. She asked questions which Art answered easily. More than once she held her breath as she looked at him.

When her turn came, she talked in a low confidential voice, and she told a mysterious story that she had overheard, and she asked Art when she was finished if he thought it was true.

Art said it might quite well be true, simply because there was many a strange thing in the world.

Even the world which they were now passing through was strange to him, though he did not tell her that. For the secret truth was that Art had never been to the River, much less to the fabled Hazel Pool.

The hollow that the stream ran through grew deeper and bigger. It was full of bends and round each bend was a place they had never seen before. The sun shone out of a summer sky, but it was not too hot because of a wandering wind that came round the corners, and ran over the bracken on pale feet, and eddied here, and died away there, a soft cool gentle wind that invited the body to run into it.

But Art did not run now, because his eyes had to command so many strange things and he had to be wary. Moreover it was clear to him that Mary Ann was not at all frightened. She thought everything was marvellous, and sometimes she came very close to him for safety, and sometimes she cried out at the sight of flowers and ran towards them. Art ran after a rabbit and it went into a hole. If he had had a spade, he said, he would not have thought twice of digging the rabbit out of the hole. He explained to Mary Ann how to kill a rabbit. "Do you like being off with me like this?" he asked.

"I love it," said Mary Ann.

"Love" was a soft word that Art himself would never use, but girls thought nothing about using it. They were like that. Art was glad he was different, but he refrained from comment. At the same time it was not unpleasant the way Mary Ann had used it.

Adventuring into the unknown was very exciting, but a moment came when sheer wonder fell upon them, especially upon Mary Ann. They were in a deep rounded hollow, a wild-looking place with a still pool, when up on their right hand they saw a ravine with a small burn of its own and crowds of tall purple foxgloves.

It looked like a fairy dell. It was so magical a place that the foxgloves themselves seemed to have faces of their own. Mary Ann could hardly believe her eyes. With a cry she ran towards the flowers which were so tall that their purple bent high above her red-gold.

Art watched her for a little, and then, as became a leader, decided to investigate this wonder spot for himself. He moved here and he poked there and finally he came to an opening under a heather-lip, a dark mouth into which he had to stoop. A strange smell went into his nostrils, a rotting smell like what he had sometimes got near the mill. It must be a cave. Then he saw a thin shaft of glittering light inside and grew afraid. There was a step behind him and he swung round with a cry. It was Mary Ann.

"What is it?" she asked.

Art ran away and Mary Ann did her best to keep up with him. When she screamed, he turned and said: "Give me your hand." Mary Ann gave him her hand and they ran on together.

When they had left that place well behind them, they flopped down on the grass, panting. Art described what he had seen and said it must be a wild beast's den.

Mary Ann looked behind her and suggested they might go on a bit yet. And though Art said there was no need to go farther, he went.

They had now been through danger and were allies. Their friendship increased. They talked of wild beasts, like wolves and bears and lions. The sun shone, and Art smiled when Mary Ann found with dismay that she had dropped all her flowers. "The world is full of flowers," said Art. "Thousands and thousands of them. And I'll show you stranger ones yet."

"Will you?" asked Mary Ann.

"I will," said Art, nodding strongly.

After a time Mary Ann said: "Perhaps it wasn't a wild beast's den."

"What then would it be?"

"Perhaps," said Mary Ann in a very low voice, "it was a little house."

"Who for?"

Mary Ann glanced at him and glanced away.

Art felt uneasy.

"Who put the foxgloves yonder?" she asked. "They were like a garden."

"A garden!" said Art. "That's silly."

"They were lovely, weren't they?" murmured Mary Ann. "They were the loveliest sight ever I saw."

"That's nothing," said Art.

"Do you think *they*—planted them there?" asked Mary Ann, fearfully but wonderingly, too.

Art scoffed once or twice at this oblique reference to the little folk as they went on their way, but in spite of himself a great desire came upon him to tell what he knew of them.

Perhaps the only real treasures Art possessed were his secrets, and if so, the greatest of them all was his traffic with the little folk over Henry James. That was so terrible a secret that Art had made up his mind no one in the broad world to the end of time would ever find it out.

Sitting on a narrow meadow-flat by the little stream, Art told Mary Anr that secret.

Thereafter their conversation was interesting, and often surprising, for it was very long.

Some said there were little folk, and some said there

weren't, but it was queer however it was, because you could feel it was queer, particularly after listening to Mary Ann. Art had had no idea that Mary Ann could talk so much or in such a quiet friendly way, her voice solemn, her eyes looking into the distance, or sideways at the stream, but seeing all the time what was moving in her head. It was *and* this, *and* that, *and* the other, on and on, her head giving a little nod after each *and*.

The *ands* began to creep over Art like small ants. He realized (as a leader must in such circumstances) that he was too far from home to permit this creepy feeling to get the better of him. So he lifted his head and brushed it off, saying: "I don't believe all that. Old Hector told me that the little folk are good folk. They are the folk of peace. They like peace. It's 'the man of peace' and 'the woman of peace'. That's what they're called, so it's bound to be true. And they like music, too, and they like dancing. They are the great ones for the dancing. They can dance for a year and a day. And that's as true as true can be. You can take it from me that's right."

"I like dancing, too," said Mary Ann.

Art was astonished, for he had expected her to argue, as he would have done himself, but apparently she had already forgotten all she had said. Which was just as well.

"And they dance in their own house, and once a year the side of it opens, and you can see the light coming out and hear the music," explained Art. "And then——"

"I would like," said Mary Ann, "to have a little house of our own."

Art looked at her. "What sort of a little house?"

She looked at Art. "Come on," she cried eagerly, her eyes very bright, "let us build a little house!" She jumped to her feet. "Come on!"

Art got more slowly to his feet. "What sort of a house do you want?"

"You have a pair of good hands," she said critically.

Art looked at his hands. Mary Ann measured one of hers flat against one of his and Art's was longer (and he had hardly pushed it forward at all). So Art was pleased at that, and repeated, objectively, Tom the shepherd's dictum that he, Art, would yet have the best pair of hands for carving in the two townships.

So he took command as a man should and laid Mary Ann under his instructions. From the edge of the stream they carried up stones and on the green grass Art laid the foundation of their home.

He kept the lines straight, both the gable-ends and the sides, nor did he forget to leave a blank space for the door, and when the lines were completed the house was built. "Watch your head!" he cautioned Mary Ann as she entered at the door.

The sky seemed all the bluer now for the small white clouds suspended beneath it in sunny ease. As they sat by their own fireside, Mary Ann looked happily about her, until suddenly she decided she must have more space at her back.

"Whatever for?" asked Art.

"For the cradle," said Mary Ann.

The breath went clean from Art. "That's one thing," he said with powerful decision, "I won't have on any account."

"But we must have it."

"We must not," said Art, rising from his chair. "I have had enough of that."

"But I want it," said Mary Ann.

"I don't care whether you want it or not."

"But I want it."

"Want away!" cried Art.

"I want it!" Mary Ann got angrily to her feet. "And I am going to have a family of thirteen!" she announced in bold defiance.

Art turned round and looked at her. "God be here!" he said.

For one awful moment they felt the coming of God.

"Oh-h-h-h!" said Mary Ann, her shocked mouth narrowing into a very upright "O". Art left the house. Mary Ann followed him through the wall. "Oh-h-h-h!"

Art began to laugh recklessly. Mary Ann's face slowly collapsed in appalled mirth. Art waded into the stream for a big stone, and as Mary Ann shook and rolled with laughter, Art threw his head up the better to laugh, too. At that, his feet went from him, he sat down abruptly, and his kilt floated around him like a water lily.

On her knees, Mary Ann wrung his kilt. Art said: "It's nothing."

"You stand still!" commanded Mary Ann.

Over the green they ran, weaving patterns in the warm drying wind.

And the clouds hung still, through the whole sunny day, until they grew faint with hunger.

On the way home—for Mary Ann had forgotten about the River which they never reached—Art said that they should take the other side of the burn for a change. Mary Ann agreed, for she knew that Art did not want to pass too close to the wild beast's den. But she herself wanted to have one more look at the foxgloves, and when they saw them in the distance from high up on the bank above the sunken pool, Mary Ann, standing still, asked in a quiet voice: "Do you know what made me say yon, yon time?"

"Say what?"

"About—it might be a little house."

"What?"

"Do you know," asked Mary Ann, "the other name for the foxglove?"

"No. What is it?"

"The thimble of the fairy woman," said Mary Ann.

It was black night that night and no fairy woman helped Art through his bitter agony and renunciation of all women and especially of Mary Ann. For, sure as fate, Donul and Hamish, the hunters, the scoffers, sent to look for the lost children, had found them coming wandering home, with Mary Ann holding to Art's hand.

Never would this bright day be forgotten now; never in all time would it be washed out; always and forever like two in a terrible story would himself and Mary Ann in the broad daylight of eyes wander down the Little Glen over the green grass under the blue sky; and the awfulness of this came upon Art in the darkness of the night.

9

Art Runs a Great Race

For boys there might be a more exciting event than the Day of the Games, but if so they did not know it. Weeks beforehand on the level green of each township "practising" went on—at running and jumping and throwing the hammer and putting the shot. Art was late often for his meals and had hard words said to him, but that did not put him much about, and a wallop in the by-going only toughened him. It was great to see Duncan slip up the piece of string between two posts a full foot beyond what had defeated Donul and Hamish and then clear it with ease. It filled Art with the profoundest admiration. In fact it was nothing for Art to be walking quietly along the path and then, as if stung behind, to break into a terrific burst of speed. Once he took a flying long jump from a peat ridge and, landing in the belly of the bank, did so hit his jaw with his knees that the daylight flickered and nearly went out on him. He practised running secretly, and in a private mile-race round and round below the barn was surprised and mocked by Janet and Neonain. But if he was, he gave them mountain torrents.

There was, however, another side to the Games, so fascinating in thought, so brimful to the imagination, that Art could not ponder it long at any one time. There were stalls at the Games, stalls with heaps of gooseberries, red and green, and ginger-bread, and toffee in long round stalks, in flat cakes, in little squares, in tiny balls, in paper and not in paper, and sweets of every kind in the world, including "conversation" ones which caused great laughter among young men and women because a fellow could hand a girl one with the red writing on it asking "Do you love me?" and the girl would hand one back with the writing asking "Would you like to know?" or some silly remarks of the kind, and nuts and apples and oranges and juicy things too numerous even to think about with the water already around the teeth, not to mention the wonderland of comical toys from little mannies that popped out of a box to monkeys that did the cat's twirl on top of a stick, and to ignore—for excitement can be too terrible—the numerous games of skill with ball or marble when for a penny a fellow might win not only a coconut but a beautiful painted gold-rimmed vase or even a clock itself, a real one that went.

Those days through which the whole world moved towards this divine event had accordingly for Art one supreme difficulty and its name was money. Donul mocked him mercilessly over this, for Donul had two-and-twopence saved up of his own. Art had one penny, and it would cost him threepence to get in, for the Games were run by a Committee who had to make all the arrangements and pay the prize money. The first person to come to his rescue was Old Hector.

"I'll give you the twopence now," said Old Hector, as he returned from the kitchen, "and that will ease your mind on the main count."

"It will," said Art. He wanted to add that if he could do anything for Old Hector at any time he would be only too pleased, but he was overcome and did not say it.

"You'll probably get more before the Day," nodded Old Hector. "It's always like that."

"I have no-one to get it from," replied Art. "But I don't mind now. I can get in whatever. I—I thank you very much."

"Hots! tots!" said Old Hector, "it's nothing. To tell the truth I never handle money now. Agnes does that and even buys me my tobacco. I found that twopence in a little jug on the top shelf of the dresser. It was all that was in it."

"Will she miss it?"

"She will," said Old Hector, "but she's out at the moment, and worry never did anything but kill the cat."

Art's eyes glanced in a merry smile. "Do you like money?" he asked.

"I never think about it," answered Old Hector.

"I would like to have so much of it," said Art, "that—that I could hardly handle it all. With all that much, as big as would fill a room, you could get anything in the world you wanted, couldn't you?"

"I couldn't," said Old Hector.

"What couldn't you get?"

"I couldn't get your youth, for example," said Old Hector, smiling.

"That's nothing," said Art; then he thought again and looked at Old Hector. "Would you like to be young like me?"

"Well, now, I wonder! Perhaps on the whole I'm as well as I am. What do you say?"

"I like you as you are," said Art, "best."

But it was not talk that would solve Art's difficulties now. Nothing would solve them but cash down in round copper coin of the realm. On a day when he was tired running below the barn and had given himself up to thought he saw

Morag come out with some clothes to bleach. He edged nearer to her. She spoke to him pleasantly. Art mumbled.

"What's that?" she asked, bending her head.

"I was only saying," he tried to remark casually, "that if ever you were wanting me to run a message to—to—anywhere, I'd run it."

Her face flushed somewhat and her eyes shone. "That's uncanny," she murmured, "for I was just wondering whether—whether——" She communed with her thought. She looked far away. "Wait here," she whispered to Art and hurriedly returned to the house.

Art was very fond of Morag. In truth, she was the only woman he would now permit himself to be seen near. And presently she handed him a note and told him that she would give him a penny on the Day of the Games if he delivered it without anyone's knowing.

"You can trust me," said Art.

Tom the shepherd saw Art from a long way off and came across the vacant moor to meet him. When he read the note, his anxious smile turned into a happy laugh. "You'll be collecting for the Games," he said, and thereupon presented Art with threepence.

In short, the day they set off for the Games, Art possessed no less a total sum than eleven pennies.

And it was a fine day. Folk said they always got a fine day for the Games. Which showed that Whoever looked after the weather had a pleasant smile for that day. And no wonder, when everyone was so happy, with smiles, and greetings, and loud shouts, and laughter. Art could hardly contain himself, and when Morag offered to take his hand, asking him, "Are you tired?" for it was over three miles by the short-cut that the young bunch of them were following, Art told her not to be silly and nearly treated her like an ordinary female person.

But then and at last—there was the wonder place itself, below them, with more houses together than Art had ever seen at one time. Without thinking, he took Morag's hand. She smiled down to him, but he was hardly aware she was in it. She pointed out the field. He saw the great circle of roped posts that made the ring for the "athletic events". Folk were gathering in crowds. Music, bagpipe music, came from here and from there, wherever a piper found a lonely corner to listen to himself in order to get his pipes running sweetly and his fingers supple.

Art hung a little on Morag's hand because there was a melting in his breast and it was difficult to take everything in. Hitherto he had seen the Games only through Donul's eyes when Donul was wanting to astonish him and make his teeth water. Information had come from other sources, too; and in his time he had received a conversation sweetie with "Do you love me?" on it and eaten it. If a sweetie was soiled on the outside all you had to do was to spit out the first one or two sucks, unless it was soiled with black-twist tobacco when you had to spit out three or four.

And so they came to the gate in the low dry-stone dike which was the "entrance gate". Anyone could look over the dike and see the Games, but everyone crowded about the gate in order to pay to get in. "Have you your three-pence ready?" asked Morag privately. "Yes," whispered Art, in whose right hand the three pennies were already hot.

Suddenly there was a gay shout: "Is that yourself, Art?" And here was Tom the shepherd pressing up to him. And just as Tom was paying Art in, didn't he see Morag, so he was fairly caught and had to pay her in, too, and she was sixpence.

Art wondered if he should offer Tom the threepence, but Tom was laughing, and as Morag made no move to offer her sixpence, Art politely followed her example. But now he saw Donul and Hamish and one or two others hurrying away into the great field and Art ran after them forgetting Morag in an instant. He was frightened Donul would turn on him and drive him off, as he always did when on a ploy with Hamish, and presently when Donul felt Art's hand hanging on to his jacket in the press of folk and turned round and saw it was Art, he asked: "What are you doing here?" But in a moment he laughed and took Art's hand. Art gulped down his pleasure, for at the end of the day Donul was his leader. Hamish patted him on the back and laughed, too. "We'll show you a few things," said he. "But let's go canny with the spending, it's early yet."

And so he saw the wonders of his imagination come real before his eyes. There was a stuff he ate that melted in his mouth, and ran about his gums, and slid down his throat, and the taste of it was good beyond all belief, so that it was incredible, yet the next mouthful was even better. Hamish bought gooseberries after that. They were soft with ripeness and warmed by the September sun. If you pressed them hard, they spouted. So you left it to your mouth to make them spout inside. Nothing was lost that way, and the throat choked gently with delight before it let the flavoured goodness down. "See that fellow spitting out the skins? He's showing off," said Hamish. Art did not show off.

"Three balls a penny! Three balls a penny! Every time you break a pipe you get a coconut!"

The pipe was a white clay pipe stuck upright in the wide mouth of a cardboard clown. There was a swagger on Hamish and he presented his penny and received the three round wooden balls. He threw the balls with great force and the nearest was a foot away. Donul felt he could do better than that. His first two shots were wild, but the third broke the pipe to bits.

"Come away," muttered Donul urgently, his eyes glistening, "I know the secret." When they were by themselves, he explained: "You threw too hard, and that put you off your aim."

"I felt that," said Hamish.

"Of course!" said Donul, and in demonstrating with the coconut how to bring the hand back he hit a man in the jaw. The man laughed. They all laughed.

"We'll have a dozen coconuts this night," said Hamish.

"At least," said Donul.

Art might have been on his head until his feet were trodden on. But he said it did not hurt at all, and the stranger gave him a penny for being a brave little fellow.

A great urge came upon Art to do something with his money, but Donul and Hamish were such big men so far that when they bent down and caught the import of Art's whisper, they laughed. Plenty of time for that, they assured him, for the present round was apparently of an exploratory nature with a view to ascertaining where wealth might most profitably be invested later on.

And they hadn't finished it when the distant beating of the big drum shivered their hearts, the rhythmic beating: *boom! boom! boom!—boom! boom! boom!* and up behind the last *boom!* rose all the bagpipes of the world in stirring, marching unison. Donul and Hamish rushed for the ring, and Art with them, and gallantly they fought their way, Donul leading ruthlessly and Hamish bringing up the rear, and when anyone asked who they were shoving at, they shoved on, until they came to the rope itself, and Donul told Art to duck under it and lie down, which Art did.

The pipers would have been tall enough if Art had been standing, but now it was legendary they were, with their heads against the sky, and their bonnets and their drone pipes and the tartan ribbons floating behind, all against the remote sky. On they came, in step and in line, knee and knee, and the kilt on the swing, many men as one man, with pride and precision and glory. A terrible oncoming sea of ever-swelling sound, irresistible and splendid, surging up and up, breaking over human heads like boulders on a flat strand. But the minds of the heads were not drowned, and they left the old heads, and they took the crest of the wave where the spindrift was flying, where the ancient glory was streaming its banners.

Art's breast began to melt on him. He knew the march, he knew the tune, and such knowledge was nearly too much, for the horror of tears at that moment would never be washed out in all time. But fortunately there was also in this march of the pipers a terrifying element, the element of fear, faced and breasted and overcome, and that kept the melting from going too far. When the pipers formed into a sylvan ring and played a reel, a merry hooch! rose here and there and Art was saved.

No sooner had the music stopped than a bell was rung and a voice roared. The "athletic events" were about to begin.

There were thrills for Art then, and when he heard Donul shouting encouragement to a competitor, he shouted the competitor's name, too, and followed his progress with breathless anxiety. When a man won who had once spoken to Art, Art's pride was so great he danced and he waved.

The bell clanged. "Competitors for the high jump!" And here was Duncan, Art's own brother, walking calmly into the ring.

His own brother Duncan. It gave him a queer feeling to look at his brother with his bare knees and his black shorts and his black head, tall and slim, walking out there. Art was quietened, and stood up to be against Donul. But Donul was laughing and saying he did not expect Duncan to win, because Ian from Clachdrum had held the championship for three years, and the only person Ian was frightened of was a Hector Munro from down the country. Art felt relieved that Duncan was not expected to win. Duncan could try all the harder now, and it wouldn't matter if he wasn't even third.

There were nine competitors and four of them wore trousers tucked into their socks. They all got over the first jump. Donul and Hamish made a joke, saying they could do that one themselves. Art tried to join in the laughter but found it difficult. There was a man at each post, and they now pegged up the stick between the posts no less than three holes. Two men went out at the very next round, but Duncan was still in. Art breathed, for Duncan was not the worst now. At the next hole, two more went out, and in the succeeding round, one. Four competitors were left, and two of them, including Hector Munro, took off their jackets for the first time. Duncan was still in. The competition was a great strain on Art because Duncan was jumping last. Accordingly when his three opponents cleared the new height and Duncan began to square up for his short little run from the left side, Art found the gooseberries and the toffee and the ginger-bread gathering into a ball in his breast. But Duncan went over like a bird.

Art had just taken a deep breath when there was a great commotion behind him, with Morag's anxious voice crying: "Donul, did you see Art?"

Art looked round Donul and Morag saw him. "Oh dear," she laughed, "I thought we'd lost him!" Her face was flushed with excitement, but Art was very annoyed. Tom the shepherd was there, and one or two others, including a dark-eyed girl whom Art had never seen before. She had a pale, rather grave face, and Art caught her looking at him. Hector Munro, the first competitor, cleared the next jump. Then Ian from Clachdrum cleared it. Art found it difficult to bear the situation, so to create a diversion within him, he stood on his tiptoes towards Donul and asked him: "Who is she, that one?"

Donul, after a look round, bent his head. "That's Peigi Maclean."

Art brought his lips to Donul's ear: "Is she Duncan's one?"

"Hsh! She is," whispered Donul.

Art had another look round at her. The dark eyes met his own and smiled, and Art would have been very embarrassed if the third competitor at that moment had not knocked down the stick. So there was Duncan, padding the ground lightly with his toes, measuring his distance. He was off—off—up—and over. They all cheered, except Peigi Maclean and Art. The third competitor was given two more tries, but he failed, and Duncan was now certain of being third and "in the prize money".

"It doesn't matter now," said Art to Donul with a big breath.

"Not a bit," cried Donul, straightening himself and laughing, his eyes very bright.

But there was no respite. Here they were getting ready for the next round. Hector had a supple graceful body and ran in from the right. He got his feet over, but his right hip brought the stick down with him. Ian ran straight in like a bull at a gate and, tucking his legs under him, skimmed the stick with nothing to spare. And here was Duncan again, padding the ground with his toes, measuring his distance. Off he flew, up went his legs, his whole body curved and arched and turned in the air, and there he was neatly on his feet below the untouched stick.

"By God," said a man's voice, "Duncan has a beautiful style."

Art could not look at anybody now. Hector failed in his two extra tries. Duncan was bound to be second.

At his next jump, Ian kicked the stick clean before him. And here was Duncan again, padding the ground with his toes, measuring his distance. It was hard on Art. It was difficult to bear. Duncan ran in, up . . . and over. There was clapping of hands all round the ring.

Ian kicked the stick before him a second time. At that he grew very serious. He stood under the stick, measuring its height, and placed a white handkerchief on the ground. It was his last chance. He backed away. He spat on his hands. Down he raced. His ankles grazed the stick—but he was over.

"By God," said the man's voice, "that's the highest ever he has done." The round ring was cheering. Up went the pegs to the next hole.

Ian stood under the stick and placed his white handkerchief and spat on his hands as before, but he brought the stick away with his knees. He was finished and knew it.

And here once more was Duncan on his toes, like a restive horse, like a leashed hound. But too swiftly he ran, too anxiously, so that the ground refused to hold the foot that would have sent him soaring over. He slipped, rose a very short distance, and knocked the stick away with his shoulders.

Folk shouted that he had slipped and that helped Art. But Donul said that Duncan would now lose confidence in the ground. And Duncan indeed seemed worried, for in his second jump he misjudged his distance badly. After the third attempt, Ian was knocked out; and here, oh, here was Dunan, searching for his right distance with his toes, his hands clenched, his head up. The whole ring waited for this last decisive jump. Off went Duncan . . . up . . . over slid his feet, and his legs, and his arched lithe body, his arms streaming behind him, but—ah!—a fold of his jersey below the shoulder, a little bulge, a crease, touched the stick—no more—and it quivered. On his feet, Duncan looked up, waiting. Hundreds and hundreds of people waited, watching the stick quiver. Would it hold? The off end slid from its peg and the stick fell. There was a loud groan.

"By God, that's luck for you!" said the man's voice, and it was bitter.

But wait—the master of events was running towards the two competitors. They might have another round to settle it. He spoke to Duncan, and Duncan nodded. He spoke to Ian, but Ian shook his head. So the event was over, with a tie for first place.

There was talk then.

Beautiful it was to watch the dancers bouncing off their toes, and one tall gay fellow in Macpherson tartan to his hose seemed to live in the air itself, so light his movements were, so full of abandon, yet so intricately patterned, so delicately precise.

"Isn't he perfectly built, that chap!" said Hamish.

And Art saw at once that the dancer's shoulders were broad and his flanks lean and his legs all strength and grace. His toes flexed and down-pointed like the beaks of geese, like the heads of adders, but, oh, swifter than they, swifter, and the boards beneath tapped back the rhythm of the reel, and the piper played better than he had done in his own competition itself.

The sun shone and from the crushed grass arose a green scent, more penetrating than the scent of haymaking, and never more would Art get that scent but he would think of this day of days.

For it was moving now to its climax, and justly the introduction to climax came with the ringing and the clanging of the bell. "Boy's race! All boys under nine years!" What's that he's crying? asked those beside Art. "Special race!" roared the voice. Usually the race was for boys under fourteen, but apparently there were so many children on the field that the Committee decided to make two races of it. No sooner was this clear than Art heard his name being shouted by Donul, by Hamish, by Morag, by Tom, ay, even by Peigi Maclean, not to mention so many others that his heart rose clean into his throat and would not go back. Donul was pushing him, and Hamish, and Morag ducked under the rope. "Go on, Art! Go on! . . ." And here was a man coming and hauling shy children out. Art turned blindly against Donul, wanting to escape, but could not. "I'll hold your bonnet," said Donul. "Off with your jacket!" Donul had him ready in no time, and Art could have danced with rage, for he was not wanting to go, but he was wanting, too. "Come along," said the man, and Art was swept off.

The handicapping was a tricky business, for there were some youngsters of no more than five or six, but Art being over eight was placed scratch on the outside of a long line. On the inside, near the little flags, was one fellow so big that Donul said he must be eleven. Donul was mad, too, at Art for being on the outside. The race was lost for Art already. Any fool could see that, said Donul. Morag said nothing. She was laughing, a little beyond herself, and her eyes were brilliant.

"Get ready!" came the roar. "Off!"

And off they ran. Up went Art's chin and out went his chest, and twinkle-twinkle went his bare legs for all they were worth. And lucky it was for Art now that he was on the outside, because the big fellow, who was the swiftest, found himself, for all his cunning in choosing the inside berth, inconvenienced by the youngsters in front so that he pushed one of them and all but fell himself. Donul roared at that. Art was in a little bunch, but presently he came clear, lying third. The long line was stringing out. Up moved Art, foot by foot. He was lying second—and moving up.

"By God," roared the man's voice, "Art is taking the lead!"

"Art!" yelled Morag, not knowing she had opened her mouth.

Art was lying first, and close to the flags now.

But the big fellow was coming up in long strides, overtaking the third, overtaking the second, his mouth wide, his eyes staring, all out. Three yards behind Art . . . two yards . . . one.

"It's a sin!" cried Donul. "He's twelve if he's a day!"

But Art's speed did not slacken. The practice for the mile helped him now. His little elbows were flashing like shuttles. Other children had fallen out, panting, but Art would run until he dropped.

They were coming up now on Donul's group, and the shouting for Art rose to a wild yell. But the big fellow closed the yard and lay abreast of Art, with the finishing tape twelve yards ahead. "Art! Art! Go on, Art!"

The big fellow made his supreme effort, but he had overshot his staying power; his legs suddenly weakened, his breath sobbed, and Art ran clean away from him into the tape.

"By God," rose the man's voice, "Art broke his heart!" And Morag might well have embraced the man, if he hadn't been smelling of drink, early in the day as it was.

There was pandemonium then, and Donul had to lay his hands on Morag, to keep her from running into the ring, for well Donul knew what a terrible thing it would be for

Art to live down if Morag kissed him before the assembled multitudes.

And anyway, look! there was Duncan, crossing over to Art. Duncan was always cool and collected, and now with a smile, without any fuss, he stretched out his arm, and Art and himself shook hands.

That was a bit better, indeed. Donul nodded, moving restlessly on his feet, gleaming-eyed, and said to Hamish, for he had to say something or burst: "He'll get two shillings for that at least. It looks like being a good day for us!"

And a memorable day in truth it was, a fabulous day, before they came home through the gloaming at its close, and Art saw Old Hector standing by his peat-stack, the smoke of his pipe in his whiskers, waiting for the first news.

10

A Minor Operation

"I wonder what's wrong with my hero now?" said Old Hector to himself as he watched Art slowly limping near.

"What's gone wrong with you at all?" he cried to Art from a distance.

Art did not answer until he came quite close. "Something's gone into my foot," he said at last in a forlorn and bitter manner.

"Hots! tots!" exclaimed Old Hector. "That's not so good! How did it happen?"

"It just went in when I was walking."

"It would," said Old Hector. "Will you let me see it?"

"It's no good seeing it," said Art. "I looked for it myself."

"It'll have gone in a good way in that case," nodded Old Hector. "Whereabouts is it?"

"In m-my heel," answered Art.

"Well, you're a brave fellow not to cry if it's there, for that's an awkward place." He looked around and shouted: "Agnes! Will you bring me my glasses?"

"No, no! I'm going home," said Art. "I'm in a hurry."

"Och, what's all your hurry? It'll do no harm just to have a look at it."

"I'm going home," muttered Art, with difficulty keeping his bravery from breaking.

"Where were you that you're in such a hurry?"

"I was away off," muttered Art.

"Was it off to the River you were going?" asked Old Hector, with the deep interest of a conspirator.

Art looked at him—but just then Agnes came hurrying. "Here's your glasses," she said; "and I've brought a needle, for I saw you limping, poor boy."

"I'm going," said Art hurriedly. "They're waiting for me."

"Let me have a look at it at least. I promise not to touch it," said Old Hector. "Lie on your back now, and put up your foot."

Art at first refused, but in the end he got on his back and put up his bare foot. Old Hector, on his knees, peered through his spectacles at the heel; but Agnes, who was only forty-two and did not need spectacles, squatted lower and her head pushed his whiskers to one side.

"You're in my light," said Old Hector to her sharply.

"I'm seeing it!" she cried with decision, ignoring them both. "Wait a minute!"

Art's foot by a spasmodic movement hit her in the face.

"Steady!" she called, taking a good grip of the foot.

"No, no!" cried Art, his voice breaking.

"If you don't get it out now," said Agnes, "it will fester, and then your foot itself will have to be cut off."

"Will not!" shouted Art, struggling.

"Art," said Old Hector, gravely, "you must show if you have courage in you now. This is the time."

Art tried to avoid Old Hector's eyes but in the end he looked at them. Agnes took his foot in her lap. Old Hector smiled to Art. "Did you ever hear this conundrum?" he asked.

"If you lie like that," said Agnes, "you'll hardly feel it."

"Did you ever hear this conundrum?" repeated Old Hector. They both knew it was a trick, but it was a trick, they also knew, for withdrawing them into the male region of stoical courage. "It's not an easy one," proceeded Old Hector, "but here it is:

I went to the wood and I sought it not;
I sat on a hill and I found it not;
And because I found it not,
I took it home with me.

What was it?"

"I don't know," said Art.

"Try to think," said Old Hector.

"Oh-h-h!" yelled Art. "You're hurting me!"

"Just a minute!" cried Agnes impatiently.

Art looked at Old Hector's face, and after he looked his trembling lips muttered: "Say it again."

Nodding with deep understanding of Art's courage, Old Hector said it again.

Agnes squeezed the little hole she had made with her thumbnails, but the thorn refused to come out.

"Don't you know what it is yet?" asked Old Hector.

"No," said Art. "But I feel my heel better now. I'll be going."

"Lie still," ordered Agnes. "That's a brave little fellow."

"You're doing grand," said Old Hector. "I bet you Donul couldn't——"

Art leapt as the needle went into the tender flesh.

"God bless me, woman, can't you find the thing?" demanded Old Hector strongly.

"Will you keep still both of you," cried Agnes impatiently. "I'm seeing it, but how can I get it out if you keep jumping like fleas?"

"Shut your teeth, Art, for one second," said Old Hector, grimly.

Art shut his teeth, for he saw they were both in the grip of the woman.

"Wait now, wait now," went on Agnes in a voice of incantation. "I'm seeing it. I'm seeing it. It's coming. It's coming. Don't move now, don't move. That's a clever boy. That's a brave boy. . . ."

Art's body squirmed upward, but he held hard to Old Hector's hands, letting only small yelps past, until all at once he heaved in a wild blind spasm.

But Agnes's voice rose in triumph. "Look! I've got it! There it is!" And she wiped the tiny black thorn from the point of her needle on to her palm.

There in truth it was, and all in a moment Art had the lovely free feeling of no pain.

They both complimented him on his behaviour and Agnes said she would run now and get a glass of creamy milk. He deserved it, if anyone did.

"I—I cried," explained Art confidentially to Old Hector, "just because I—thought it was going to be worse."

"Naturally," agreed Old Hector. "And I can assure you I have heard many an older one cry more for less."

"Have you?"

"I have that."

"Isn't it fine," said Art, trying his heel, "having no pain?"

"There is no greater blessing in this life than just that," said Old Hector with profound conviction.

Art smiled. "I didn't catch your conundrum properly," he murmured politely.

"How could you?" agreed Old Hector, so he repeated

the conundrum once more, adding: "You did not look for it, yet it got into you, and because you could not find it you took it home here with you."

"A thorn!" cried Art.

"Good for you!" exclaimed Old Hector.

Art laughed. "Was it clever of me to find that one myself?"

"It was indeed," nodded Old Hector.

"I'll give *you* one," said Art.

"I'll do my best," promised Old Hector.

"What is it that is higher than the king's house, and finer than silk?"

Scratch his whiskers as he would, Old Hector was stumped now.

"Surely you're not beaten?" cried Art.

"Not yet," answered Old Hector.

"I can see it from here," cried Art.

"From here?" repeated Old Hector, looking abroad upon the world with care and surprise. When, however, his eyes turned upon his own house, Art felt sure he was going to get it, so he could not wait, and shouted:

"Smoke!"

"Ah, smoke!" said Old Hector, nodding. "You beat me that time."

Art was so delighted that he pivoted, without noticing it, on the heel that had held the thorn.

11

Going and Coming

1

Art's father turned on the jetty and said in his quiet way that perhaps they might as well be going. Everyone was smiling. The moment had come for farewells, and quickly and light-heartedly they were spoken. "We won't be wishing you luck," said Old Hector, wishing it by not wishing it, so that the old dark ones, who can be vindictive, might be deceived. His father turned to Art, and Art saw the face he knew break in a gentle smile, so that the eyes, considering him, grew deep and kind. Thus set apart in that still moment, Art became awkward and could not find his right hand, but his father found it for him.

Shaking hands with his own father induced so strange a feeling in Art that he could not say good-bye, and when it came to Duncan's turn he was like a stiff toy. Then there they were going into the open fishing boat, five men and four wooden chests.

Jokes were called, and those in the boat answered with a laugh or a witty word to increase the good humour. The oars were shipped. The brown sail went creaking up and was filled by the gentle wind. It was always considered a good omen when they could thus depart by sea for the bus at Clachdrum instead of lugging their heavy kists over the land. Soon they were no more than faces and shoulders in a boat whose stem rose and fell, cutting through the water with a lively eagerness. As they made the Point, the stem fell away on its new course. Presently the Point, holding firm, slowly ate up the whole boat, but Art knew the boat was still sailing the sea, for look! there were the tip of the mast and the peak of the sail beyond the dark rock, dipping and rising and still going on. This appearance of peak and masthead excited Art so profoundly that he cried out to Donul, pointing with his right hand towards the existence of the unseen.

"I'm seeing," said Donul. "Don't get excited."

Art was damped by Donul's voice. He wasn't excited! He looked around to make sure that no-one was laughing at him. He heard a man say: "Well, I suppose if they have a good season at the herring, Duncan will be marrying when he comes back," and two or three smiled at the odd but not unpleasant way life had of carrying on. Art saw their eyes light up in a humour so old and understood that no more words were needed for it.

But all this was outside his excitement, and he felt impatient with it, and he wanted to run up on to a height where he could still see the boat going away. Suddenly, however, he did not like to do this, because Donul might not be pleased, moving as he was among the others in a grown-up manner. And now he wanted to stick to Donul. He did not even want to go with Old Hector. The blood feeling of family was heavily upon him, holding him fast within its circle.

At last when the group was breaking up, members of each family to go their separate way, Art whispered to Donul: "Let us climb up the brae-face and see if we can still see her!"

Donul went on as though he had not heard, and presently when Art repeated in a moody tone that he would like to climb up, Donul asked, "What's that?" not sharply, but very nearly.

Again Art said that he would like to see the boat, and Donul paused and looked about to make sure they were not being observed. For a moment the old adventurous glimmer came into his eyes, but it faded, and he asked: "What would be the sense in that?"

"I would like to go," muttered Art, the fun chilled in him.

"I doubt if you could see her even if you went," said Donul calmly. "And in any case, we haven't time to go. There's work to do."

Art looked up at the side of his face as he strode on. Donul had never been a great one for work on the land, and many a row Art had heard him get from both Father and Duncan for stealing off on one of his expeditions at the wrong time. The only work that Donul could do, and do well, was look after the cow and the calf or stirk. He understood what went on in the heads of the beasts better than anyone else, and often he would make Art laugh by his predictions. "Now watch!" he had said the last time from the corner of the barn. "She'll have a look round, then she'll lick her lips, then she'll switch her tail, then she'll give a small sort of angry moo as much as to say 'What do I care?' and then she'll go down round the knoll as if she wasn't making for the off corner of the corn. Now watch!" And Neonain, a small red cow, not unlike Old Hector's one, and called after their sister Neonain, did exactly what Donul had foretold. Art had laughed and rushed after Donul, who had shouted the most terrible sounds at Neonain as she, joining in the race (seeing her intention had been discovered), galloped for the corn patch. There were heels in the air and a wildly swinging udder as Donul closed the distance between them with a stone that made exact allowance for the relative motions of two moving bodies. Art had laughed until he was sore.

But now Donul was quite different. This was not the Donul who had first given Art the courage to put his hand in a calf's mouth or hunt peewits' eggs on a Sunday morning. Keenly had Art been looking forward to the time when Father would be away, and Duncan, too, because then it was certain life would be much more free and full of fun. Donul and himself would have the greatest times and, in particular, Donul would be able to take him to the fabled River and the Hazel Pool—the River that he sometimes thought he would never be allowed to reach in this life.

Such bright hope Art was unwilling to let go, so he tested Donul by saying confidingly: "We should have good times now by ourselves, shouldn't we?"

"How do you make that out?" asked Donul. "Are you glad they have gone away?" He smiled in a calm but mocking manner.

"No," said Art, "but—but we should have good times?"

"Seeing Father and Duncan are away, surely it stands to reason that there will be more work to do?"

Art did not answer. The thought of work was dull. A brightness went out of the landscape, and he saw his home and the coloured fields around it go still and lonely as if they were aware that Father and Duncan had been withdrawn from them. Where there should have been an overflowing there was, instead, a draining away.

As they were walking up to the house, Donul said: "The corn is coming on well," but Art did not answer. Donul paused to look all around him and his eyebrows gathered in the way his father's did. He muttered and Art turned to follow his look. Neonain, the herd, was sitting in the grassy ditch, making something, probably a string of daisy-heads. "Hey!" shouted Donul. Neonain lifted her head and then swung away like a frightened rabbit, but the cow, though well down, was still in the ditch. Donul went on and Art slowly followed him.

Inside the house, Mother and Morag were sitting by the fire having a cup of tea, and Janet was softly rocking Henry James in his cradle. There was a cheerfulness about them as though they were having a picnic. As the boys entered, the faces met them, and Mother said: "Well, are they off?"

"They are," answered Donul, looking here and there as if he had lost something important, like a scythe.

"Come and have a cup of tea," said their mother, her voice friendly and inviting.

"No," answered Donul calmly, "I'm not wanting it." He was distant and preoccupied.

"Have you lost something?"

"It's all right," answered Donul, and he turned and went out.

As Art saw a faint smile dawn in his mother's face, he turned and followed Donul, though he was very fond of a fly cup of tea, because often then the butter was laid thick on a piece of oat-cake, and sometimes on an abernethy biscuit if Morag had been to the shop.

Donul went into the byre and, lifting the hoe that was used for raking the stalls clean, handled it as though it were new to him and he wished to estimate its exact weight. "The other one is down in the barn," he said. "It's lighter."

Art followed him to the barn, and Donul, after taking the feel of the hoe, handed it to Art. "That should suit you," he said. "Would you like to help me clean the potatoes?"

"I would," said Art, and as he walked after Donul with

the hoe over his shoulder, he was conscious of a small access of eagerness and happiness. He made up on Donul. "It's fine going to work, too, isn't it?"

"It'll do," answered Donul. Then he gave a dry but friendly smile. "Perhaps you won't think so when your back is like to break."

Art smiled, too, now all eagerness to be with Donul working the croft. "I didn't want the tea either," he said.

"Women are always at the teapot," answered Donul. "They wouldn't let it get cold if they could help it."

Art nearly laughed. "That's what Red Dougal said yon night, remember?"

"I didn't need to hear Red Dougal say it," replied Donul.

"I know that," said Art. "I was only just remembering."

"It's all right," nodded Donul. "One would need to have a good memory to remember all Red Dougal says."

"Doesn't he say a lot!" agreed Art, anxious before all else now to please Donul. "Tell me this: why does he grow barley as well as oats? We don't grow any barley."

"You're asking me!" replied Donul. "All I know is that barley is not so valuable a human food as oats. That's enough for me."

"It should be enough for anyone," agreed Art. "But Old Hector has a small patch also. I'll ask him."

"You can," said Donul. "We start here. I'll show you how to do it on this drill, and then you'll follow me up on that one."

Art watched Donul very carefully and asked many questions, and Donul explained how necessary it was not to cut down a potato shoot when pulling away the weeds with the corner of the hoe.

It seemed easy to Art until he got going, when he found that the blade of the hoe answered him very awkwardly or not at all. As often as not he was on his knees, pulling the weeds away with his fingers. Donul was gaining on him. Yard by yard Donul withdrew from him, and Art grew so anxious to keep up that he slew a potato shoot. At once he was assailed by the feeling of having committed a crime and by an urgent need to hide it from Donul. This affected him so deeply that his skin burned all over. On his knees, he began hand-picking the weeds again until, little by little, he managed to scoop earth over the slain potato shoot. When it was well covered he got up and, looking towards Donul, trod down the earth above it. Then he took up his hoe again.

But he was tired of the work now and desperately afraid he would slaughter more potato shoots. As it was, he felt certain Donul would discover the buried one.

Presently Donul came down. "You're doing fine," he said. "You needn't try to keep up with me. Every little helps. Are you feeling dry?"

"I am," answered Art.

"I'll tell you what," said Donul, more in the voice Art knew, "you go and get some oatmeal and sugar and mix it with well-water in the little milk-pail. Then we'll have a good drink. How would you like that?"

"Fine!" said Art. It was the drink men had when reaping the grain. "Will Mother give it to me?"

"Tell her I told you," said Donul firmly.

"All right," said Art, and he ran off.

As he approached the house, he paused, touched by an obscure feeling that his mother would smile at him. He looked around and saw Neonain busy crawling about the grass at a game of her own. He had never cared much for herding, but now he saw how lucky she was. Then his eyes lifted to where Donul, all alone, with bent head and moving hoe handle, was doing the work of the croft. Something in this vision of Donul touched him more obscurely and more profoundly than his premonition of his mother's smile.

But his mother did not smile. "Surely," she said quite naturally, and put a good lot of sugar amongst the meal. "You need it when you're working."

Whereupon Art became all impatience to get the pail and be off. But his mother told him to wait a minute. She richly buttered two bannocks of oat-cake.

"Heavy weather on us to-day!" said Morag.

"You shut up!" said Art.

"What way is that to talk to your own sister?" demanded Morag with bright teasing eyes.

"Perhaps you deserve it," said her mother, as she handed her son the bread.

Art did his best not to run too hard lest he spill some of the contents of the pail, so before he reached the potato plot he let out a great shout at Donul. Donul heard it and, laying down his hoe, came to meet Art.

2

Dear Wife,

This is to say that Duncan and myself are both well, hoping you are all the same. We had a good season so far. The weather has kept open and the herring are on the ground, a big improvement on last season though the prices have not been so good. Duncan is with a very good man. Their boat has fished fully better than ours. We should be sure now of our hired money and maybe a fair bit over and that's something to see the winter through. The quality just now is extra good and I am trying to arrange about a barrel of salt herring for I must say they are special. If we are not home this next week, we will be home the week following if all goes well.

I hope everything is going well with you at home and that the child is coming on. I will be glad to see you all once more.

Your loving husband,
DONALD MACRAE.

When the mother had read out the letter, they were all delighted with the good news, for it was the only letter they had received in six weeks, and once outside Donul and Art got a lot of fun from mouthing the English words "extra" and "special" in such a way that they thickened with meaning, for English itself was a formal polite tongue, lacking the merry warmth of life.

"You'll be back at school!" scoffed Donul.

Art paused, hit in the wind. "I will not!" he cried, but without conviction.

Donul scoffed harshly. "You won't be in when they come home!"

"I will so!" cried Art, flying into a rage.

"You won't see the presents taken out of the kists!"

"I will! I will!" Art danced.

Donul walked down to the barn, laughing. Art ran bellowing into the house and awoke Henry James.

But as good luck would have it he was not only at home but the first to see Alan Maclean's cart coming, with Father and Duncan sitting on their kists. Though they waved to him, he did not go to meet them but, on the contrary, bolted back to the house shouting, "They're coming! They're coming!" beside himself with excitement.

Movement and bustle beset the house then, with the blue peat smoke in a dance of its own and Henry James adding valiantly to the volume of sound. Art rushed out at the door—and was suddenly smitten by a terrible shyness.

His hands went down to his sides and then behind him, and he leaned hard against the wall of the house, trying to back into it, and, not succeeding, started edging and scraping away. A desire to run off and hide overwhelmed him. But he could not run. And because he could not run he wanted to cry.

Morag came dashing out, followed calmly by her mother with Janet on one side of her skirts and Neonain gripping hard the other. Alan's two chance passengers leapt from the cart.

"Welcome home!" the mother greeted them.

Her husband shook hands with her, his face creased in smiles. "Well, well, so here you all are," and he looked upon them with gladness, shaking hands. Duncan behind him, was also shaking hands. Donul came slowly round the end of the house and they shook hands with him, too.

"Where's Art? Oh, there he is!" cried their father.

They all looked at Art, and Art bolted, but Duncan soon caught him up and lifted him high in the air. Art struggled and screamed but by the time Duncan said a few words in his ear the fearful tension in him broke and he came forward to meet his father, who bent down and said: "Is this my own little boy?"

There was a noise now of the cart turning and the father at once stood upright and shouted, "Alan! Don't go yet, man!" and he walked up towards Alan with strong gestures of hospitality.

Morag nudged her mother. "There's a good smell," she whispered with restrained humour, referring to her father's breath.

But her mother said calmly: "Why wouldn't there? It's not every day they come home. . . . Come away in, Alan!"

"Och, look here, you won't be wanting me——"

"Come away in, man!" said the father, gripping Alan by the arm. "Where would we have been without you?"

"Oh well, there's no saying!" replied Alan, with a bright glance at the woman of the house.

So in they all went, and there was Henry James, and when he had been inspected, with much complimentary comment on the fine lungs that were in him, whatever else, Janet got down to her nursing and the father drew a whisky bottle from an inside pocket.

When Alan was offered the glass of whisky, he made a polite gesture towards the woman of the house, and when she refused it with a pleasant smile, he took off his bonnet. "Well, I'm very glad that you have had a good fishing, and you too, Duncan. And here's my very best respects to yourself, mistress. May your store increase, and health and happiness be with you always. Good health!"

"Good health, Alan, and thank you," said the mistress.

Alan drank off the glass and smiled. "Ha-a-a. It's a good drop."

"It will see you on your way," said the father. "And I'm sure we don't know how to thank you."

"Thank me, is it?" said Alan. "I only wish you were coming every day!" And with a laugh he put on his bonnet and turned away. The man of the house accompanied him to the cart, and there they talked warmly and confidentially together. Art had never seen his father so full of pleasant energy.

Duncan opened a large cardboard parcel that contained bacon and tea and a fruit cake and other unusual eatables. Janet and Neonain each accepted a fancy biscuit, so Art took one too. As he nibbled the biscuit, he watched all that was going on, careful not to miss the least thing.

With the frying-pan sizzling and other preparations afoot for a feast, the men straightened themselves and said they would have a look round while the bacon was cooking. Out they went then and Father and Duncan seemed much taller to Art, and as they stooped, going in at the byre door, they spread their feet wide and lurched slightly like men on a boat at sea.

Art waited for them to come out, and when they did they moved leisurely round the gable-end until they could see the crops. Donul had nothing to say and seemed awkward, his head restless on his neck. Art saw the quiet look of pleasure come glimmering into his father's eyes, as if there was nothing more lovely in this life than the calm of good crops growing.

As his eyes took in the way the potatoes were cleaned and heaped, he nodded. "Yes, you have done well," he said to Donul.

Donul's face darkened as in anger, he was so pleased. Then he tried to make a joke of his awkwardness by saying: "Art gave me a good hand."

"Did he?" His father looked at Art in order to see him properly, but the affection in the look was held in a man's restraint. Art was glad he had helped Donul now.

Duncan in a light scoffing tone said: "Things might be worse." These words released Donul and he scoffed back at Duncan, who laughed.

The table was laden and the smell of fried bacon sharp in the nostrils. In a circle of peace, the father said the Grace Before Meat, and the mother sat where she could reach for the teapot, her hands in her lap, more calm than the others, as if they were all her children, including her husband. Her face was smooth with beneficence and her provident eyes quiet with peace. Before her husband's hand was down from his brow, she said in pleasant practical tones: "Now be eating, bairns."

At last, when all was eaten and the gravy licked up, the table was pushed away and the kists produced. "Oh, you needn't be expecting much," said the father. He lifted up his face to the small window. "It's getting dark, woman."

"So it is. Light the lamp, Morag."

And in the lamplight, the ferlies, the bonny things, the presents, were produced one at a time. If Art was bursting with excitement, he was nothing to Neonain and Janet. Even Henry James insisted on a view, and from his mother's lap surveyed the whole scene, including the brightness of the lamp, with an impartiality that nodded and occasionally adventured on a chortle of amusement, befitting the only one present who achieved a reasonable degree of detachment.

And when the father had handed out something, he must relate an incident or other that suddenly came back into his mind, for the good food was mellowed by the whisky that had gone before. And if he did, never had he had a more attentive audience, even if they failed to grasp his full point, so eagerly were they waiting for what was coming next. For Art he had a rubber ball, half as big as his head, painted over with Edinburgh Castle and houses in the most beautiful colours. Art had only once seen a ball like it and t but half the size, and only with lines, not a castle and houses.

"I don't think it will bounce," said Donul.

Art hugged the ball and muttered that it would so bounce. There was a laugh as they all looked at Art. So Art tried the ball there and then, and it bounced right up through his arms, and Donul, in trying to catch it, knocked it straight towards the fire, but Duncan with a lunge fisted it clear so that it smacked against the wall, rebounded, narrowly missed the lamp, bobbed off Henry James's head, and was caught by Art as he fell over a chair. Henry James was about to make a few comments, but his mother dandled him and asked if that wasn't a lovely ball. Morag addressed to him the same question and so did Janet. Henry James, thus directed towards the brightly coloured sphere, off which Art was blowing invisible dust, began to struggle violently, having already forgotten the mysterious knock on his head in his anxiety to possess the sphere itself.

But Art would not give up the ball for anyone or anything, and held it in his hands behind his back. Morag explained that the ball had gone far far away, and Henry James, trying to follow the mysterious movements of her hands, saw the lamp and considered it thoughtfully. A strange thing, this light.

From present to present, surprise to surprise, time hurried so fast that it stood still. And now here was Duncan about to act the magician. The mother first, and then Morag. The trinket Morag got was so unexpected that she could hardly believe it. It was a brooch of two four-leaved clovers, for luck, bright as silver, and had cost Duncan all of one-and-sixpence.

"You don't keep it in your mouth," said Donul.

Morag closed her mouth and joined happily in the laughter. "It's lovely," she said to Duncan, and very lovely she looked herself.

"It's for luck," said Duncan, and if Morag blushed she didn't at that moment care who saw her.

Art was not deeply impressed by a mere brooch: he was waiting. And then it came, wrapped in paper, a small hard thing. They watched his fumbling fingers. It gleamed and lay on his palm, its handle whiter than ivory and inset with a small rectangle of silver. A knife, smoother to his fingers than anything he had ever touched. Two blades. Two. There was a hubbub of sound somewhere around Art as the ancient sphere of the earth wobbled appreciably on its airy foundations.

12

What is Good Conduct?

Many were the difficult subjects discussed round a peat fire, and if the fire happened to be Old Hector's, one could depend on it that the subject would be discussed reasonably and illustrated with wisdom, for at the very hottest moment Old Hector would smile, enjoying the heat, and so turning it naturally into pleasantness.

One evening when Art was there with Donul, the subject of money cropped up. Old Hector maintained that money wasn't everything, that there were more important things than money, and that in his young days people didn't hanker after it so greedily as they did now.

One or two in middle life scoffed at that and told Old Hector he was a back number, for times had changed entirely. "Had they been keener on the money and their own interest when you were a boy," said a man with a laughing red face and a quick temper, "our forefathers wouldn't have been cleared out of the Clash in the times of the evictions."

"The boot's on the wrong foot there," replied Old Hector. "It was the lairds and the factors who were keen on the money, and it's because they were keen on the money that they drove the people forth."

"Yes, yes, but if the people had been keen, too, they would have put up a fight. Damn me, if I would have lain down to them!"

"Perhaps not," agreed Old Hector. "But if you hadn't lain down they would have knocked you down. They had the power."

"Had they! We had power, too."

"Not enough," said Old Hector. "Not enough—to fight the sheriff, the police, and the soldiery, backed by the law."

When the red-faced man had worked himself into a heat, another man with thin dark hair, a sallow skin, and a tidy mind, said: "Hach! we have heard all that before. What I want to know is this. Here I am now, with whatever sort of qualities go to make me up. Well, do you mean to say to me that if I got money over and above, I would be other than myself then? I would still be myself——"

"Only more so," said a voice sadly.

"I would still be myself," proceeded the sallow man, "but I would be easier in my mind and in a position perhaps to help my neighbour."

"I have not observed," replied Old Hector, "that it's the people who are out to make the money who are the helping kind. Indeed we know, many of us to our cost, that the more they make the grippier they become."

"True for you, Hector!" said a man who had suffered from a merchant.

"Yes, but you don't get my point," persisted the sallow man.

"I get it," said Old Hector. "We can only talk of what we know and see. Money is needful and a fine thing in itself, but it's not everything. The more you think about money, the less you think about other things, until in the end you would betray your own father to get it."

That was deemed by some to be going a bit too far. There were voice and counter-voice and several voices at once. "No! no!" and "Yes! yes!" and "Listen to me!"

. . . . .

What is Good Conduct?

There was once in times long past (said Old Hector when his turn came) a farmer, and he was about to die. It was a large-sized place he had, and fertile. All his life he had been a decent man, and his store had increased. Well, as his hour drew nigh, he called his three sons about him, told them that he was not long now for this world, and asked them to listen to his last words and to abide by them. It was a solemn moment, and the old man imparted to them what he considered were the virtues which no man should be without if he was to live at peace with himself and therefore at peace with his neighbour. The words needed were not many and they were enough. Then the farmer said: "You will find all my money in the shottle of my kist"—and he pointed to the kist which made a low table by his bed—"and you will find the key in the blue jug on the mantelpiece there. It's all in gold, and it is my wish that when my body has been committed to the grave you will open the kist and divide the money equally among you. In the same way, each of you will have a third share in the farm and all that belongs to it. May you prosper and above all be honourable one to another and at peace among yourselves." Then he gave them his blessing and he died.

When the funeral was over, the three sons entered the room where the kist was, and they opened it, but they found no money inside, neither in the shottle nor elsewhere.

They stood up in astonishment then, as you can well imagine. "Perhaps his mind was wandering," said the youngest, "and there was never any money in it at all."

"His mind was not wandering," said the second son, "and there was money in it. I'm certain of that."

"He never told a lie," said the eldest.

Yet here was the kist and it was without money. They

did not know what to do, for it was strange indeed, seeing no-one had been told where the key was but themselves.

Now the farmer's oldest and greatest friend was a man who lived at some little distance. He was a wise man, this man, and the eldest son said they would go and tell him what had happened and ask him for his advice. The other two agreed to that, and off they set.

The man welcomed them to his house and took them in and gave them refreshment. When they had eaten his bread and spoken together, the eldest son told the man of their father's last words and how when they opened the kist there was no money in it. The man was surprised at that and looked at them, but he did not say much at that time, for what had happened was unusual and could not be judged without thought. So he invited the three sons to stay with him for a short while.

Well, in the darkening of the third day, as all four of them were sitting round the fire and talking, as we might be talking ourselves, it came naturally to the man to tell them of a thing that had happened long before then; and this is what he told them:

There was once a young man who was very poor, and he loved the daughter of a rich neighbour. Because he was poor he could not marry her. One night when they had met secretly, their love was very strong upon them, and they made a vow of their love to each other, and pledged themselves in solemn promise. And then they parted at that time, for part they had to.

Presently there came a rich suitor who grew enamoured of the girl and pressed his suit strongly. Because he was rich he could marry her. The father supported his suit and told his daughter that marry him she must. At first she refused, but a father had great power over a daughter at that time, and in the end she gave in, for give in she had to.

The wedding followed, and a splendid and sumptuous wedding it was. Well, when the feasting and dancing were over and the guests all gone and the bride had been put to bed by the other women, as the custom was, up went the bridegroom to the bridal bed. But his bride was not in bed. She was standing in her long nightdress by a heavy curtain, and she was weeping.

At first he thought it might not be very much, but soon he saw how strange and pitiful the weeping was and knew there must be something on her heart. So he questioned her, and there and then she told him the story of the poor lover to whom she had pledged herself.

"Dress yourself," said he, "and come with me."

So she dressed herself in her wedding clothes, and quietly she followed him down the stairs, and he drew back the bar of the door.

"Don't be afraid," he said, and he led her round to the stables. Then he went in and brought out his horse. He put her behind him on his horse, and off he rode without talk between them, until at last they came to the house of the poor lad. There he dismounted and helped his bride down and led her to the door. He rapped on the door, but spoke no word; then he turned and mounted his horse and rode away.

By this time the lad had struck a light inside, and when he came to the door and opened it, there on the step, dressed in her wedding clothes, was the girl he had loved and thought he had lost.

"What's brought you here?" he asked, for it might well be that the ends of the world were giving way.

She began to tell him, and before she had told him much he took her in, and he listened to what she had to say until the end.

"So he did that," he said, looking past her. "Wait here."

He got up, and he went out, and he leaped on his horse and rode to the house of the priest. There he explained to the priest all that had happened, and he brought the priest back with him.

Pleased the priest was to come, and not much questioning did he put them through, but there and then he broke the pledge that was between them, and absolved them of it. Oh, it was properly done and the poor lad had it put in writing.

Well, the priest rode off, and the poor lad and the girl prepared to ride off, too. But when it came to the bit, and the poor lad had handed her the piece of writing, he mounted her on his horse, and said that it might be better for her if she rode home alone.

She said it would be better.

She rode away into the night on the poor lad's horse, in her wedding dress. The moon was up now and a fine night it was, and there was nothing for her to be frightened of except a dark wood, and she had only to skirt that.

She was passing it midway, when who should leap out but three robbers, and one of them caught the horse's bridle.

"Ah," they cried, "we have waited all night and got nothing, but now we have caught the bride herself!"

They were jubilant at that, for they had heard of the rich wedding and had come a long journey from their den, hoping to waylay some of the guests. But if their luck had been out, it was in now!

"Let me go!" she cried. "Let me go!"

They laughed at that.

"Let me go!" she cried. "The man I was pledged to let me go. Let me go!"

"We'll let you go," said they, "when we get all we want to get." And they laughed again, for they thought it was a good joke capturing a bride all dressed in her wedding best on her first night.

She beseeched them then, telling how it happened she was in the plight she was and how generous the poor lad had been in releasing her from her pledge. There and then she offered them ten golden sovereigns which was all the money she had on her at that time.

One of the robbers was touched by her story, by the generous way in which good men had dealt by her, and he said: "As others have done this, I will take you home myself." He refused the money.

But the other two robbers did not refuse, and one of them cried: "I will have the money, for that's the one solid thing in this life!" And when he had made sure there were no more gold pieces on her, he let her go, and the good-natured robber then mounted her on the horse behind him and rode with her to her husband's house.

Right glad her husband was to see her again, for he thought he had lost her for good, and when she showed him the writing over and above, there was more than content between them in the bridal chamber that night.

Well (proceeded Old Hector), that was the story the man told the three sons. And when he had finished, he turned to the eldest and he asked: "Whose conduct do you think was the best of these men?"

And the eldest answered: "I think it was the conduct of the husband, for he showed himself an honest and a generous man in sending her back to him to whom she had been pledged."

"What do you think?" asked the man of the second son.

And the second son answered: "No, I think the conduct of the pledged man was still better in sending her back to her husband."

"What do you think?" asked the man of the youngest son.

And the youngest answered: "I don't know myself, but it seems to me that out of it all the only ones who got something real were the robbers who got the ten pounds."

Now this man, who was their father's friend, had been observing the sons for three days. He looked at the youngest son and he said: "It was you who stole your father's money."

When it was put to him like that, the youngest could not hold the wise man's eye, and guilt came, despite him, and wrote its name on his face, and he confessed that it was he who had betrayed his father's last wish in order to steal his father's money.

Those sitting around Old Hector got tied up in the story for a bit, for it was not easy just to see and estimate every incident of it both at once and in relation to the whole, not to mention the relating of the whole to points in the earlier discussion.

The sallow man began a story which he said would show what he meant, but his mind was so tidy that every detail in it had to be made clear, and so it grew up all detail and no point, and when that's the case the best detail can turn arid. But no-one could interrupt him in another man's house, and Old Hector would sit there attentively until the day broke.

But the red-faced man shifted restlessly on his hips as though the seat of the chair was harder than its bare wood, and suddenly he could not help saying: "Ay, take that point itself before you go any further, and I'm not interrupting you."

They argued that point until the sallow man was put off his story, and as he shaped up to come back on to it, the red-faced man, with a hearty laugh, said: "So, you see, you're wrong. And that's what I've been getting at all along. The man of the house here is wrong, too. You're all wrong. For why?"

"Excuse me," said the sallow man, "but I was about to finish my story——"

"One minute," said the red-faced man, "just one minute," and he extended his arm with the open palm towards the sallow man's mouth, and he looked at Old Hector, his eyes glinting. "It's all very well telling stories and this and that, but the fact remains. And the fact is, we're here, and the Ground Officer is yonder in the Clash with the good land. All the rest is in my eye. And more than my eye. Because the more we talk and talk the more we close up our eyes until our ears are bung-full. We're like seals barking on a rock, but whenever anyone heaves in sight, watch us taking headers into the quiet ocean then. Ay, ay, it's a fine day! We're against the robbers in the story but we touch our bonnets to the robbers in life."

"Good for you!" said Old Hector with a nod. "It's talking you are now, and no mistake. But that sort of talking I have also heard all my life, and the Ground Officer is still yonder and we are here."

"Yes, but he wouldn't be yonder if we stood up for our rights. Unless we stand up, he'll always be yonder, and we'll be here. The rest is just soft soap."

"And with the soft soap we blow bubbles," said Old Hector, and he smiled. "That's good, too. But the trouble is that the word you used was rights—not money. Now——"

"But without our rights we can't make money. Surely that's clear to half an intelligence."

"Yes—but the rights come first. It is right and fair that the people should have the land back. For untold generations our folk cultivated the Clash, and the Clash was theirs. Whether they made money out of it or not is beside the point. Indeed there wasn't any money to speak of in the old days, and even the laird was content to get such dues as he could in butter or cheese. It's when the greed of money-making started that the lairds got their charters, through laws made by lairds, and cleared our folk off the land. It was money-making they were after. And whenever the prime concern in life is money-making, then you have trickery and brutality and wrong. I'm saying that, not from what I have heard, but from what I have observed in a long life among our own folk."

"No doubt, no doubt," said the red-faced man, "but how are you going to alter things now unless we combine to fight?"

"Let us get one thing clear at a time," replied Old Hector. "We have to combine, certainly, but if we combine to fight on the idea of each man making more money for himself, then we end by fighting one another. And that's the trouble now. Why haven't all the people combined long ago if it's as easy as you think? Let any one of us be left a bit of money, let him get an extra croft, let him get a little shop, let him be more thrifty than his neighbour and have a few pounds in the bank, let him get a share in a boat without going to sea himself, let him get an extra horse and do a bit of carting or contracting—but you know fine what I mean, and how quick the knife can be stuck in the back of friendship. No, the first thing we have to learn is that our claim is fair and just as between man and man; human dealings are founded—*founded*—not on money but on what is fair and just all round. The wise man was maybe not so far wrong when he asked the three sons for their opinions on the conduct of the characters in his story."

"Talking of that story," said the sallow man, "reminds

me that I didn't get finishing my own. Now you'll remember that I was at the point where. . . ."

On their way home through the darkness, Art said to Donul: "Weren't there the arguments in it to-night!"

"There were," said Donul. "Did you like them?"

"I liked them fine. Old Hector is good at it, isn't he?"

"He put Red Dougal on his back by the end, anyway. And that was something."

"Why? Don't you like Red Dougal?"

"Ach, I like him well enough, but the trouble is he's got too much mouth. He's never yet been on a grazing committee or anything else but there was a fight. Yet he's a fine fellow in many ways, and often kind. But even when you agree with what he says, he somehow makes you feel that he's always in the right and you in the wrong. It's vexing, often."

"I could well believe it," said Art. "He's that sort."

"He is," said Donul, and laughed at the way Art's words cleared his mind.

Art felt the access of friendliness in Donul and presently he asked:

"Who did you think was the best?"

"The best where?"

"In yon story of Hector's—you know, about the conduct?"

"Oh, that. I haven't thought about it. Who do you think was the best yourself?"

"I was thinking," said Art, "—of course, I'm not saying he was, I'm only just thinking it. Remember the robber who wouldn't take the money, and mounted the girl behind him and rode home with her to her husband? Do you think he might be the best?"

"Well," said Donul judicially, "he certainly was very

good, now that you mention it. I wouldn't have thought of that."

"I thought of it at once," said Art. "Do you think he was the best?"

"If he wasn't the best, he was very near it," agreed Donul.

After a thoughtful pause, Art said in a low but clear voice: "I know one thing whatever."

"What's that?" asked Donul.

"I wouldn't have liked to have been the youngest son."

"Mind your feet here," cried Donul. "Isn't it dark?"

"It's dark, but I'm not frightened."

It was lovely to be in the dark walking home with Donul, and not to be frightened.

13

Art's Wedding Present

"There will be great excitement at home," said Old Hector as he sat on the little knoll, with one eye on the red cow.

"There is," said Art. "Morag is dancing about like a hen on a hot griddle, and if she is, Janet and Neonain are not much better, and Mother is ironing. It's no place for a man yonder."

Old Hector took his pipe out of his mouth the better to enjoy a soft note or two of laughter.

"And Neonain," continued Art, "said she was going to get married, and she is only ten past, and when I asked her who she was going to get married to, she said it was none of my business. I told her she hadn't anyone to get married to. Boy, didn't she grow wild then!" declared Art, his eyes dancing.

"She would."

"She did. You would think," added Art, "that a wedding was a great thing."

"Well," replied Old Hector, "it's not a small thing, as a rule. They contrive, one way or another, to make a lot of it."

The cunning-shy smile came to Art's features and he half looked away. "Do you think," he asked, "that—that women use it to make fools of men?"

"What's that?" asked Old Hector sharply. Then he observed the confused innocence breaking into merriment as Art pivoted on his bare heel, and he inquired: "Where did you hear that?"

"I heard Father saying it."

"Did you indeed? He must have been exercised beyond his usual, surely?"

"He was. The Dark Woman was in and she and Mother were talking round the fire."

"In that case," said Old Hector, "I have some sympathy for your father. He would have had a hard time of it."

"That's what he said. He said he didn't know his own house."

"He wouldn't," agreed Old Hector. "They would be joking and taking fun out of him."

"They were," said Art. "And then the Dark One said something to Father, and Mother and herself laughed out loud, and Morag gave a small laugh, too, but I didn't catch what it was."

"It was maybe as well," nodded Old Hector.

"I would like to have catched it, though," said Art. "You don't know what it might have been?"

"How could I," said Old Hector, "seeing I wasn't there?"

"Why are you smiling like that, then?" asked Art.

"A man can smile if he likes, surely?"

Art smiled too. "And do you know what Father said about Duncan?"

"No."

"He said, 'You would think he had a sore head.' "

"Ho! ho! ho!" laughed Old Hector.

Art laughed too. "Is that a good one?"

"Fair to middling," replied Old Hector with bright eyes.

"Do you actually think," asked Art, "that Duncan has a sore head?"

"Oh, I shouldn't think so."

"But perhaps a man has a sore head when he's going to be married. You never know. He might have."

"He might, of course."

"There's something wrong with him whatever. Donul asked me to ask him last night if his head was any better, and when I asked him he turned on me and gave me a blow that flattened me."

"Did he indeed? There would be trouble then."

"There was," said Art. "And Mother took his side, and Morag, too, and Janet and Neonain, but Father took my side."

"And what about Donul?"

"He ran away," said Art, "laughing."

"The rascal!" Old Hector bushed up his whiskers to scratch underneath, but Art saw he was smiling in them. "It's a difficult time altogether." Old Hector shook his head. "It's not often I get lumps in my porridge, but lumps there were this morning."

"Is Agnes great about the wedding, too, then?"

"Who isn't? Three of our young hens have been named for thrawing. It's nothing but presents, presents, and clothes, clothes."

"Are you making a present yourself?" asked Art.

"Oh, I'll have to give something, I suppose, but it's not much they have left me after many years. All my feathers are gone."

Art looked at Old Hector's whiskers. Old Hector looked back at Art. Art flushed very slightly and, to change the thought, said: "They won't be expecting a present from me, will they?"

Old Hector chuckled. "I doubt if anyone in the two

townships will be let off, but the best present you can make is to stay about your home during this difficult time, so that you may do any little thing that's required of you and run a message when you're asked."

"Why is it always me? It's queer it should always be me who's got to do that," remarked Art with some petulance. "There's Donul: he was off the whole day yesterday, and early this morning he was off again, and he said to me—for I woke up as he was going—he said, 'I'll murder you if you try to follow me.' It's queer it should always be me."

"Never you mind," said Old Hector soothingly. "You'll one day be fifteen like Donul, and then you can be off, too."

"You were off yourself," said Art moodily, giving his friend at the same time a suspicious glance.

"I was only off on a visit or two. At a time like this, many strange things have to be done. Indeed I've got to be busy this very minute," and he looked far around the countryside as if his knoll were a watch-tower. "Now you be a good boy, and run off home, and. . . ."

But it was all very well. Art no sooner put his nose inside his home than it was shoved out. "Can't you run away and play yourself?"

With whom was he going to play? The whole world had gone queer and hidden things were on foot. A fellow could see by the look of the earth itself that things were moving in silence.

Art went down to his own secret place behind the little barn, and sure as he came there the idea struck him. Donul and Hamish had gone off to the River to catch salmon! Not to poach in the ordinary way—he could think of that readily enough at any time—but to get salmon for the wedding feast *as a present!*

It was a thought, and two thoughts. Ducks, hens, butter,

cheese, bakings, cakes with currants, a side of pork, a leg of mutton, eggs and more hens, from this one and from that, from here and from there, puddings and shivering jellies, little pastries and big pies, things Art now heard of but had never seen, much less tasted. And Donul and Hamish were adding to this communal feast the distinction of salmon!

Art looked about him and saw the cat. He had nothing in the world that he could give even to the cat itself, barring a kick. And he never kicked the cat. It wasn't safe.

The distant River slowly drew him by the nose. The farther he went on, the more clearly he saw Donul and Hamish actively engaged at the Hazel Pool.

Skirting Old Hector's cottage at a discreet distance, he paused to spy out the land. There was no sign of Old Hector now. Only women and cows and children here and there. The country was deserted.

He slid down into the hollow beyond, and so entered the Little Glen.

In the Little Glen he was all alone, going away off to find the fabled River and the Hazel Pool, and because this fatal mood was upon him and there was no help for it, he wanted to cry. It was hard on him, having to do all this alone. When the cry mounted he took a little run to himself and the tears that came out bounced off.

Presently he noticed that the glen was quieter and more watchful than when he had gone down it before, perhaps because Mary Ann had been with him then.

But the glen itself seemed to have changed, too. There were curious little places which he had not noticed before, and one or two bends which he could have sworn were not in it the last time. And then he observed, on the other side, the small ravine of a burn which issued in a noisy trickle of water. He certainly had never seen *that* before, so he stood and stared at it until it began to stare back. Whereupon he went on, but with the corner of his left eye on the ravine to prevent a surprise, and while he was thus politely not really looking at the ravine, the earth itself bobbed clean from under his foot and he went face first into a ditch. It was the one he had told Mary Ann how to jump.

So he was on the right road, and even if things could be enchanted, as he had heard Donul say before now, they clearly had not been enchanted entirely.

All the same, they had gone a bit strange, and even if Mary Ann——. The thought of her brought up a vision of the foxgloves which she had called the thimbles of the fairy woman—the foxgloves that grew in front of the wild beast's den, which could not be so very far ahead of him now. Art suddenly stopped.

Mary Ann had said it mightn't be a wild beast's den at all, but the house of the little folk who had planted the foxgloves in front of it for a garden. To Art at this moment there didn't seem much to choose between a wild beast's den and a house of the little folk.

Back he couldn't go, and forward his feet wouldn't budge, so he went sideways down to the stream in the glen, crossed it without misadventure, and climbed the opposite slope until at last he drew himself up through a tongue of heather and lay on his belly peering all round.

And it was lucky for him that he did so, for now striding across the moor towards the side which he had just left came three strange men. Even at a distance Art could see that they were dressed like the Ground Officer when he went to meet the Factor on the day of the collection of rents. And if it came to a choice of passing close to these Great Ones of the earth or to the wild beast's den, Art would rather take a chance on the den.

So it was fear mostly that held him where he was, while

the strange men strode down into the glen. By the stream they paused, glanced about them, and debated together, one pointing this way and one another. The oldest took off his cap, scratched his head thoughtfully like an ordinary man, then looked towards where Art lay. But if he was expecting Art to move he was disappointed, for Art was beyond movement now. He had a heavy dark-grey moustache. The youngest man took a thin book from an inside pocket, opened it, and kept on opening it until it grew into a large bright sheet which he laid on the grass. They grouped round this, and the young man moved his finger along it, glancing up and down as he did so. They all nodded, and the oldest said loudly: "I told you so." When the young man had folded the map and put it back in his pocket, they crossed the stream and moved down until they came to the mouth of the ravine which had not so long before stared back at Art. They now stared at it. They nodded. Then, the youngest leading, they proceeded in single file, silently, stealthily, to enter that place.

No sooner were they out of sight, than Art got to his feet and ran on as fast as he could, indeed a little faster, but when he fell he let no yelp out of him now. The next time he fell was from fright at a big black bird that flapped up from below him. As he gazed down the short steep slope, he saw the body of a dead sheep. Where the wool was off its side, the skin was black, and white maggots were crawling over it. A rotten smell attacked his nostrils, and, pushing back his head, he saw, fair across from him on the other side of the small glen, the ravine of the foxgloves and the wild beast's den. He would have run then, but for one infernal circumstance—the roots of the heather above the den breathed out a faint but unmistakable blue smoke.

Art's mind became a whirling place of wild beasts' dens and little houses of fairy folk and legend and dread that set the world itself going up and down and round like the machinery in the meal mill. Then out of the little door, which Art had discovered on the day Mary Ann and himself had set off to find the fabled River, out of the little door that gave entry to the dark den, came the shaggy head of a great beast, and all at once, O torrents of the mountain, it was not a beast's head, but the hairy *oorisbk* itself, the fabulous beast-human. There were legends of this human monster that could chill the heart's blood of grown folk. On all fours it came forth, and slowly it reared itself, and looked around, and Art saw, as in a strange and powerful dream, that the *oorisbk* was Old Hector.

And Old Hector surely in the living flesh, for who else could scratch his whiskers in that wise and friendly manner while contemplating the heather breathing smoke? But now, like the *oorisbk*, Old Hector got down on all fours and crawled in again.

"It's not much," said Old Hector, as he stood upright in the cave, "and ten yards up, the smoke disappears entirely."

"Good for it," answered Red Dougal, who was switching the froth off a tub of wash. "You'll believe me now when I said my peat clods were the blackest and best."

"I believe you," said Old Hector, smiling. "You're stoking well, Donul—but go canny. Hold your hand. She'll be coming near it now." Old Hector lifted a piece of stick and tapped the head of a large enclosed copper pot with a funnel top to it like a chemist's retort.

"Humour her," chuckled Red Dougal, switching the froth flat. "The great thing is to humour her first." His face was blown red and sweating, and charged with hearty mirth and a heavy brown moustache.

Presently Old Hector said to Donul: "Come here and smell this."

Donul bent down and smelt the end of a small copper pipe that issued from the foot of a tub. After sniffing once or twice, as though he couldn't believe his own nostrils, he glanced up at Old Hector, saying: "It's like the scent of roses."

"The same, but keener," nodded Old Hector.

"More searching," said Red Dougal, getting down to have a sniff himself. "That's the scent of her coming, Donul, boy. Isn't she the lovely one? And when she's kissed you once or twice in the mouth and put her long white arms round you, it's dead to the world you'll be then, my boy."

Old Hector set a glass jug whose handle was broken under the end of the pipe. And presently there was a crystal drop, another drop, a quick succession of drops, a pause, a trickle in a small gush.

Old Hector smiled as Donul asked him if that indeed was the true spirit.

"Not quite yet," he answered. "See!" From the jug he poured a little of the crystal liquid into a coarse tumbler and added some water, whereupon the whole turned a milky blue. "She's not clean yet."

"Is this weak, then?" asked Donul.

"No. This is the strongest of all," answered Old Hector, "but impure. This is the famous 'foreshot'."

"Is it?" said Donul wonderingly.

"It is," said Old Hector. "There's nothing like this in the whole world for taking the heat out of an inflamed part, and it's capital for the rheumatics."

"Do you hear him?" Red Dougal asked the chastened wash. "Damn me, do you hear him?"

Donul smiled, his face red from the heat of the fire. He had never cared greatly for Red Dougal, whom he had hitherto considered to be mostly "all mouth", but now, somehow or other, the mouth was richer, mellower, and even those references to white arms which would normally leave Donul awkward were here less aggressive. Red Dougal was in his element.

"See how she's clearing," remarked Old Hector, adding water to a fresh drop. And Donul saw that the milky-blue tinge had all but gone. In another minute or two, Old Hector slipped a small cask under the mouth of the pipe, a copper filler in its bunghole, and fixed it securely in position. "You can put on your fire now," he said to Donul.

When Donul had placed the peat clods in a way that gave the greatest flame with the least smoke, Old Hector nodded approval: "You're coming at it!"

Donul, flushing with pleasure, straightened himself. The crystal liquid was running in a small but even trickle into the cask. The rumble of boiling was in the fat-bellied pot. Donul's eye ran up the pot to the head that narrowed like the head of a retort, bent over, and was continued in a thin pipe that would have stretched a long way had it not zigzagged upon itself in so parallel and compact a pattern that it was contained in little more than half of a gross barrel or tub. Into this tub, near the foot, water flowed through a piece of lead piping from the burn outside, the overflow being drawn away by another piece of piping. The constant supply of cold water about the zigzagged copper pipe, or "worm", was sufficient to condense the vapour inside the worm as it was forced through from the boiling pot. Donul followed the whole operation and considered it very neat. Suddenly his eye landed on tiny bubbles breaking on the surface of the water in the tub. "What's that?" he asked.

"Ah, dear me," said Old Hector, stripping off his jacket, "she's started leaking again. She's done."

It was a very old worm, lead-soldered in many places,

and when Old Hector had stopped the pin-point leak, he spoke of ancient days. Red Dougal made a seat for himself of five uneven peats; Donul sat on a ledge of flat rock, and Old Hector on an up-ended wort-tub.

"I'll hear you better," said Red Dougal, "if we try the new run."

So Old Hector raised the filler, ran some four inches into the tumbler, and replaced the filler without having spilt a drop.

"No, no, try it yourself first," said Red Dougal, politely shoving back the proffered tumbler.

Old Hector sniffed, and sniffed carefully, and nodded to himself thoughtfully. "There's no guff in this," he said. He smoothed back the left wing, the right wing, above his mouth, and then drew down an open hand with natural dignity over his beard.

"Take off your bonnet," said Red Dougal solemnly to Donul, as he removed his own.

If only a few drops went into Old Hector's mouth, he pondered them with some care before ejecting them with precision into the heart of the fire, where they disappeared like an outraged devil in a wild flash. "Ha-a-a," breathed Old Hector, both out and in. Then he nodded finally. "She'll do," he said, and handed the tumbler to Red Dougal.

Red Dougal took two heavy sniffs. "Here's my best respects to you," and he took a mouthful. He held it for a little as if he didn't know what to do with it, and then let it down in a gulp.

He tried not to show any choking, took in air noisily, and smiled through a flow of tears. "Boys, it's a good drop," he remarked huskily. "I'll say that for you, Hector. It's—kha-a-a—special." He handed the tumbler to Donul.

"No, no," said Donul, embarrassed.

"Taste it whatever," suggested Old Hector.

So Donul, pleased at that, warily lifted the edge of the tumbler to his mouth.

"She won't bite you!" cried Red Dougal, glowing now and laughing at Donul trying to take a few drops without taking many.

This was a more difficult operation than Donul expected, for he was used only to drinking water, and indeed it seemed there was a lot in his mouth once he got it in. Round his teeth it went, stinging his gums not unpleasantly.

"Let it down like a man," said Red Dougal.

"Spit it out," advised Old Hector.

Donul didn't know which to do, and at last did both. When he recovered, he breathed out and in quickly, smiling and wiping his eyes. "It's burning," he said, "but it's fragrant still."

Old Hector looked upon him and smiled with a benign humour. "It's young," he explained. "It has still about it the innocence of creation." From the tumbler he swallowed a small drop and nodded. "Yes. Youth itself, as yet unspoiled. The fragrance is the fragrance of the yellow barley under the sun and of the wild flowers in sheltered hollows. It has not yet begun to get old, Donul. With the days it grows rank a little, going through all the green humours as man himself does. Only in advanced age does it get back the original innocence, with something added besides." Old Hector took another small sip.

"In all languages," said Red Dougal, "it's called 'the water of life'. Isn't that wonderful?" He winked openly at Donul, with a sideways nod towards Old Hector. "He thinks himself innocent at this moment. Isn't that wonderful, too?"

"It can be abused," said Old Hector, "but then so can life itself. So can everything."

"It can be dear," responded Red Dougal, "and so damn dear that the folk who first made it in history—our folk—can now neither make nor get." Thoughtlessly he stretched for the tumbler, and added: "That's why I made up my mind we'd have a drop for Duncan's wedding, supposing the whole heaven of the gaugers came down upon us in small bits. So I persuaded Hector. And was I not right? For he is the last of the great makers. Good health to you, Hector, and long may your worm leak in the right place."

"Thank you," acknowledged Old Hector with pleasant grace.

"Kha-a-a," said Red Dougal, pleasantly. "He's a fine fellow, your brother Duncan, Donul; an upright, decent lad. And his wedding is a time when a fellow is shy and needs—when he needs——"

"We're all the better of a little gaiety at such a time," interposed Old Hector. "Indeed we suffer from the lack of it, and sometimes I see a sadness on the land."

"Sadness bedam'd, and if so who is to blame for it but ourselves? Isn't that what I have always been telling you? But would you listen to me? Not you! You would always say that everything should be measured by right conduct, by what is fair and just. To hell with that, say I! It should be measured by action. And this is the kind of action I mean. We're *doing* things now: not sitting and talking and grieving over the past." Red Dougal cocked his eye at Old Hector. "Would you say our conduct is fair and just, now?"

Old Hector's eyes glimmered thoughtfully.

"Here," said Red Dougal, "have a pull at this before you answer."

"Put it round with the sun," said Old Hector.

Red Dougal laughed and handed the tumbler to Donul. "You're not frightened of leading the lad astray?"

"Open trust never led a lad astray," murmured Old Hector, "in all my experience. And I am sure of Donul."

With a warm smile of pleasant embarrassment Donul investigated the liquor curiously and handed the tumbler to Old Hector.

"Now you can speak," said Red Dougal, "and I'll try not to interrupt you."

Old Hector shook his head. "What I have to say, you already know."

"Are we deceiving the Revenue?" demanded Red Dougal.

"We are," responded Old Hector.

"Are we breaking the law?"

"We are."

"What would happen to us if the three gaugers were to descend upon us at this moment?" pursued Red Dougal.

"Because the largeness of the fine would be far beyond us, you and I would be put in prison for a very long time, but Donul would not be put in prison, for he had not anything to do with this, but only happened to light on us by chance. And you will both remember that story carefully," said Old Hector.

Red Dougal laughed. "Have I not cornered you now, hip and beard?"

"Not that I have noticed," replied Old Hector mildly.

"Haven't I proved you the very fount and origin of law-breaking and all that's wrong?" demanded Red Dougal.

"Law-breaking, yes," said Old Hector. "But wrong is a difficult word. Many a day I have pondered over it, but I am not sure that I have found the answer. I only have a feeling about the answer and sometimes I go by that feeling. For, you see, laws are necessary, and to break them is wrong. Yet a law can be wrong."

"And is a law wrong just because *you* find it wrong?" scoffed Red Dougal.

"Yes," answered Old Hector.

"But the law that's wrong to you is sure to be right to the other fellow, or it wouldn't be in it. How then?" demanded Red Dougal.

"I still must judge for myself, just like the other fellow. That he may have the power to make me suffer does not, of itself, mean that he is right. It just means that he has the power to make me suffer. But it remains with me to judge for myself the outcome of all the elements and to come to a decision on the matter."

"What are the elements here? Eh?"

"Many and varied they are," replied Old Hector. "This is our old native drink, made in this land from time immemorial. We were the first makers, as you have just said. For untold centuries we had it as our cordial in life, distilled from the barley grown round our doors. In these times, because it was free, it was never abused. That is known. Deceit and abuse and drunkenness came in with the tax, for the folk had to evade the tax because they were poor. The best smuggler in my young days was an Elder of the Church. Before he started making a drop, he used to pray to God, asking Him not to let the gaugers come upon him unawares."

"I have heard of that," said Red Dougal. "Tell me," he added with a curious look, "did you put up a few words yourself before we started here?"

"I did," replied Old Hector, looking back at Red Dougal with his gentle smile.

The laugh that had been ready to come out died inward in Red Dougal, and he looked downward.

"For we do not make this drink to profit by it at the expense of the tax," proceeded Old Hector. "We do not sell it. Just as Donul does not sell a salmon he takes out of the River. Nor would we even make it thus for our own use if we could afford to buy it. But we cannot buy it. We are too poor. The men who have made the law have taken our own drink from us, and have not left us wherewith to buy it. Yet they can buy it, because they are rich. I have the feeling that that is not just. I do not grudge them their riches and all it can buy for them."

"And do you think," said Dougal, lifting his head, "that the Sheriff in his court will listen to your fine reasons?"

"I have no foolish notions about that," replied Old Hector. "But I am a man whose eightieth birthday is not so far distant, and I had to decide for myself whether my reasons might meet with understanding in a Court higher than the Sheriff's." There was a pause, and Old Hector looked at the fire. "There is only one thing," he added quietly.

"What's that?" asked Red Dougal, eyeing the old man.

"I should not," said Old Hector, "like to die in prison."

There was a little silence, and upon it fell a small sound. The sound came from outside. It was no more than the rattle of a tumbling pebble, but it might have been the sounding of the Trumpet of Judgement upon bodies grown rigid and faces that stared. There was no more sound. Then sound came again, and came nearer. The low doorway was slowly darkened, and before their awed eyes a small human figure uprose in the dim chamber and gazed at them, and the figure was Art.

"God be here!" exclaimed Red Dougal harshly, and though the unstable peats upon which he sat now threw him on his back, projecting his heels into the air, yet he contrived to stare from the ground.

Because of the brightness outside, Art at first could see

nothing but terrifying faces in an infernal gloom, and he began to whimper where he stood.

"Art," whispered Old Hector at last. "Who brought you here?"

"Is there anyone outside?" whispered Red Dougal harshly.

Terror mounted to a wild cry in Art, but Old Hector soon had him by his knee, soothing him. And presently to the question, "Is there anyone outside?" Art managed to answer: "No."

"Who brought you here?"

"M-myself."

"Did anyone see you coming?"

"No."

"Glory be to God," said Old Hector.

"Holy smoke, you gave us the fright there! Phew!" breathed Red Dougal.

"How did you know we were here?" asked Donul.

Art at first could not answer, but at last he told how he had set out for the River and how he had seen Old Hector from across the glen.

Relief was such that they were all smiling now as at a miracle.

"All the same," said Old Hector, "we ought to have had Hamish posted where I said."

"If I put him where I did," replied Red Dougal, "it's because he can command a better approach from the south, and that's the way the gaugers must come. Surely that's sense."

Old Hector turned to Art. "And you never saw anyone?"

"Yes," replied Art, "I saw three strange men."

Red Dougal, who had been twisting round for the tumbler, stopped in his twist like a man struck by lumbago.

When they had got Art's story, Old Hector nodded

with finality. "They'll be here in one hour. They're combing the glen."

"Some rat has informed on us!" cried Red Dougal. "Some bloody rat must have given us away!"

"Let us think," said Old Hector.

"Think, bedam'd! We've got to get the stuff away, and double quick. Come on!"

"It's too late now," said Old Hector, sitting quietly where he was.

Red Dougal raged, ready to tear asunder and save what he could, but Old Hector arose, saying: "It's all or nothing. We'll take the chance."

Red Dougal gaped at him. But Old Hector was very calm now. "Come outside," he commanded, and went before them with an empty malt sack. They followed, and he turned to Art. When he had given Art instructions how to climb up and crawl along the ridge a little way until he could command the glen, and how to watch and report back, he concluded, "Will you do that?" with a smile that in its great trust moved Art profoundly.

Art nodded, his chest thick with excitement and fear, for well he knew now who the strange men were.

"You two," commanded Old Hector, "take this sack and bring back on it the rotten sheep yonder."

"What's the sense——" stormed Red Dougal, but Old Hector turned from him and, gathering a nest of decomposing undergrowth, placed in it a pile of sheep droppings. Whereupon he crawled back into the cave.

For a moment he stood looking about him thoughtfully. It was a natural cave, open parts to the front having been built in with solid turfs on which the heather outside grew naturally. The long narrow vent above he would close with a couple of divots, once he had flapped the smoke away.

After covering Red Dougal's wash, he withdrew the cask, placed a wooden bucket under the pipe, draped a sack over both pipe and bucket, and bunged the cask with its small drop of whisky. Into the fire he fed some of the nest until an acrid stench got him in the throat. Raking out the fire from under the pot, he threw the remainder of the nest upon it, and, in due course, stamped out the red embers until the dry putrid stink choked him. Rolling the small cask before him, he reached the outside air, where he lay for a little, gasping and wiping his eyes.

By the time Red Dougal and Donul came back carrying the sheep on the sack, Old Hector was sitting by the mouth of the leaden inlet pipe which ran underground, wiping his forehead. The mouth of the pipe he had choked with a sod and concealed with accidental boulders. The wild contortions Dougal and Donul were making to turn their noses away from the sheep sent a smile into his whiskers as he got up and guided them to where the entrance of the cave had been. As the carcass landed with a sickly squelch, the two bearers grunted in concert.

There was little fight left in Dougal now, for the aroma from the sheep had set up an internal argument with the fumes from the liquor, but still he gaped combatantly for the entrance which had disappeared under Old Hector's hands. "I'll have—*hic!*—the cask though, though the heavens—*hoc!*"

"Don't *hoc* here," commanded Old Hector sternly. "There's the cask. You and Donul clear up the burn. Collar Hamish. Get home. Quick!"

Donul, who had crossed the burn and was sitting amid the tall withered stalks of the foxgloves, his head between his knees, arose and followed Dougal.

Old Hector looked around, smothered an abrasion here, smoothed a heel-mark there, then took out his knife and cut a hole in the black tough skin of the sheep. Whereupon he retreated hurriedly across the burn, stabbed his knife in the ground to clean it, and climbed until he saw Art, to whom he beckoned.

"Come with me," said Old Hector, "and we'll cross over to the other side of the glen."

This they did, and soon they were lying in the place from which Art had recently seen his friend emerge like an *oorisbk*.

Art had a thousand questions in him now, but Old Hector whispered that even whispering would keep them from hearing. Presently he dug Art in the ribs. "Do you see my heroes?"

Art could see nothing but an old raven sitting on the cave above the sheep, croaking at another old raven, both looking all round. But in Old Hector's eyes Art saw a primordial mirth so warm that he nestled into it.

Time passed.

"They're a long time," whispered Art.

"Time is longer sometimes," whispered Old Hector.

It got so long that it must have stopped, and Art was about to formulate his own view of time when Old Hector's hand came gently on his back and pressed him into the heather.

Art was frightened to look at first. Then through the heather roots he saw the three strange men coming down the off side of the glen. They stopped, they talked together, looking this way and that. The young man took out his map, but the man with the moustache waved an impatient arm and strode on. The young man returned the map unopened to his pocket. They drew near, they paused, and, rounding the last bluff, surprised two ravens that rose heavily, croaking, from a dead sheep.

They looked at the ravens, they stared at the sheep, they

went slowly through the withered foxgloves and peered into the water. Then the young one lifted his head sharply and stared at the cave. As if struck in the face, he backed away among the foxgloves, a hand to his nose. By the way he made up the burn, an unmentionable disease might have been after the fibres in his throat. The others followed, but more slowly.

They had not proceeded many yards, however, when the man with the moustache, going last, paused, turned slowly round, and sniffed the air like a stag. Old Hector lay very still now, for this was the only one he feared. Art felt the large hand grip in his back.

The man swung round as if to recall the two who were fast disappearing in front. With a hoarse croak of laughter, one of the ravens circled down and alighted above the sheep. The man gave it one look, then followed the others out of sight.

Old Hector's head drooped among the heather. Art asked him if they would come back the same way.

"No," answered Old Hector, lifting his head slowly and regarding Art with a profound and tender smile. "You saved your old friend from prison that time."

"Did I?" Art was deeply moved.

"You did. And you saved Duncan's wedding present into the bargain. Indeed, I doubt if such a great wedding present as this of yours was ever made before. All that remains now is for you to hold it *as secret as the grave.*"

"*As secret as the grave,*" murmured Art, his heart like to burst with the amount of life and loyalty in it.

14

The Secret

It is a terrible thing to be bursting with a secret you can't tell. Art could not rest. Any odd time when he got Donul alone, he would find relief by going over the smuggling adventure and setting once more in clear perspective the manner in which he, Art (like one of the heroes in a legend of old) had arrived just in the nick of time. When Donul fell in with this mood they had the greatest talk and fun, and Donul would then tell Art about the distilling and other processes he hadn't seen until Art was like to burst once more. But the part Art liked to hear best of all concerned the emotions aroused in the breasts of Old Hector, Red Dougal, and Donul himself, when they first heard Art's approach as *the sound outside.*

"What did Red Dougal look like?"

"Like this," replied Donul, giving a fair imitation.

From the horrific gape, Art fell away, shaking merriment over the world.

Most times, however, Donul would gloom on Art and tell him never to speak of the adventure even to himself, lest the ears of the invisible should overhear and so bring the heavens down upon them in small bits. "For someone must have told. The gaugers must have got an inkling, or how did they turn up just then?"

"What an awful thing—to tell!"

"It's the worst thing in life. It's worse than—killing a man."

"It is," said Art. "I wouldn't tell, supposing I was offered the whole world."

"I should hope not," said Donul. "What's being offered the world?"

Art agreed it wasn't much, and Donul said darkly: "Besides, they may come back."

"When?"

"Perhaps when the fun is on at the wedding itself."

"No?"

"Oh but yo. So shut up, whatever you do."

"But seeing the whisky is made and the pot hidden, what would they find now?"

"Wouldn't they find the whisky and it being drunk? And wouldn't that be a disgrace on Duncan, seeing it's his wedding?"

"Would it be a disgrace?" asked Art. "Why?"

"Never you mind why. I'm telling you. There are queer people in the world."

"I wonder why there are queer people like that?" asked Art, looking far away.

"Oh, who knows?" said Donul impatiently. "But there are. Red Dougal was saying last night that it wasn't always so. He was saying that when Prince Charlie was wandering the hills after the battle of Culloden, £70,000 was put on his head, yet not the poorest Highlander gave him away."

"Who put it on his head?"

"He wasn't carrying it on his head. That was the sum that the English Government offered to anyone who would tell where Prince Charlie was so that he would be captured and his head taken off."

"And no-one told?"

"Not one. In fact many a poor Highlander risked his

life to save Prince Charlie, much less not take the £70,000."

"Did he? Tell me——"

"Shut up! Here's Father."

So that the secret sometimes grew until the bursting-point could be seen through, like a piece of stretched elastic.

The worst place of all was school, for here there was no Donul to whom Art could turn and let off some of the pressure. He just had to walk among his fellows, conscious of the abyss of knowledge that divided him from them. If only they knew! If only they could get an inkling of the immensity of the adventure and of the thrilling fashion in which Art had saved grown men from prison! If only they could know, without being told! If only! Art sometimes shot away by himself to keep his laugh in, and he didn't always keep it in. If Art had thought them his equals before, he now saw they were far from being that. Indeed at moments he was touched by pity for them, if not scorn, they were such children, carrying on in the old silly way. And one of them, in particular, Dan Macgruther, was now seen to be what he was, just a big windy fool. Nothing in him but brose. And he thought he was so important! It was difficult often for Art to keep from laughing.

When Dan began to follow him with a hard combative eye, the position became very complicated. Dan was eight months older than Art and fully two inches taller. He had brought off a sufficient number of battles to make him cock of his class. Art was in his class, but so far had avoided combat, had even refused to contradict Dan when Dan had said he could fight any one of them "with one hand". "I'll tie the other one behind my back," Dan had said. But they knew the meaning of a figure of speech where Dan was concerned, if they didn't know it in their grammar.

"What are you laughing at?" asked Dan.

"I can laugh if I like," replied Art.

"I'll make you laugh out of the other side of your mouth," said Dan.

"Well, you had no right to say that about Duncan's wedding."

"Oh, indeed! And who is going to stop me saying what I like?"

Art did not answer, and boys who had been scattering on their way from school now gathered round, their eyes glistening. "Is it a fight?" asked one, coming panting up.

Dan pushed his body up against Art. "Who is going to stop me?" he inquired a second time.

Art fell back.

Dan laughed a harsh note or two. "I said it would be a rotten wedding and no whisky at it."

"There will so be whisky at it," cried Art, trembling with rage.

"Oh, there will, will there?"

"Yes, there will," cried Art, maddened.

"You're a liar," said Dan.

"I'm not a liar."

"Did you see them making the whisky?"

"I did," cried Art. "I was there!" The urge to tell them of his glorious deeds, and so put them in their place, came over him in such a flood that even his ears were drowned—but they rose out of it to hear Dan's voice, Dan's horrible voice, saying:

"You saw Old Hector making the whisky?"

Art could not speak. His jaw began to tremble.

"You said you saw Old Hector——"

"I did not!"

"You said——"

"I did not!" screamed Art, tears bursting from his eyes.

"You——"

"I did not!" And before astonishment could draw a breath, Art let out a fist at Dan's advancing face. The distance was just right and the nose caught the full impact. Not that Art stopped then. In his madness, he rained blows, weeping and shouting savagely as he did so.

"Blood!" yelled a voice. Dan's nose was bleeding. The blood was on Art's hands. Dan felt the running of his own blood and stopped. Art did not stop. "Blood! Blood!" Dan turned away, but Art followed him. Dan ran, and Art ran after him. The noise of Art's rage was as terrifying as his blows. Art was a practised runner, and he tripped Dan. When Dan fell, Art sat on him and pummelled his head, yelling at the top of his voice. Never had such a spectacle of fury been seen. When they pulled him off Dan, he fought those who pulled him off. If the minister of the church hadn't happened to be coming along the road, there is no telling to what lengths Art would have gone. As it was, he remained on the deserted field until the minister was nearly upon him. Then he turned and walked off across the bog.

He was in truth the prey of conflicting emotions now, for the exultation of having walloped the blood out of Dan was riddled by the horror of having told. In that telling was disaster, disaster to which there was no bound. It swelled in his mind like a dark and horrible bladder. The *secret of the grave* was given up. Doom. Doom. Doom ever swelling. Rage being spent, his face grew white and his eyes furtive. He would not go home. He would never more go home.

He struck up on to the moor, moving slowly, sometimes pausing to look around. If there was anyone he did not want to meet in this world, it was Old Hector. Though Donul would be nearly as bad. £70,000 on his head, and no-one told. Art had told—for nothing.

Perhaps the abyss of vanity has never been sounded because its ultimate misery has no bottom. He lifted up his eyes, and there was Old Hector at a little distance, letting the red cow have a last bite or two on the moor before he slowly drove her home. Art turned away from the hand raised in welcome, and kept moving away from the voice that called "Art!"

Nevermore, said his mind. Nevermore. And he closed his ears against the crying of Old Hector and went up over a rise and down out of sight. Nevermore. It was hard on him, and bitter. For no-one knew, as he knew now, the end of everything; no-one but himself. There were dry sniffs in his nose. He saw blood on his hands. He pressed the sniffs back into his nose with the back of a bloody hand. He could afford to do it now, for what was blood? Nothing.

He sat down by a boggy pool where he could wash off the blood. But he did not wash off the blood. He would leave the blood to be seen. The great blue sky was a domed window over him through which looked down the eyes of God. The moors stretched far to the boundaries of the world, silent as the grave. Lifting up his eyes against the stillness that is crime's nightmare, Art saw advancing towards him the three strange men.

They came with the inexorable rightness of three who had been appointed. Their legs pushed darkly one in front of the other, and their bodies were tall and upright.

Because no others could have come but them, Art could not move. Through a long period of time—perhaps ten seconds—Art regarded them with a pale and alien face. Then his nostrils sniffed, a twitch of living fear darkened his eyes, and, pushing up on to his feet, he made off as fast as his trembling legs would carry him.

"Hector! Hector!" he called as he topped the rise and raced down. "They're coming! They're coming!"

"Who's coming?" asked the old man, folding Art against his knees.

"The gaugers! They're coming!"

"Hush, now! Let them come. Old Hector is not frightened. Hush! Don't cry. Stop it! . . . That's my hero. That's my own lad. Say nothing. Leave it to Old Hector. . . ."

The three strange men topped the rise, striding swiftly, but when they saw Old Hector their pace slackened and the oldest of the three, the man with the heavy dark-grey moustache, approached with a smile in his narrowed dark eyes, and said: "How do you do, Mr. Macdonald?" and shook hands with Old Hector.

"Very well, thank you, Mr. Macdonald," replied Old Hector, for they were of the same clan. "It's a fine day."

"It is a nice day. This is Mr. Ramsbottom." Though the youngest of the three, Mr. Ramsbottom was clearly the officer in charge. With expressive affability, he shook hands, and Old Hector said he was glad to meet him. The third, a smooth-faced man, shook hands without being introduced, as Old Hector and himself were not unacquainted.

"Yes, it's a fine day," repeated Mr. Macdonald agreeably.

"It is indeed," nodded Old Hector. "We have had a good spell of weather lately, and there was need for it."

"It would let you get at the harvest," nodded Mr. Macdonald. "How are the crops?"

"Pretty fair, thank you. We can't complain this time!"

"Started threshing yet?"

"Oh, just enough to keep the womenfolk quiet, but it's early enough."

"Well, the folk can't complain about the barley. All over, it has been heavy in the ear. It should thresh well."

"Och, it's not much barley we grow. But I will say the grain crop on the whole was fair, and at least we'll have good straw. And that's a blessing."

While this pleasant discourse continued, Art, who was holding to the slack of Old Hector's trousers and now and then peeping from under his eyebrows round Old Hector's haunch, saw the affable smile grow stiff on the face of Mr. Ramsbottom and the long legs with the stylish boots grow restless. Once this man inquired smoothly if the folk in these regions still used the hand-flail for threshing, and Old Hector replied: "Yes, they will be using it sometimes."

At long last Mr. Macdonald, with the smile back in his narrowing eyes, said: "I suppose you know what we are here for?"

"Well, I suppose you will be going about your lawful occasions," replied Old Hector, with so natural and polite a smile that even the most astute might be forgiven for failing to see that he had won the first round.

"We are," said Mr. Macdonald. "You haven't heard of anything doing hereabouts?"

"Well, it's not much I hear. I'm getting on in years and stick pretty close to my own fireside."

Through this manœuvring for position between the two clansmen, Mr. Ramsbottom, who deeply disliked the devious ways of Celtic discourse, cut in directly: "We have information to the effect that smuggling is going on here. Do you know anything about it?"

"Indeed, if it has been going on, sir, no-one came and told me."

Before Old Hector's raised eyebrows, Mr. Ramsbottom's speech momentarily deserted him. Whereupon Mr. Macdonald, in astonishingly simple tones, inquired: "You have no idea—where the still is?"

Old Hector looked at Mr. Macdonald, a faint gleam in his own eye. They were old opponents.

"Whose still?"

"Any still," replied Mr. Macdonald. "If only we get the still, we mightn't bother about anything else—or anyone."

"There would be a reward, of course—five pounds," said Mr. Ramsbottom pointedly.

"Five pounds. It's a lot of money." Old Hector was clearly astonished.

"It's waiting for you. Just say the word," urged Mr. Ramsbottom, feeling he had the true measure of the situation at last.

Old Hector smiled and slowly shook his head.

"As the oldest inhabitant you are at least bound to know where a smuggling bothy would be," Mr. Ramsbottom pressed him.

"Oh, I can remember", said Old Hector, "talk from the old days. I can even remember, as a boy, being pointed out where, it was said, smuggling had at one time been carried on. But that wasn't yesterday! And there are no folk there now."

"Was that over at the Clash?" asked Mr. Macdonald.

Old Hector nodded. "I was sure you would have been over there."

"But we haven't been over there," said Mr. Ramsbottom, taking out his map. "Have we?"

"No," answered Mr. Macdonald.

"Haven't you?" said Old Hector, with something more than surprise, as if indeed he were disconcerted.

"Ah, here it is!" exclaimed Mr. Ramsbottom, his finger making a hollow in the map.

"I'm glad you've found it," nodded Old Hector, relieved. "You won't need me now."

"What's that?" demanded Mr. Ramsbottom. "How

are we going to find the bothy if you don't show it to us?"

"Indeed," said Old Hector, "I doubt if I could find it myself now. It's probably fallen in and disappeared these many years." His manner was still as pleasant as ever, but his self-possession was touched by a faint concern.

Mr. Ramsbottom got the impression, very subtly, that Old Hector was sorry he had mentioned the Clash.

"But, look here, I don't want you to walk all that way and back for nothing," he said. "I——"

"No, no!" interrupted Old Hector, with a glance over his shoulder. "I don't want to have anything more to do with it."

"You needn't be afraid anyone will ever hear about it," pursued Mr. Ramsbottom. "You can be dead sure of that."

"No, no!" said Old Hector. "I'm not afraid of anyone. I never was. But I like to mind my own business. If people care to do anything that's their concern."

"By my official commission here, I can call upon any one of His Majesty's subjects to assist me in the execution of my duties," said Mr. Ramsbottom quietly but very clearly. "I don't want, of course——"

"No, no!" interrupted Old Hector, so concerned now that he gripped Art's hand hard.

"Is that your grandchild?" asked Mr. Macdonald amiably.

"Yes. At least, no," said Old Hector. "He's just a neighbour's son. And they'll be missing him."

"He seems to have been in the wars," said Mr. Macdonald. "Couldn't you take the cow home?" he asked Art with an engaging smile.

"That's it!" said Mr. Ramsbottom. "And here's twopence for him."

Art clung to Old Hector and would not take the money. He was terrified, for he could see they were cornering his friend, who was now clearly distressed, though smiling still.

"The little fellow is wanting home," said Old Hector. "If—if to-morrow would do, I, perhaps, I could take you then."

But Mr. Ramsbottom knew a trick or two better than that. A whole night for these wily natives to fix things? Not on your life!

"To-morrow will not do, I'm afraid," he said with an official smile. "I've made up my mind I'm going to get this still. I'll get it. Now I don't want you to misunderstand me, but I have to say that your name has not been unconnected with—uh—with these operations."

"Mine!" exclaimed Old Hector.

"Yes, yours. I'm not making any personal allegations. But now is an opportunity for you to clear yourself in official eyes. If you take us——"

"But I tell you I don't know what folk may have been doing in the Clash," interrupted Old Hector with some force. "Are you trying to trap me, or what?" And he glanced strongly at Mr. Macdonald, who now, however, seemed to be concerned with the colour of the sky.

"I hope you won't compel me to use my official powers," suggested Mr. Ramsbottom. "It will be to your interest—not to."

"My interest? What's it got to do with me?" Old Hector looked about him wildly.

Mr. Ramsbottom waited for a moment. "I think," he said, "the little boy will take the cow home."

Old Hector looked at Art, then at the distance, and he grew still. "Very well," he said calmly. He put his hand on Art's head. "Take the cow home. Tell Agnes I will be back in a little while, but don't—don't tell anyone where I've gone. Do you understand me?"

"Yes," muttered Art.

"Go, then," said Old Hector.

Art moved away a short distance and turned, his teeth in his thumb. Old Hector gave him the friendly salute of farewell, and walked away among the three men like a prisoner.

Going half by the back, Art watched the four tall figures march away. As their heads lifted against the sky, Art was tripped by the earth. The yelp came out of him and he reared sharply from the earth and ran away after the red cow, his eyes blinded. The red cow was obstinate and would not go the proper way. Sometimes through his tears she wavered into an immense size. This brought his rage upon him, and he danced before her with such terrifying sounds that first she looked at him, and then, as he clawed at the earth for a missile, turned and made off home.

When Agnes saw the cow coming, she yelled at Art not to make her run. "Do you want to shake the milk out of her?"

Then she saw the tears and the blood and Art trembling. Her face opened. "What's happened?"

Art hiccupped, pale and wild with distress.

She ran forward and caught Art. "Where's Father?"

Art's guilt now came profoundly upon him. He wept where he stood, a horrible dry weeping.

"Tell Agnes. Where's Father?"

His body leapt in her arms from the explosion of a hiccup. She soothed and caressed him. He tried to tear himself from her.

Donul appeared, breathing heavily. "What's happened?"

"Oh, I don't know," cried Agnes. "He's got the hiccups. Hold him till I get some cold water." She ran down to the house.

"What's happened? Where's Old Hector?" asked Donul in the low voice of a confederate.

Art looked around. "He's—he's gone away. The—the gaugers——"

"Have the gaugers got him?"

Art hiccupped. "Don't—don't tell her." He gripped Donul hard.

Donul caressed him. "Leave it to me," he murmured.

As Art took a mouthful of cold water, his teeth knocking against the glass, Donul said to Agnes: "It's all right. Your father will be home soon."

Agnes searched his face. "Have they taken him away?"

"How could they take him?" frowned Donul.

"Oh, they've tâken him! I knew it would come to this!" She raised a keening cry.

"Be quiet, will you!" shouted Donul, his frown deepening. "Don't you open your mouth till I come back." And he led Art away.

When they were by themselves, he got Art quietened, and among the dying hiccups Art told of Hector's capture.

"You run home," said Donul. "And remember——"

But the thought of home was terror to Art now. Donul looked at him. "All right. Come on, then." Taking Art's hand, he started hurriedly on a short cut to the Clash.

Presently Donul could see that Art was labouring under a dread that made his feet lag, and to cheer him up, said: "I heard you gave Dan Macgruther a great hammering!"

Art did not answer. His hand grew heavier.

"What's wrong with that?" asked Donul. "You ought to be proud. He's older and bigger than you."

But Art plainly did not want to hear about the fight. This astonished Donul so much that he stopped.

"What's wrong?" he asked. "What's happened?"

Art could not speak and would not look at Donul.

"You needn't be frightened for Old Hector, if that's what's worrying you. They haven't taken him away. He's only gone to show them an old place." His tone was bright and even full of hidden humour, as if it were all a joke.

But Art, with the terrible knowledge of betrayal deep in him, could see no joke. In his inmost being, he knew that what he had said to Dan Macgruther would surely in the end drive Old Hector into prison. He began to feel sick.

"What's wrong with you?" Donul was now concerned for his brother, but he was also growing impatient and angry. "Come on!" If they did not hurry, they would be too late.

Art went, but began to lag again before they were yet half-way. As Donul grew desperate, Art curled up on the ground. "Leave me," he muttered, and his head shot forward in a spasm of retching.

"Have you eaten anything? Tell Donul."

But Art would not speak, his face pale, his eyes turned away.

Donul was at his wits' end. So anxious was he to spy on what was taking place in the Clash that his brows gathered in anger as he looked at Art. Would he leave him? His anger mounted. "Why won't you speak?" he demanded.

Art sank his head deeper toward his curled-up knees. He looked utterly exhausted and more miserable than anyone Donul had ever seen. Donul's rage increased at being thus baffled. Then something in the sight of his little brother, something white and remote, all at once touched him with fear. He lay down in front of Art and put an arm over his shoulder. "Tell Donul," he whispered softly.

Art stirred towards Donul.

"You needn't be frightened of me," whispered Donul. "You can tell me anything. You can tell me the most desperate thing and I won't be angry. Speak to me." Donul was now so moved by his own compassion that his voice nearly broke.

"I—I—didn't tell," muttered Art.

"Tell who?" whispered Donul.

"D-Dan Macgruther. I—I only said that—that there would be whisky at—at the wedding."

"Of course. That was quite right."

"And he said—that I said—that—that Old Hector——" Art choked.

"He would," said Donul. "He's a big mouth if ever there was one."

"But—but I said I did not."

"And he said you did?"

"Yes. And—and I said I did not. And—and he said I did. And then——"

"And then you hammered the life out of him?"

"Yes."

"My hero!" breathed Donul. "That was the stuff to give him! Boy, I was proud of you when I heard it. I couldn't tell you how delighted I was."

"I—I would rather die than—than anything should happen to Old Hector or—or anyone——"

"Of course. I would die, too. But instead, you blooded Dan Macgruther's nose! Ho! ho!" laughed Donul softly. "But in any case, whatever you said doesn't matter a docken blade now. It's all over and no-one can prove it. Is this Dan's blood on you?"

"It—it is," said Art.

"Boy, you must have given him a terrible hammering! Wait now, and I'll rub some of it off with this moss."

Art sat up and Donul wiped his face, spitting on the moss to make it more damp. There was deep affection between them.

As they continued on their way, Art clove to his brother,

and Donul's hand was firm and companionable. Moreover, Donul said such cheerful things, that Art felt perhaps the carefree world he knew long ago might come back again. Only, the terror would not go away because they were advancing towards the three terrible men who had Old Hector in their power. This power, Art felt, was greater than all other power in the world. And though Donul might pretend he was gay, Art could see that he was moved by a desperate excitement.

When Art could bear going forward no more and was trying not to say he wanted to go home, Donul clapped in the heather, pulling Art down with him. Donul crawled into a little hollow, Art beside him.

"I saw them," whispered Donul. "They're hunting all round."

"What for?"

"Hush!" said Donul with a queer gleam in his eyes. Pressing Art into the heather, he crawled up a yard or two and lay still, watching.

In a little while, he turned his head slowly and beckoned Art to come up.

Through the heather, Art saw the three men and Old Hector standing in a group. One of the men had a twisted thing like a gate on his back. Presently the group broke up, and the three men went off towards the road beyond the Clash. Old Hector drew nigh on his short-cut home. When he would have passed by, Donul whistled. Old Hector saw their heads and looked back over his shoulder, but the revenue men had disappeared. He came and sat down beside them with his usual welcoming smile. "Well, well, and what's brought you here?"

"Did you manage?" asked Donul, his voice thick with excitement.

"I did, but it was a job indeed."

"Was it?"

"It was. I'm afraid Sandy Macdonald yonder does not now what to make of me at all, at all."

"Doesn't he?" Donul exploded from the pressure inside him.

"Ah, he's the clever one, is Sandy."

"He met his match to-day, then!" cried Donul, the excited laughter bursting from him.

"Well," said Old Hector, scratching his beard, "that's as may be. But they pushed me to it. Indeed, in the end the officer himself—he's a new fellow, by the name of Ramsbottom——"

"Of what?"

"Ramsbottom," repeated Old Hector. He nodded over the grovelling body of Donul. "I agree it's not a known name with us. However, he got very forceful in the end, and go I had to, or he would have the law on me, he said. And then on the way, while we were having a few words, didn't he out with it that he had a search warrant."

"To search you?"

"No, but to search my house! I haven't been nearer being angry since I was a young man. I stopped then. I wouldn't go a foot. I told him he could search my house till he was blue in the face. And I meant it. What's the world coming to when a man can walk in on you and search your own house? He saw he had made a great mistake then. He apologized, and said he didn't say he had a search warrant, but that he could get one if there was enough suspicion. Oh, we had a few more words, but in the end I went with them. He has the makings of a gentleman in him, but I'm afraid authority will go to his head one day."

"And what then?"

"Och, then I showed them the old bothy in the ravine up above the ruins, where whisky hasn't been made to my certain knowledge for forty years. Man," and Old Hector's eyes glimmered, "Sandy got the smell! And then he saw the peat ash."

"No!" said Donul, hugging himself.

"Yes, and then he found the draff you put in the off corner."

"Did he?"

"There was such a tirrieho then," said Old Hector, "that I was nearly more astonished than any of them."

Donul shook. "What did they do with it?"

"Stuck their noses in it. 'They're fresh barley husks,' says Mr. Ramsbottom. 'I can smell the wash off them.' He was fair dancing with excitement."

"What did you say?"

"I said I couldn't believe it, and stuck my own nose in."

Donul now caught Art and knocked him over. Art began to laugh in shy bewilderment.

"And what then?"

"Och, well, then," said Old Hector, pleased to be amusing the boys and feeling not much older than either of them, "then Mr. Ramsbottom wanted to carry some of the draff away with him, but found he had no place to carry it in, so what did he do but ask Sandy and Silent Willie to cram their pockets with it. And Sandy had on a fine new suit. Sandy wasn't very willing at first, and indeed I was concerned for him, as it was a nice bit of tweed. So I suggested that perhaps he could carry it in his bonnet. Sandy looked at me, because indeed he is very bald when his bonnet is off."

Donul gave Art another push, and Art gave him a small push back.

"Well, when their pockets were crammed, they began hunting for the still. But hunt high and hunt low, they could find no trace of anything. I was beginning to think we had hidden the old worm too well."

"I said that," cried Donul, "at the time!"

"You did. But it wouldn't have been hidden too well for Sandy, if he hadn't been put out by having to cram the draff in his pockets. Mr. Ramsbottom is a curious man. He believes he is cleverer than Sandy, and is inclined to grow impatient with him. That, I think," said Old Hector thoughtfully, "is funny, too. However, this Mr. Ramsbottom had now got the idea that I was worth the watching. Where he got it from, I don't know, I'm sure. But when they had been clawing and digging inside the bothy, I got a little tired watching them and went out for a breath of air. I heard Mr. Ramsbottom coming quietly out after me, but of course I was not so rude as to look round. I stole a quiet glance at the cairn of stones and then went and sat on them and took out my pipe. He came over, and I was just asking him for a match when he told me to get up. He hadn't removed six stones, when there was the top end of the worm. Man, he let out a shout then!" Old Hector shook his head solemnly at the memory.

"Were you astonished yourself?" asked Donul huskily.

"You would have been astonished, too, if you'd seen them," nodded Old Hector. "I just gaped at the old worm there in the light of the broad day. For do you know, and this is true, I had the odd feeling that, of us all, it was the worm itself that was the most astonished. Man, somehow, with its old soldered spots, it not only looked done—for done it is—but sad. As sure as I'm telling you, it affected me. We were old friends."

There was a short silence. "So when they began hunting for the pot, I said to them that I felt they could save their pains," continued Old Hector, "and when pressed to it, I told them that when I was a lad, the pot they used was an iron pot, and when the distilling was over, the pot would be taken home to its usual job of boiling clothes for the washing, or potatoes for the family and hens. And that was true. Sandy admitted the truth of it. The copper worm was the only important thing, and they had that."

"And they were quite pleased!"

"Delighted," said Old Hector. "At least Mr. Ramsbottom was. And he said to me that he would not forget to send on the reward. I said that anything I had done to help them was done for no reward."

"What reward?" asked Donul.

"Five pounds," said Old Hector. "To anyone who helps them——"

"Five pounds!" breathed Donul, stricken to stillness at last. "But—but a new worm wouldn't cost that?"

"Barely," said Old Hector with so profound a gleam in his eye that Donul rolled over and, lifting up his legs, pedalled the vacant air.

For a little while they gambolled in the small hollow, and Art even climbed up on Old Hector's back, for he was burning now to tell of his great victory over Dan Macgruther. And as he could not keep it in, he told of it himself, and Donul embellished it, and Old Hector, seeing far into Art's mind, withdrew the last sting of betrayal and left in its place the sweet balm that strengthens loyalty for the future.

"Ah well," said Old Hector at last with a sigh. "It's young you make me feel. And, indeed, to tell the sober truth, I've seen the day I would have thought the reward of money a good joke. But now I don't think I would care to touch their money. The only reward I wanted was a happy wedding for your brother Duncan, with no interference from the outside, and at least I have made sure of that. God is good, too. Come, we will be going home."

15

The World Beyond

There were two worlds for Art: his own and the one beyond. He lived in his own world, as inside a circle, and here things happened but never changed. The crops moved about on the fields as he did himself, but the fields remained where they were. So did the braes and the hollows and the outlines of the land against the sky, whether in snow or summer sunshine, in dryness or in flood. From Shivering Eye to Loch of the Rushes, from the lonely grey ruins of the Clash to the smuggling cave in the Little Glen, he knew the feel of the earth under his bare feet. Sometimes his legs tucked themselves beneath him while he made things with his knife or created fables with his mind, and sometimes his legs rushed in panic from that which seemed more real than the knife itself. But whatever happened, the earth remained in its abiding outlines, the houses in the same place, and men and women tall and secure and moving about. Here was the permanent, changeless as Old Hector's whiskers.

So much for his own world. Beyond its known rim there was, however, the other world, the world outside. Folk talked sometimes in solemn voices of great changes taking place in it, and now and then they would shake their heads in wonder. Still, it was the world outside, and though men like his father or Duncan might go away into it, they always came back, as the peewits and other birds came back to build their nests and lay their eggs, to cry in the darkening or whistle in the daylight. Art knew why the peewits came back. They came back because they liked this place best. And even if they cried and swooped and grew angry, it was no more than he himself did often. And if there had been any doubt in his mind, Old Hector had settled it. "Why do they come back?" he had asked. And Old Hector had answered: "Because they feel at home here." Art had nodded to that with such understanding that the next time he came on a peewit's egg he did not take it, because it was the only one in the nest. He marked the spot and waited till there were three in it.

Now between these two worlds the boundary line was a circle vague as what lay beyond the horizon—except in one place, and that place was the River. Many times Art had tried to reach this River, but he had never succeeded, yet so much had he thought about it that it ran clearly through his own mind. It had indeed the clearness of a stream in a story, but with more body to it. A brightness was on its dark waters, and the ground that bordered it was green. Hazel trees hung over it where it formed the Hazel Pool. There were rocky points, and smooth still sweeps, and rushing shallows up which the salmon flashed, knocking spindrift off their bows—to rest in the quiet of the Hazel Pool. Once Old Hector had talked at a ceilidh about "The Green Isle of the Great Deep", and though that paradisaical isle had haunted Art for a time, it was readily drowned in the flow of the River.

And now and at last here was the day, and in the evening of this day Art was going to the River.

Donul, before Hamish as witness, had drawn his forefinger across his throat in solemn promise, for, as they said themselves, it was the least they could do in view of Art's great service at the time of the smuggling. The very least, said Hamish. And Art said nothing.

But he could have said a lot this morning at school—if he had liked! Ho! ho! it was little everyone knew! And less they would learn!

"What are you staring at?" asked the master.

"Nothing, sir," mumbled Art, caught for the second time.

"Well, I'll give you something to stare at." And he took Art out to the floor and marched him to a corner where he could stare at the wall.

But after a few bitter moments, Art had his secret revenge and stared once more at the River. His enemy, Dan Macgruther, wouldn't have looked so pleased as Art was marched out, had he known what was going to happen to the herring net over his father's screw of hay! He would have smiled out of the other side of his mouth then! For off that screw Donul and Hamish were to take the net and use it at the Hazel Pool, and then bring it back and put it on the hay again. What a joke! Art could have laughed where he stood.

He even remembered a joke against himself almost with pleasure. Donul had said that the salmon now were not silvery but brown, yet though they were brown they were still good eating because they had not spawned.

"Why are they brown?" Art asked.

"Because they are always brown at this time of the year," Donul answered.

But Hamish and himself had then started an argument, for Hamish had the idea that the brownness came from the length of time the fish had been in the peaty water.

Donul had admitted there might be something in that but Art, remembering a talk with Old Hector, said suddenly: "I know. It's because they eat the nuts that fall off the hazel trees, and ripe nuts are brown."

"That's one of Old Hector's yarns," said Donul, and Hamish and himself had laughed.

Art had tried to laugh, too, for in the company of Donul and Hamish he was prepared to laugh even at his secret dreams.

Donul had been in such good form because to-day he was going to help the man who came into the country to buy a cattle beast here and there, and drive them off to Clachdrum. Last year Donul had got half a crown from this man, and had given two shillings to his mother and kept sixpence for himself. Donul knew the gamekeeper had at least a stirk for sale, and it was his idea that, what with the money and excitement knocking about, not much attention would be paid to the River at night.

Freed from school at last, Art made a dive through the gate, and one or two of his companions, who tried to keep up with him, soon fell out of the race. Not until he saw cattle grazing on the slope near his own home, did he draw to a standstill. The man must be in the house! Art did not care to meet strange men, and somehow the sight of these beasts was a little frightening. But perhaps his father and the man were just bargaining. Art ran on again, but warily. On tiptoe he approached the door, and, listening, heard:

Mother: It's for yourself to say, Donul.

Donul: Oh, I'll go all right.

Father: It's a chance for him, as you say, and indeed there's nothing much for a young fellow here; nothing at all.

Man: That's what I thought. And Donul is very good with cattle. Mr. Maclennan asked me to keep my eye open for a likely lad, and there's no lad I could recommend sooner than Donul. Whether he'll like it or not is another story, but you can't find out anything without giving it a trial. And, anyway, he could always give notice he was leaving at the next term.

Father: That seems fair enough. What do you think, Donul?

Donul: Oh, I'll go all right.

Mother: Would you like to go?

Donul: Oh, yes, I—I think I would.

Mother: It's come so suddenly on us. Couldn't you give us a day or two to think over it and get him ready? We have nothing ready. He would need——

Man: I know. But there you are—I must have someone to help me with the cattle now, and if he came straight away, it would be an obligement, and I would pay him, of course. I'd pay him—I'd pay him—ten shillings. You could send anything on by the post, and for the rest he could take a small pack on his back.

(*Silence*)

Man: Well, it's got to be yes or no, for I must have the cattle at Clachdrum before the dark. I don't want to force you, but . . .

Mother: It's very kind of you, Mr. Nicolson, to think of us. Believe me when I say that. But—it's come so suddenly on us. If only I could be sure he would be all right. . . .

Man: All I can assure you is that Mr. Maclennan is a big farmer and well spoken of by everyone. The boy has got to make a start in life some time. However, it's for you to say.

Father: It's for Donul himself. If he thinks—I don't know——

Donul: I'll go.

Mother: Are you sure—you would like——

Donul: Yes, I'll go.

. . . . .

At the sudden scraping of chairs and movement of feet, Art turned and bolted for the corner of the house. There had been that in and behind the tone of the voices that affected him more than holy words spoken on a Sunday, for fear was not now vague, it was here and immediate, it had come. It had come upon the land in an invisible darkening, in a terrible stillness, in a drawn-out remorseless waiting. He saw Janet and Neonain afar off. They were coming slowly, walking across the landscape, all by themselves, small withdrawn figures, unaware. The colours of the earth affected Art's sight. He glanced here and there, feeling light-headed. He could neither run off nor go back to the door. And in this mood of suspense, this terrifying feeling that something was about to strike, he could not think, could not think that Donul was going away, wanted only to gather himself into a great cry. Janet and Neonain stopped, their heads lifted, gazing at the cattle. A few slow steps they took, then Janet broke into a wild run, Neonain after her.

As they came by the corner of the house, panting, Janet saw Art's face. Her eyes widened to a stare. "What's wrong?" she asked in a whisper.

Art's face began to work. Janet thought of Henry James, and turned for the door, followed by Neonain. Art now took a little run down towards his secret place behind the barn, but half-way he stopped and came back with stealthy awkward movements, trying to keep his feet against the swirls of an invisible tide.

Voices suddenly came rocketing out. Art saw a tall big-boned man emerge from the door, straighten himself, and look over his cattle, talking at the same time to Father, who followed. Art drew his head back, and the place where he stood went naked for any eye to see. Art's breast was in such a tumult that he could not listen properly to what they were saying. He was waiting. He leaned against the wall, turning his back to the world, and picked mortar from between the stones, waiting. All his forces pressed against themselves until they locked and stood still and drained away into this waiting.

At last his mother's voice, and Morag's. . . . They were all there. A shout. Something had been forgotten. Morag found it. Many voices. His mother's calm voice: "Good-bye, Donul. You will remember always that this is your home. Look after yourself——" And Donul's voice, breaking in, quick and sharp, with a laugh in it: "Good-bye, Mother. Good-bye. Good-bye. . . . Where's Art?"

The surge mounted from low in Art's breast up into his head.

"Round the corner," said Janet.

When Art heard the steps coming, he bolted for the barn. Donul called after him: "Good-bye, Art." But Art did not stop until he was hidden behind the barn.

Morag went down and found him there picking moss off a stone. She regarded him for a moment. "Why didn't you say good-bye to Donul?"

Art, paying no attention to her, slowly got to his feet.

"Donul has gone away," she said in a remote sad voice, partly to herself. But, if she was expecting to comfort Art or get comfort from him, she was disappointed. Without looking at her, Art walked slowly away.

He heard the man whistling to his dog, and he saw the cattle being driven. Donul was walking behind them with the man, a round pack on his back.

Art got to his knees and looked about the land, picking a grass from the ground as he did so, then he began secretly to stalk Donul and the man, using his ingenuity in order not to be seen by them or by any other.

Soon this stalking engaged his full attention and all his

forces. Up on the moor he used whatever cover he could find, and once raced with all his might along a shallow fold, and was actually less than thirty yards from beasts and men as they passed. He heard Donul and the man talking together. In this way he had gone over a mile with them, before Donul saw him. Donul did not shout. He waited until he could surprise Art at a suitable place, a queer secret smile playing on his face, but he did not tell the man he had seen Art. Donul walked away to his left all of a sudden, and there was Art caught in mid-stride.

"Hullo, boy!" Donul smiled in the old friendly way. "Come to say good-bye?" He stepped down over the brow of heather and held out his hand.

Art put his hand shyly into Donul's, but did not speak.

"I knew you would want to say good-bye," said Donul. "Man, it's a pity about to-night. I wanted to see you about that. You'll be disappointed."

"No," muttered Art, valiantly lifting his head but not looking at his brother.

"Never mind. We'll go sometime when I come back. I've got to hurry now. Look here. Tell Hamish how quick I had to go. He may not hear. That's what I had to tell you about. Will you?"

"I will," muttered Art.

"Good! Well, well. So-long."

"So-long," said Art.

"So-long, boy," said Donul gently.

Art turned and rushed away, and not until he was well out of Donul's hearing did he let the sobs and the tears through.

When he came off the moor and saw the few houses that he knew so well, they lay close to the earth as if something had passed over them. They were where they had always been but they were not the same. Once Art had got an odd feeling when the minister said that some place in the Bible had had "a visitation". Once he had come by himself on the wreckage of a wild bees' hive the day after it had been robbed. There was something desolate now about the world he knew, and for the first time he saw clearly that his own home was the innermost of all the houses, the farthest away; it was, what it was often called, "the last house".

While he gazed upon it, he saw Hamish leave its door. Art had no keen desire to meet Hamish. He did not want to see or speak to anybody. The River flowed on in its darkling waters, remote and sad. He had never been able to reach that River, and its flow held no urgency for him now.

All the same, he let himself be seen by Hamish, who came rapidly towards him, calling: "Were you seeing him off?"

"I was," answered Art.

Hamish looked at him. "You'll miss Donul. I'll miss him myself desperately. I don't know what I'll do without him. Did he say anything?"

"He said he could not see you because he had to go so quick."

"I wonder what made him go?" Hamish sat down and began plucking at the grass. His face was flushed, his eyes glancing. "I wish I had seen him. We often talked about going out into the world. I wish I had seen him." He looked like one who had been left behind but might have gone if only he had been told in time. He was very restless, and presently got up and left Art without even mentioning the River.

Art wandered home, and when he went inside, there was his mother sitting beside the fire. She lifted her head and looked into his face for a long time as if he were a stranger or someone she had never rightly seen before. And her voice, though cool and normal, was not part of her, asking: "Why didn't you come in for your food?"

Donul was gone. The house knew it. The land outside was aware of it. The mouth of the night was darker with it, and a small wind, issuing forth, whispered it round the edge of the thatch.

The path Donul had gone over the moor became the path of the man from the outside world. The path not only went away to the outside world, it also came in from the outside world. And as Art lay, unable to sleep, with no Donul beside him any more, the path changed into a long, dark, menacing arm.

For days thereafter a feeling would suddenly come over Art that he had lost something, and at once he would thrust a fearful hand into his pocket. The knife was there. Then he might realize that what was missing was Donul.

But by degrees the feeling of loss delicately changed into something else. When a school companion would say to him, "So Donul has gone away," Art would answer: "He has. He's gone to a great farm where there are hundreds of cattle, and he drives them about with dogs, and he drives them to the market in a great town, and in that town there are streets and streets without end." If the companion was a special friend, they would sit and talk about the size of the town, and the distance between one horizon and another was little enough then.

In this way the outside world gathered a certain brightness for Art, and he grew proud of Donul for having adventured into it. Donul was bound to get on in that far realm, for who could beat him when it came to an adventure? Not many could be his equal in that respect, and perhaps one day he would be a rich man, with great herds of cattle, he would be a farmer with great possessions, like one in a story. There was nothing here for a fellow like Donul, as his father had said; there were only just little places.

Art liked the little places because he felt at home in them, like the peewits. He did not want to go away and excused himself by saying he was too young as yet in any case. So he wove all his stories round about Donul. And when in imagination he saw him having the greatest times and the most wonderful adventures, he was glad for Donul's sake and proud to have him as his brother.

Once, when Morag and himself had been discussing the outside world, a little silence fell upon them. Art started out of this silence, and in the tone of marvel, coming from as far away as his thought had been, he said: "I wonder what Donul is doing at this minute?"

16

The Little Red Cow

Donul was leaning against the dike that separated the Home Park from the farm steading, his head down watching his fingernails as they slowly broke into minute portions a piece of grey lichen which they had just scraped off a coping stone. The brown of his face emphasized its self-conscious warmth as he listened to the three men on his left, who were also leaning with their backs to the wall, discussing the love affairs of a local farmer with a freedom of expression that was new to Donul.

The talk and his own silence left him uncomfortable, and as his head jerked up and stared at the steading-wall or at the collie dog curled in the dry dust by the cart-shed door, his thought in spurts became lost in the bellowing of the little red cow in the park behind them. Into a rich lull in the talk, the bellowing intruded.

"She's persistent, I'll say that for her," the shepherd said, and they all laughed in the carry-over of their thought.

The cattleman nodded. "She's all that. But what could you expect, coming from the West?"

The three men glanced at Donul, who reddened as he tried to smile. They chuckled.

"Never you mind, Donul," said the shepherd. "Good men have come out of the West before now."

"As good maybe as came out of the East," replied Donul, trying to hold his own.

They laughed again.

"He's coming on," said the second ploughman. "He'll soon be having as much to say as the cow herself."

"Let us hope not!" cried the cattleman, jabbing his stick in the ground and tilting up his lean face.

"Where does she come out of?" asked the shepherd.

"Where would you expect but the back of beyond?" answered the cattleman, still intent on his fun, for his assistant was inclined sometimes to be a little dour and a bit livening up might do him no harm. "I believe," he added, "it's from somewhere in the Clachdrum country."

"Isn't that where you come from yourself, Donul?" asked the shepherd, who was native to the wilds of Sutherland, and believed he had some understanding of the boy.

"I do," answered Donul.

The other two grinned, for they had not yet got over the novelty of Donul's lack of plain yes or no.

"What sort of country is it?" proceeded the shepherd in a conversational, helpful tone. "Mostly crofting, I suppose?"

"It is," answered Donul. "But there are sheep farms as well, and some of them, like the Clash, are bigger than any you have on this side."

"Good!" declared the cattleman, jabbing his stick.

Donul reddened again, but held his ground. The brown in his dark hair glistened and his eyes looked stormy. The men about the farm rather liked him, and if they poked fun at him now and then and mimicked his speech, it was with the intention of bringing amusement into the passing hour, not of really hurting him. Donul understood this, even if it did not help him much.

The red cow had come back to the gate and now let out

a prolonged broken bellow at their backs, ending with a choking gust.

"Gode, she'll roar her guts out," said the ploughman, taking his haunch from the wall, and turning round.

The cattleman laughed. "For the size of her, she fair beats the band!"

"I think she hurt her throat that time," said the shepherd interestedly.

They all looked at her. She was small, a shaggy dark-red, and getting on in years, but her brown eyes were deeply glittering, youthful, full of wild mad fires. A tuft of hair on her brow let drop a few coarse strands over the left eyebrow, giving her a ferocious look. One could fancy that what was troubling her might drive her insane.

"What do you think is really wrong with her?" asked the ploughman.

"She's just strange," said the cattleman. "She's finding everything strange. That's all."

"I think she's hurt herself," said the shepherd, watching her.

"Not she!" said the cattleman.

The red cow opened her mouth and bellowed lustily five times in succession. They thought she was never going to stop, and even the shepherd, who was a quiet man, laughed. "No, her throat seems all right," he said.

"What do you think is wrong with her, Donul?" asked the cattleman. "You should know, seeing you come from the same country."

"Och, she'll just be finding herself strange," answered Donul, looking over the dike at the cow, and smiling in an awkward grown-up way, pretending he hadn't seen the cattleman's wink.

"Gode, she doesn't believe in keeping her breath to cool her porridge," said the ploughman.

This gusty humour made them feel friendly to one another, and for the moment almost tender to the little red cow.

"She's for the butcher, I suppose?" said the shepherd.

"Where else?" answered the cattleman. "Did you think she was for Kinrossie's prize herd?"

"You never know," said the shepherd dryly. Regarding Donul with his considering eyes, he added: "You wouldn't care for a trip out to the Argentine with her, would you, Donul?"

"I might do worse," said Donul.

They were drawing the lees from the fun of this new thought when the red cow bellowed until the steading echoed. "Aw, shut up!" said the ploughman. Stooping, he picked up a muddy stone and threw it at the cow. It hit her in the flank and she turned her wild eyes on them, but did not move. "Man, ye're dour!" said the ploughman. "Get off! Whish! Get out!" But though he raised his arms in a threatening jerk, the cow did not move. "Ye for a stupid bitch," said the ploughman, summing her up without heat as he rubbed his fingers against his hip.

"She does look dour, does she no'?" said the cattleman. "They're like that, them that come from the West."

"It's in the breed," said the shepherd, not thinking of Donul. "Actually they're mild and gentle brutes, though they look wild."

"I've known them very treacherous," said the cattleman.

"Ay, but only when they've young calves following them," answered the shepherd.

They discussed this until the bellowing distress of the brute forcibly claimed their attention again. "Put the dog at her," said the ploughman.

"Here, Toss!" called the cattleman. The old collie

with the grey mouth got up from the dry spot by the cart-shed door and came across. "Hits! Drive her off! Get into her!" The dog leapt on to the wall, saw the bellowing beast, and knew what he had to do. As he barked, the cow swung her head, but he easily avoided it, and in a very short time had her careering madly before him. When he thought he had driven her far enough, he stopped, without any shout from his master, and came slowly back.

"He's a wise old brute, that," said the shepherd. They straightened themselves, and the shepherd said he must be getting home. The others went along towards the farm cottages for their food. Their day's work was over and they had enjoyed the talk by the wall.

In the darkening, Donul slipped away from the bothy where he lived with three other men, wearied of the look of their bodies and the sound of their talk. The red cow was still bellowing, but now with longer intervals between each outbreak. The other beasts in the field paid no attention to her, had paid no attention from the beginning. They were of a group that had travelled together for tomorrow's sale. The little red cow was all alone.

Donul knew quite well why she bellowed, knew it as though she were kin to him and were moved by the same emotions. She was of the breed of Old Hector's cow and of their own. He could see her moving about her home croft, tethered here, enclosed there, or herded by someone like Art or Neonain. A girl like Morag had milked her, after first clapping her, then speaking to her, and finally helping her to let down her milk by humming an old Gaelic air. The crofter who owned her had probably decided to sell in a hurry, because the young cow was coming up, and the problem of wintering was difficult. Or perhaps he was of the kind who thought he would get a better price by taking a chance in the market, for it was being said that Mr. Nicolson was making a pile of money by not giving anything like the right price for the cattle he bought on the spot. And certainly, to Donul's knowledge, he had made a large profit off the beasts they had brought from Clachdrum. But it was another matter to call the man "a robber".

Or was it? The irruption of the bellowing red cow into his new difficult life had disturbed him deeply, had irritated him, and at times during the day had maddened him. In a moment of involuntary listening, he had heard the sound of her in the distance give out a curious echo, as though the field were encompassed by high prison walls. Actually he had had to turn and look at her to dissipate the fancy, and when he did, there she went, padding the ground, restless, wandering, seeking a way out.

Now in the deep dusk falling into night, the fantasy came back upon him; the prison walls grew higher and darker than ever, and echoed the sound into a distance remote and forlorn and terrible. The only way he could bear this was by shutting his heart in anger against the cow. He knew what the beast was shouting for. He knew only too well, damn her. He knew all right. Shut up! Oh, shut up!

Then a thought came to him. If he opened the gate and quietly drove her out, she would go straight home. He felt this with perfect certainty. She would go down glens and cross rivers and swim lochs and climb mountain ranges, day and night. That she had come part of the way by train made no difference. Certain beasts had the instinct that found the way home from any place. Men had told him of dogs and cattle that had done it, and even sheep. This beast was one of that kind. He now realized for the first time the nature of the instinct itself. It stirred in his own breast. He stopped, turned half round, and knew with a profound inner conviction that he was facing directly home. He sniffed the air and got the faint but distinct home smell of peat. Nostalgia went crinkling over his skin in a shiver. He had a swift blinding dislike of the cattleman and the other strange people. In a bitter spite he decided it would serve them right if he let the cow out. He was full of spite. He spat. And suddenly in an involuntary but clear vision, he saw the cow nearing home, stumbling a little on her weak legs because she was now in such a hurry, mooing softly through her nostrils, her wild eyes shining, a slaver at her mouth.

His body was trembling, his forehead cold. Those on the croft did not want the cow back. They needed the money. Dismay stood in their staring faces.

The little red cow bellowed far over on the other side of the field. Beyond the dark wall the sound went into the night, into regions of fear and terror. The primeval forces of fear and terror lurked and convoluted there, formless but imminent, and the little red cow went baying them like a beast of sacrifice.

Donul turned and made back for the bothy, holding himself with all his strength against running, his chest choked, his legs trembling. At the gable-end he paused, took off his bonnet, and wiped his forehead and his damp hair. He faced the horrific black formlessness as long as he could; then he went into the bothy.

In the morning he was sent into the field to round the cattle up and take them to the market in the county town. It was a very busy day, for the farmer had many beasts of his own for sale in another field. The cattleman was shouting. The dogs were barking. As Donul drew near the red cow, the brute looked at him with her shining eyes, her head lowered, waiting, dumb. An intense anger swept over Donul. "What way was yon to behave, you bloody fool!" he said harshly and drew his stick with all his force across her buttocks. He was ashamed of her, the fool that she was, and tried to hit her again; but with a sudden snorting, a queer sound, not of pain, she started running, like a cow in heat, towards the gate. "Canny with them!" shouted the cattleman as he opened the gate and let them through. Donul controlled the dark emotion that assailed him, by gripping his stick hard and not looking at the cattleman.

He had great difficulty driving the red cow along the main street. The other beasts grouped together and let vehicles past, but the little red cow hadn't even the sense to get out of the way. With splayed forelegs and head down, she waited. Once when Donul gave her a resounding whack, a fur-clad townswoman winced, her face suggesting that surely there was no need for such brutality—beasts were best handled by kindness. The cow went up a side lane and knocked over an empty perambulator and a message-boy's bicycle with a full load of groceries. Out of this pandemonium, after a final savage "Shut up!" to the message-boy, Donul got her back to the main street. She went into a shop. The rest of the beasts had meantime overshot the right hand turn to the auction mart.

By the time he had them penned, Donul was blown and red in the face.

As the sale proceeded, the cattleman and others he knew came round the ring. The incident of the cow in the shop provided a subject for amusing talk under the high urgent voice of the auctioneer.

"Did she offer to buy anything, Donul?"

"No, man," said Donul, trying to make a joke of the question by taking it seriously, but his smile was awkward, his face congested.

"Leave you Donul alone."

"I'm not caring whether I'm left alone or not," replied Donul.

They laughed, throwing a wink or two, and as one man mimicked his voice, his heart went black. But he did not walk away from them, and presently they scattered, each to get his own lot into the ring. "I'll leave the red cow to you," called the cattleman.

He heard them laugh as they went and knew they were laughing at him.

What should he do now? The cattle were being sold a few at a time. He saw dealers marking their catalogues. Was the red cow a "lot" in herself, or what? He went out and began to ask one of the mart men how he would know when the red cow was due to appear. The man gave him an abrupt look, shouted at someone, and hurried off. They were very busy. Donul decided he would go and wait by the pen, where he was astonished to find the red cow now all alone. She mooed at him, her eyes shining, a slaver at her mouth. But the moo was one of distrust, though in it, too, there was an incredible something that spoke to his flesh and his bones. The half-pedigree heavy stock were new to him, with a certain strange indifference about them, and he was not dismayed by this; but the crofter's cow was intimate to him as his inner self.

After a discreet glance around, he spoke to her. "Ah, you fool, what was the sense in behaving like yon, with everyone looking at you?" He spoke to her in Gaelic, and she answered him at once through her nostrils, her mouth shut. The sound of understanding, of longing, gave his heart a turn. "Be quiet!" he ordered, turning his back on her.

He leaned against the wooden rail of the pen, his elbows resting on it. Men came and emptied pen after pen, with shouts, and the whacking of sticks on hides. He felt the red cow's head between his shoulders, pushing him. "What the devil are you up to?" he demanded in English as he swung round.

Time passed. He suddenly saw the cattleman and two others at the other entrance to the mart. The cattleman raised his stick, pointing Donul out, and they laughed. A great voice roared: "Hurry up, there!" from the near entrance.

"Are you wanting her now?" called Donul.

"What the hell!"

Swiftly Donul opened the gate of the pen, but now the little red cow was dour and would not move. "Get out!" yelled Donul, pushing her fiercely.

"Damn it, do you think we can wait for you all day?" bellowed the man at his back. But the little red cow took an astonishing amount of punishment from the man before she went along the passage-way, hit into the opened gateway of the ring, and had to be shoved bodily through it, followed by Donul.

"She's not so tough as she looks, gentlemen," cried the gentlemanly auctioneer. There was a laugh. "Well, who'll start me at ten pounds? . . . eight? . . . seven? Come along, gentlemen. Well cared for, plump crofter's cow." He made a gesture to Donul: "Show her round."

Donul tried to get her to move, but she had her forelegs splayed again and her head lowered. By sheer force he heaved her hindquarters round three inches, but that was all. He felt red and hot; sweat broke out on his forehead. He became intently conscious of the tiers of faces surrounding him under the roof of the mart. The sting of the watching faces maddened him as he struggled in the ring with the little red cow. There was a tittering laugh from one corner. He knew that laugh. Soft snorts broke out here and there from the amphitheatre.

Smiling, the auctioneer swung round, lifted a glass of water from the clerk's table behind him, and drank in a gentlemanly way. He generally had to provide his own humour, and humour at any time was a godsend; it lightened the proceedings and brought bids more readily.

Donul lost his head. "My curse on you, get round!" The Gaelic words tore harshly through his straining muscles and produced at once a general laugh. The unexpected Gaelic fitted the scene so precisely! Donul drew back and hit the little red cow a wild wallop with his stick. His fierce earnestness was something to behold. Push and hit, push and hit, but she would not be ordered about. No fear! The audience chuckled. They knew her type. One of the ring men entered and, with important impatience, shouldered Donul backward. In a blinding flash of anger, Donul half swung his stick with the intention of knocking the brains out of the ring man, but recovered himself in an awkward stagger. This byplay of emotion was not lost on the audience, and when the little red cow held her own against the ring man, they felt that the score was even. Then the ring man caught her tail, but the auctioneer, in his Olympian way, raised his hand. "I think," he said, "you can all see her, and she's good stuff! Who'll bid me seven pounds? . . . six? . . . Five pounds, thank you, five pounds I am bid, I am bid five pounds, five—five guineas—I am bid five guineas, ten, five-ten, thank you, I am bid five-ten. . . ." At six pounds the auctioneer took half-crowns, and at six pounds five shillings the little red cow was knocked down to the local butcher who had a small farm. "Will you take her in the same pen, Mr. Grant?" asked the auctioneer politely, leaning from his dais. The butcher nodded. "Pen sixty-nine," called the auctioneer. The clerk made an entry in his ledger. The iron swivel was swung back with a clack, the gate opened, and Donul exerted his force. In a half-blind staggering run, the little red cow charged from the arena, Donul on her heels—a dramatic exit that left a grin on the air.

"God, don't you know how to handle a beast yet?" shouted a mart man at him when at last the gate of pen 69 was shut. As the man hurried away, Donul gripped the top rail until his hands were white. Emotion was swirling in his head, black drowning whirls of it, but he held against it, until up through it came his blind will, his voice, cursing them, cursing them all. Curse them, but I'll hold my ground! shouted his thought with such intense bitterness that his eyes suddenly stung. From deep down in her the little red cow mooed.

17

To the River

It was a clear crisp Saturday forenoon in late October. The scents of the gathered harvest and of the earth induced in Art so keen an energy that he had one or two bursts of speed down by the knoll below the barn. But there was little damage cattle could do now, and they hardly even wanted to stray, for the best feeding was by the low ditch-sides. It was too cold to sit long in any one place, and, besides, the body was restless in this keen air with its ancient tingling fragrance. Art was disturbed by the notion that something striking and wonderful could be done on such a morning if only it would "come to him", come into his mind. It seemed on the verge of coming, out of years long ago, that were not really long ago, but in the present, bright mornings in a present that was very near him but not just at him, so that he was baffled and restless, until, happening to look along the land, he saw the postman. Art stood still as a heron, lost in physical vision. Then, wonder opening his features, he showed what he could do in the way of a sustained sprint.

"Yes, one for your mother, Art," cried the postman.

"Who's it from?" panted Art.

"Who but from Donul your brother."

Art looked at the letter, took it, and, forgetting thanks and the postman, bolted.

Neonain saw him coming and ran inside and came out again, followed by Janet and Morag. But Art soon clove through them and presented the letter to his mother, gasping: "From Donul."

His mother held the letter between thumb and forefinger and then laid it down on the corner of the table. "I'll wipe my hands," she said.

"Don't shove me," said Janet.

"Who's shoving?" said Art, giving her a good dig with his elbow.

His mother sat down, opened the letter, and began to read to herself. They all stared at her, growing more impatient every moment.

"What's he saying?" asked Art.

"It's from Donul," she said. "He seems to be getting on."

"Read it out, Mother," said Morag. And, turning back to the beginning, their mother read:

Dear Mother,

This is just a word to say that I am quite well, hoping you are all the same. I am getting on not so bad in my new place. It is very big and there is a good lot to do. We are up every morning before six, and when we take our brose we go out to work and we don't finish till about six at night. It's not too heavy work, though they say it will be heavier in the winter time when the cattle are all inside and the byres to be cleaned and the turnips cut. If anybody like Red Dougal or Hamish asks for me, you can say that everybody has to work here, not like at home where there's nothing to do. Mind and tell them that.

(Every listening face smiled eagerly at Donul's fun. It was the same Donul!)

I live in a bothy with three other men. We get on all

right. They sometimes try and take a joke out of me, but if they do I don't let them off with it. The folk are different here from at home, but maybe I'll get into their ways in time. I was glad to get your parcel with the things in it. It's not much news I have except that I'm getting on fine. You can tell Art I had a funny time the other day. I was driving some cattle along the main street of the town to the mart, when what should one of them do but run in through a shop door which was standing open. She came from somewhere near Clachdrum. She was very like Old Hector's cow, and maybe she was wanting to get something, but if she was it wasn't a present that the mannie in the shop gave her.

(Oh, Donul was good! The burst of laughter passed quickly into breathless listening.)

I hope everything is going well at home. I must draw this letter to a close, as I have to walk a long way to the post. Remember me to all at home.

Your affectionate son,

DONUL.

What a pity that was all! In a moment each one wanted to get hold of the letter.

"Will you stop fighting?" said their mother.

"He wants it," cried Janet, "just because Donul mentioned him!"

"He didn't mention you whatever!" retorted Art.

Morag held the letter over their heads. "Be still, will you, and I'll read it all over again."

"Do that," said their mother quietly, preparing herself to listen.

But though he heard it all over again, Art was not satisfied until he had the letter in his own hands and, with the help of his forefinger, read his own name in Donul's own writing and read what had happened to the cow that was like Old Hector's. Janet and Neonain jeered at his slow mumbling, but Art paid no attention. Not until the letter was snatched from him did he retaliate in a manner that if it made instant flight necessary also increased to a high pitch the mocking laughter with which he barged through the door. Herding was utterly forgotten in his desire to communicate the news to Old Hector, and the keenness of the October day, hitherto without purpose, now raced him as he ran.

Old Hector saw him coming. "There's something in the wind to-day," he said to himself with a small smile.

"We had a letter from Donul," Art shouted at thirty yards.

"Well, that's good news. And how is he?"

"He's fine," said Art. "He mentioned me in it, and your cow."

"Hots! tots! You've been running too hard, man. Take a breath."

"And do you know what it was?" asked Art, who didn't need a breath.

"No."

"The cow went into a shop on him. It was in a great street and the shop door was open."

"No?"

"Yes. And the cow said—no, I mean——" Art couldn't remember Donul's words, and became distressed.

"Take your time."

"Oh, yes! yes!" remembered Art. "Donul said that—it wasn't a present the mannie in the shop gave her!"

"Ho! ho! ho! Good for Donul!" Old Hector laughed heartily. "He must be in fine form."

"He is. He's fine. I know what the mannie in the shop gave her!"

"So do I," said Old Hector.

Art doubled up.

So great was their mirth that Agnes came up to get the gist of it, and in a very short time she had drawn all that Art could remember of Donul's letter from him.

She nodded, a fine light in her eye. "I knew he would get on well in the great world," she said. "He was just wasting himself here. And one day sure enough he would have been caught at the River—if not at something worse." And down she went to the house, smiling with private satisfaction.

Old Hector looked after her with a dry private smile of his own.

Art, feeling the wind taken out of his enthusiasm, his splendid energy draining away now that all had been told, looked back from Agnes into Old Hector's smile. "What is it?" he inquired.

"Och, she was always a bit timid, was Agnes," said Old Hector. "When she was quite little she would be on pins and needles when she knew I was off somewhere." His eyes glimmered in pleasant memory.

"Off at the River, was it?"

"Ay, or somewhere worse."

"Where was worse?"

"You know where worse was yourself."

Art remembered the smuggling den, and his eyes began to glow again in a deep, secret community of interest. "She's frightened," he said, with a silent laugh.

Old Hector nodded. "You've got it now."

"All women are frightened," said Art. "I know that."

Old Hector appeared to ponder the statement doubtfully, so Art quickly qualified it: "At least they are more frightened than men, aren't they?"

"In some things, yes, but not in all things."

"What things are they not?"

"A woman will take a risk often that would frighten many a man," said Old Hector.

"What risk?" asked Art.

"Well, now," replied Old Hector, scratching his whiskers, "it's difficult to think of a woman's risk straight away. All I know is that they like to keep us on the right side of the law."

"That's because they're frightened of the wrong side. It must be. It must," said Art.

"You're getting a terrible fellow to argue," said Old Hector.

"Am I?" said Art, smiling with pleasure.

"You are. You'd argue the hind leg off the cow."

Art's eyes brimmed with merriment as he laughed. Sometimes his laughter forced itself into increase, but when it was quite natural it shook him like a swinging bell.

The calm autumn day had been affecting Old Hector himself. The scents of the earth for him were definitely in the past, but in a past so remote that it went far back beyond the beginnings of his own life, back into a time when morning was on the earth and the earth itself was young. Art's merriment came out of that distant morning.

When Art had recovered and looked at the cow and seen both her hind legs intact, he threw a glance at Old Hector.

Old Hector nodded. "They're still there."

So Art laughed again, caught in the very secrecy of merriment.

"Your mother would be glad to have the good news about Donul?" inquired Old Hector.

Art straightened himself up. "She was. Everyone wanted the letter, but I got it and read it myself. I saw what he wrote with my own eyes." He turned his face to Old Hector. "Donul is great, isn't he?"

"A fine lad," said Old Hector. "None better. You'll miss him sometimes, I suppose."

"I do," said Art. Then he regarded his friend with a certain questioning look. "I could tell you a secret."

"Could you?"

"I could. But I mustn't tell it to anyone, because I promised."

"In that case, you'll keep your promise."

"I will," said Art. "It was about—about what we were going to do the night Donul went away if he hadn't gone away."

Old Hector nodded, and a gleam came into his eye. "The herring net was left on the screw of hay that night!"

"Did you know that we were going to the River?" asked Art in a low voice, delighted to find that Old Hector knew.

"I had my suspicions," said Old Hector.

In a moment Art became full of enthusiasm; then in another moment it abruptly ceased, as if it had been sliced off, and he said in a sad voice: "I don't think that I'll ever see the River in this life."

"Oh, surely you will!"

"No," said Art. "I never will."

"Oh, but——"

"I've always been going to see it, but I never got. Something always came in the way." His voice trembled.

"You've had bad luck certainly," agreed Old Hector. "But if all goes well, I'll promise to take you there myself some day."

"You will not!" cried Art. "You will not!"

Old Hector looked down at his home, and up at the sun, and abroad upon the land.

"Have you anything special to do yourself to-day?"

Art's whole body stilled. "No." He took a side look up

at Old Hector, and waited. Old Hector looked down and said: "Why not? Why shouldn't we go just now?"

Art could not yet believe it, however.

"Come on," said Old Hector, in the voice of one who would do his best. "We'll see."

They went down to the house.

"I was thinking," said Old Hector casually to Agnes as he screwed a finger-length of black-twist tobacco off the two-ounce coil in the top drawer of the kitchen dresser, "that I might take a turn down the Little Glen to have a look at the grass. You might keep your eye on the cow."

"The grass is growing in the usual way," replied Agnes, giving her father a suspicious glance. "Is Art going with you?"

"He is," said Old Hector pleasantly. "He is going to stretch his legs. Aren't you, Art?"

"I am," muttered Art shyly.

"Well, see you won't be putting notions into that boy's head. He's too young to be led into temptation yet."

"What are you talking about?" inquired her father mildly.

"You know fine what I'm talking about," answered Agnes.

"Hots! tots! woman," remarked Old Hector. "You'll be putting ideas in the boy's head yourself."

Not until they had passed the corner of the house did Art whisper: "Was she very angry?"

"No," answered Old Hector. "Sometimes when a woman's heart is full of care for you she will speak as though she was angry, just because she's frightened something may come at you. She can't help it."

But Art did not follow the full thought, because he was now quivering with excitement, and no sooner were they down the bank and into the hollow than his body became charged with the most violent energy. Yet this he restrained and looked up at Old Hector and asked: "Are we really going to the River?"

"I hope so," nodded Old Hector.

"To the real River and the Hazel Pool?"

"If nothing comes in our way."

That last remark stopped Art from bounding on. He glanced around him with a wary excited eye, and stuck by Old Hector.

"Are you expecting anything to stop us?"

"No," answered Old Hector. "To tell the truth, it came over me that I would like to have one more look at the River in this life myself."

Art glanced up, but Old Hector was not sad, he was full of his fun. "It's interesting for me to think that what will be your first trip may be my last."

"Why do you think it might be your last? Is it because you're old?"

"It is," nodded Old Hector.

"But you can be older yet, can't you?"

"I hope so. Indeed we can't stop getting old."

"I'm getting older myself, too, amn't I?"

"You are."

Art nodded, walking beside Old Hector. "I have a long way to go yet, though, before I'll be up to you, haven't I?"

"Yes. It's a long way when you're looking forward, but it's not so long when you're looking back. I hope it will be a pleasant way for you."

"I think it will," said Art. "And I should see a lot before then. And I'll go away off into the world like our Donul."

"Would you like to go?"

"I won't be frightened to go," said Art, "will I? But of course I'm too young to go yet. It's when I'm older. Do you know what's the main reason for me to go?"

"What?"

"Because there's nothing for a fellow here."

Old Hector was silent.

"Didn't you know that?" asked Art.

"I've heard it before now," said Old Hector.

"You never went away yourself?"

"No," replied Old Hector. "I often thought of going, but I never went."

"Are you sorry you didn't go now?"

"No," answered Old Hector. "Not now."

His voice was quiet and Art looked up at him. "How's that?"

"Well, if I had gone away, I wouldn't have been here walking with you, for one thing. And for another, I like to be here. You see, I know every corner of this land, every little burn and stream, and even the boulders in the stream. And I know the moors and every lochan on them. And I know the hills, and the passes, and the ruins, and I know of things that happened here on our land long long ago, and men who are long dead I knew, and women. I knew them all. They are part of me. And more than that I can never know now."

"That's a lot to know, isn't it?" said Art wonderingly.

"It's not the size of the knowing that matters, I think," said Old Hector, "it's the kind of the knowing. If, when you know a thing, it warms your heart, then it's a friendly knowing and worth the having. In any case, you remember it, and it will stay with you to the end of your days."

"I know a good few places myself," said Art.

"What places?"

"I know the Loch of the Rushes, and the Clash, and Shivering Eye, and—and other places."

Old Hector nodded. "You're coming on. Every littl place, every hillock, every hill and slope, has its own name."

"Has it? It makes a big difference, doesn't it, when you know the name?"

"It does. There are many places, many many places, with names that no-one knows but myself, and they will pass away with me."

"Will you tell them to me?" asked Art eagerly.

"I will indeed, and gladly, for I would not like the little places to die."

"Will they die if they lose their names?"

"Something in them will die. They will be like the clan that lost its name. They will be nameless."

" 'Nameless by day,' " quoted Art from the song, and looked up with a shy, glowing smile.

Old Hector nodded in compliment. "You have it now."

"And by night, too, wouldn't they?"

"Both by day and by night."

Art was so pleased that his energy made him kick the seeds off a tuft of grey grasses in passing. "When will you tell me the names?"

"I will tell them to you from time to time. That's the best way, I think. For in that way you don't just learn them."

"Do you know," said Art, "when you have to learn things at school, it's terrible difficult to remember them sometimes, isn't it?"

"It is, indeed. And I wouldn't blame anyone for forgetting them often."

"But—but for me to get the names of the places, that's not learning, that's different, isn't it?"

"Quite different," agreed Old Hector.

Art took a small dance to himself by Old Hector's side. "And when I have all the names of the places that no-one else knows, then, when you're gone, I'll be the only one who'll have the names, the only one in the world?"

"The only one," agreed Old Hector pleasantly.

"I'll like that," said Art. "And some day, some day in a long time, I'll tell someone, too. Won't I?"

"If I thought you would do that, I would be happy."

"I promise to do it," said Art earnestly. "That's one thing I'll never forget. You can trust me."

"I do indeed. I have trusted you often."

"Did I ever—did I——?"

"Never," said Old Hector firmly.

"That time — remember — with — with Dan Macgruther——"

"You fought to save your trust, that time, and you conquered. If folk never fought for anything less than that it's a happy place this old world would be. Too often indeed, it's other things they fight for."

"What things?"

"To gain possessions and to have great power," answered Old Hector. "And then people are set upon and driven from their homes, and they die, in want and in suffering. At the core of that fighting there is only one thing, and its name is cruelty. Of all human sins, it is the worst."

"Is it worse than not going to church?"

"I think sometimes it is worse even than that," said Old Hector.

Art walked along thoughtfully. "If I saw anyone being cruel, and I was a big man, do you know what I would do?"

"What?"

"I would give him a good shot on the nose," said Art. "That would learn him, wouldn't it?"

When Old Hector laughed softly, his whole body to Art seemed to grow mellow and warm. Now, however, Art suddenly gripped him at the hip. Old Hector followed his gaze to a small ravine on the off side of the stream.

"That's where I saw the gaugers go up first," Art explained in a low voice, his eyes round.

But there was no-one there now, and, as they journeyed on, Old Hector gave Art the name of the burn that issued from the ravine, and explained how once, long ago, there had been a bothy near a spot high up the burn where stone cists, that were prehistoric graves, could still be seen. About that spot he told so fabulous a story that Art forgot to ask questions until it was finished.

And so in time they came to the place of the foxgloves and the smuggling cave. There was excitement for Art now!

But Old Hector seemed quiet and preoccupied, his eyes looking here and yonder, as if he had forgotten Art, and he answered questions absentmindedly. Art grew silent himself as they came before the grey bones of the dead sheep. The bones were a skeleton laid before the sealed door to the smuggling cave. Fear touched Art now and wonder and strangeness as if a whisper had settled like a shadow upon a known place.

"Are we going in?" whispered Art.

"No. We'll leave well alone," answered Old Hector, and his voice sounded loud and clear, it was so quiet. He inspected the mouth of the inlet-pipe and carefully replaced the boulders. He climbed up a yard or two and had a look at the divots on top of the bothy. Then, rubbing his hands slowly on his hips, he stood by the running water, and said in a slow gentle voice: "It's bonny here."

Old Hector was now a tall big man, and his whiskers were ancient as a forest. He was withdrawn from Art into a distant grown-up world, and his eyes glimmered as they looked far off. His affection for things past touched Art to an obscure turmoil of silence, as the things past came into the present, into this small wild hollow in the Little Glen, and stood beside Old Hector in greeting and farewell. Then the affection went down his arm and caught Art's hand.

Some time after they had passed into the broadening glen, Old Hector's thought left him on a short sigh of release, and as though he felt the better both of the thought and of its release, he drew a deep breath or two and glanced slowly around. "I think I'll have a smoke," he declared cheerfully. "We have the day before us. What do you say?" He sat down, took out his finger of tobacco, and then began searching one pocket after another.

"Have you forgotten your pipe?" asked Art.

"Man, I haven't a knife!" exclaimed Old Hector with dismay.

"Wait!" shouted Art, and in a twinkling he had put his own beautiful knife into his friend's hands.

Art was so delighted at the sight of Old Hector's pleasure and at the way he presently said, "Boy, she's a good cutter!" that he took a little run to himself down to the stream to inspect it and see what he could see. Sometimes he shouted back to Old Hector, who nodded in agreement as he cut and rolled his tobacco, and scraped out what had been in the bowl of his pipe on to his palm, and blew through his pipe, and carefully filled the bowl, placing some of the old dottle on top.

Because he was now in a land where he had never been before, Art was excited, and when he stood for a moment looking away down the glen, his muscles trembled somewhat because beyond where he could see was the unknown River, and he was going there. Slowly he drifted back to Old Hector and sat down beside him, overcome by the strange wonder of this day. "What," he asked, in a low eager voice, "is the most wonderful thing in this world?"

"A kind heart," answered Old Hector.

Art looked up to see if his friend was trying to make fun of him. But Old Hector's expression was wise and friendly and he started putting great blasts of the pipe off him.

"The smoke is going all through your whisker," said Art.

"Why wouldn't it?" said Old Hector agreeably. "Are you anxious to be off?"

"I'll wait," said Art, "till you take your rest. Do you think," he asked, trying to control his voice, "we'll see a salmon in the Hazel Pool?"

"There's no saying," replied Old Hector. "But I know a flagstone I can poke with a stick, and if I don't put a fellow out from under it, it will be a wonder."

"Where will you get the stick?"

"You can help me to cut one with your knife from a hazel tree. And the nuts will be ripe. We forgot that! They'll be falling out of their clusters."

"Will they?" said Art on a breath.

"They will," said Old Hector. As he looked down, the smile that was friendly paused in his eyes before it ran off along the small tracks into his whiskers. "Come," he said in a pleasant voice, "let us be going."

Because he was now a little shy and afraid of meeting the River, that dark stranger of his dreams, Art had no urge to run ahead. His eyes front, he groped up for Old Hector's hand, and thus, walking side by side, they continued on their journey.